Breaking Balls

To my father, Sidney Lebowitz —
the King of the New York Streets

Breaking Balls

A Novel of Baseball

by PAUL LEBOWITZ

McFarland & Company, Inc., Publishers
Jefferson, North Carolina, and London

Breaking Balls is a work of fiction. Names, characters, places, and incidents are the product of the author's imagination or are used fictitiously. Any resemblance to actual events, locales, or persons, living or dead, is purely coincidental.

ISBN 0-7864-1065-5 (softcover : 50# alkaline paper)

Library of Congress cataloguing data are available

British Library cataloguing data are available

Manufactured in the United States of America

McFarland & Company, Inc., Publishers
Box 611, Jefferson, North Carolina 28640
www.mcfarlandpub.com

◆ PART I ◆

1

As long as I can remember all I've ever wanted was to open the *Baseball Encyclopedia* turn to the pitcher's section and see my name: Brett Samuels. That is all I've ever dreamed of. All I've ever wanted. I didn't dream about winning the World Series or winning all sorts of awards. I just wanted to see my name in that book.

I can't remember exactly when I became a professional. Was it when I signed the contract? Was it when I got on the plane to join the team? Was it when I got my first paycheck? Or, was it when I actually cashed my first check? It really doesn't matter. The fact is that I am a professional. That means I get paid for doing this. It was totally unexpected, but hey, it's great work if you can get it. And not many get it.

I was never a "star" athlete. Never the first one picked or even the first one invited to play. But, when given the opportunity I got the job done. In unorthodox (not in the Semitic sense) ways, but the job got done. I played baseball in high school, but not until my senior year. I played in junior college. And I played on the unkempt sandlots of New York City until I received my break. A break that happened by pure unadulterated luck. I've always been lucky.

I was toiling for a team of nineteen year olds on the dilapidated fields of Prospect Park in Brooklyn called the Parade Grounds. The fields have patchy grass in the outfield with broken glass in certain spots. Outfielders have to be mindful because there's always broken glass. Usually forty ounce bottles of Budweiser with their brown shiny shards scattered all over. Diving for balls is not recommended unless the possibility of stitches interests you. The fences, if you're lucky enough to play on one of the fenced in fields, have holes in them every couple of feet. There are barely any pitching mounds on any of the fields, and in front of the rubber that the pitcher has to stand on is, routinely, a giant hole. That's where I grew up. The team I played for when I was discovered was called the Brooklyn Rockies. We had the whole get-up of the Colorado Rockies except for black and purple hats with a big "B" on them. The uniforms were quite nice. They were from the official Major League Baseball Collection, so they were exactly what the pros wore. They weren't the game uniforms; they were the batting practice jerseys. The outfit was completed with grey pants and black stirrups. They had numbers on the back but no names. That's too expensive and impractical if someone forgot his uniform top, which happened more often that you might think. You can't have LeRoy Griffin, a black guy from the Bronx, walking around with the Jewish name "Samuels" on his back. LeRoy had the habit of forgetting at least one piece of equipment or some segment of his uniform. One day it would be his hat, the next his spikes, then his glove. It was always something. We joked about it, but it was irritating. Whenever it would happen one of the pitchers would have to fork over some equipment. I got caught in that web more than once. One day he swiped my hat right off my head and I snatched it back just as he was heading out on the field. I'd had enough.

My lucky break came when I was pitching against a team called the Brooklyn Giants. There were several scouts in the stands to see a left-hander that was pitching for the Giants. There are always a few scouts in the stands at the Parade Grounds. They seem to like the Latin kids that are permeating New York nowadays. All those kids do is play baseball all day, every day. All they want to do is play baseball all day, every day. That may sound like a stereotype, but it's true. Many of them are grateful for the opportunity and that makes them coachable.

Being coachable in pro baseball is very important. The coaches and front office people don't want or need aggravation. Guys who are difficult don't last too long unless they're superstars. Superstars can be as difficult as they want. I'm difficult sometimes and that means I get into trouble. (Does it matter that I'm usually right? Probably not.) I've seen some of those grateful Latin kids cease being coachable once they receive their bonus checks.

There were scouts from the Los Angeles Dodgers, Houston Astros, Philadelphia Phillies, St. Louis Cardinals, Montreal Expos, Florida Marlins, Anaheim Angels, and Seattle Mariners at the game. All there to look at that one lefty. In the Prospect Park league doubleheaders are played on Sunday. This pitcher was going to start the first game and then he was going to leave. We didn't even know if he was a regular member of the team. I think he just came down for that one game to show off for the scouts. This is not an uncommon occurrence. The guy warmed up and the game began.

The pitcher was white, about 6'5", 195 pounds and had a funky motion the type of which are seen used only by left-handers. He would bring his arms above his head, pivot on the rubber, lift his leg and break his hands behind his raised right knee. Then he would rock back and sling the ball in a three-quarter motion to the plate. Our hitters said it was hard to pick the ball up coming out of his hand. If you were to picture a clock behind him as he releases the ball his arm would be between nine and ten o'clock. It had good velocity and movement. The scouts' radar guns were fixed on him from behind the chain link fence in back of home plate. A couple of us slid behind them to have a peek at the radar guns. The pitches were buzzing in at 88 to 92 mph. The three-quarter whip caused some unusual movement too. He could rise the ball and sink it. Or, it seemed as though he could. When you're watching a ballgame and the pitcher is making the ball move, many times it's not being done consciously. That big lefty was going pro and, unless he gets hurt, will be making money in this game for about twenty years. That's even if he doesn't make it to the Majors. Lefties always have jobs waiting for them. It doesn't even matter if they're that good. And this guy *did* seem good. Our hitters didn't make any solid contact for the two innings he pitched and then he was taken out. That was the deal. He threw twenty-seven pitches and was taken out. He took off

3

his uniform behind the dugout and left. The scouts could talk to him about anything but money. Talking about money is a violation of amateur rules. They could talk to him about his family, college, and things like that. They didn't say anything to each other though. He didn't look at the scouts and they didn't look at him. I surmised that they already knew each other.

The Astros and Dodgers scouts were the only ones who hung around to watch the rest of the games. That was where my luck kicked in. I came in to pitch the fifth inning. We were behind 4–1. This was my first appearance of the sandlot season and I wanted to do well. Intra-squad games had been good for the previous few weeks, but that doesn't prove anything. It's the games that count. We only play seven innings in this league so I had three innings all to myself. I warmed up and slowly strode to the mound. The bullpens are just small dirt piles on the side of the field. They're nothing like the bullpens you see in the big leagues. I stepped onto the mound, which was as horrible as usual. The giant hole was in front of the rubber. To pitch comfortably at the Parade Grounds was impossible, so I did the best that I could. I stood on the side of the rubber. A pitcher has to maintain contact with the rubber until he releases the ball. I stand like most pitchers, directly on top of the rubber with both feet making contact. Then, I step straight back with my left foot, step into a (usually) small divot in front of the rubber and lift my leg. I have a relatively high leg lift. My knee comes in front of my face; I break my hands and bring my right arm down behind my right hip while my glove extends in front of me. Then I raise my right arm and left arm simultaneously so that they're forming 90-degree angles and my elbows are at shoulder height. My right arm moves into throwing position and my glove is curled under my left armpit. My left foot lands in a (usually) small hole at the bottom of the mound and I turn my body toward the plate. My arm comes around and I push off the rubber with my right leg. I release the ball using all of the strength in my body. I stop and try to prepare for the batter to rifle one back at me. The power I have comes from my legs and hips. My legs are exceptionally strong. That's why I can throw hard for my size. The 6'5" guy had gravity on his side. He's pitching downhill and doesn't need his legs as much. I'm 5'11" and have no choice but to use my legs. Gravity is not my ally. I have to achieve leverage

4

without height, so I try to use my legs to make up for the disadvantage.

The first game moved along and we wound up losing 5–2. I was good but not spectacular. I wound up pitching three innings and gave up two hits and a run. I walked two, hit one and struck out three. There's a half-hour break between game one and two, so the guys try and find ways to amuse themselves by eating, hanging around in the stands, or walking around the park looking for girls. There are no clubhouses to relax in, so we just make do with what we have.

Off behind the fence in back of home plate, our coach Mark Mattera was chatting with the scout for the Dodgers. The scout is a short, stocky, Spanish looking man with glasses. Mattera is a running joke amongst the team. He's tall and fat and has jet-black hair and a thick jet-black mustache. He's either yelling or yelling very loudly. He tells war stories about his playing days. According to him, he was the greatest pitching prospect since Cy Young. With Mark, everything is someone else's fault. His path to the Hall of Fame was blocked by one vast conspiracy or another. If a movie was made about his life, Oliver Stone would direct it. The interesting thing was that for all of his supposed greatness, Mark never even played professionally. He said that he played in college, but we found that a little dubious. According to Mark, everybody who does something that he doesn't like or says something that he doesn't agree with, stinks.

"This stinks, that stinks." About three times each game he said this. He could have Sandy Koufax on his team and he would find a reason to say that he stinks. We used to make up exchanges and they would go something like this:

Player: "Mark, Koufax just signed with the Dodgers. He's going to the Majors."

Mattera: "What? He doesn't wanna play for me?"

Player: "But he's going to the Majors."

Mattera: "FUCK 'IM! We don't need him. He STINKS!"

Player: "But coach..."

Mattera: "He STINKS!"

And then he would storm off.

Scouts as a rule didn't bother talking to him. They seemed to think he was an idiot. I couldn't see why. You only thought he was an idiot if you saw or heard him.

At any rate, there was Mark Mattera standing and chatting with the scout from the Dodgers.

2

As the second game started, the guys were in the field in the top of the first when Mattera sidled up to me. There weren't too many guys in the dugout.

"Did you see me talking to that scout over there?" he asked, pointing with his ample chin.

"Yeah," I answered with mild interest. I really didn't have much to say to Mark and tried to talk to him as little as possible. I thought he was trying to impress me.

"Well, he was asking about *you*."

I turned and looked at Mark, frowned and furrowed my brow. He had finally said something that caught my interest. Why would *any* scout be asking about me?

"What'd he want to know?" I sputtered.

"Just general stuff. Your age, school, what type of kid you are. That kind of thing."

"Why would he want to know that?" I hadn't the vaguest notion. Well, I had a vague notion, but I would be living in a fantasy world if my vaguest notions were true. I left my fantasy world a long time ago.

"He didn't say. He just wanted to know," Mark said.

"He didn't say anything else?"

"Well," he paused, "he said that you have a vicious curveball and a below-average fastball. And I agreed with him."

I squeezed my eyes shut and shook my head slightly as I tried in vain to comprehend what had happened.

"Did you just say that you *agreed* with him?"

I thought I had seen the entire range of Mark's stupidity. I was wrong. I was also livid.

"Well, what could I say?" Mark asked with a shrug.

My mouth opened and nothing came out. I just turned and walked away amazed that there was someone in the world this stupid.

I told this tale to Rob Traella who was my best friend on the team. As a fellow pitcher, he would understand why I was so angry. When I was finished, he looked at me with a bemused smile and said, "Well, what do you expect from Mark?"

"Don't you think" I asked, "that someone with half a brain would have said, 'Come and have another look, it's early in the season'?"

"You're making the mistake of assuming that he has half a brain." He chuckled. "Don't worry, the guy has all your information. If he's really interested, he'll find you and come see you again."

Rob spoke from a level of experience. Being only 5'8" and having less of a fastball than me, Rob wasn't going pro but he did have a scholarship to St. Francis College in Brooklyn. They've sent quite a few guys pro. Rob knows how scouts work. That calmed me down slightly. It usually takes a lot more than that to calm me when I'm agitated.

This occurred in April, so my college team still had plenty of games left. If the scout was impressed he would indeed find me. It was approximately three weeks later when I was pitching in a game for Kingsborough Community College that I noticed the scout at the game. (That Kingsborough team was very eclectic. Team members included a pot dealer and a cocaine dealer and a guy who insisted on trying to have sex with his friends' girlfriends.) The team we were playing, Queensborough, had a big lumbering first baseman with all kinds of power. He was attracting attention from the scouts, so there were a couple of other scouts in attendance. I started the game and went seven innings, allowing only two hits. One was a 450-foot home run by the aforementioned first baseman. But I struck out eight and walked only three, which was very good. I didn't even hit anybody. When I left the game it was tied 1–1 and we eventually lost 3–1. After the game, as I was walking to my car, I saw our coach, Lou Roessler, talking to that very same Dodgers scout. *Could he be talking about me? Nahhhh.*

We had a couple of other pretty good players on our team, so he may have been talking about them. My intuition was telling me otherwise. Roessler and the scout were obviously familiar with each other because they were laughing and joking. Maybe they were just friends visiting. They were still talking as I drove off. Roessler has been a college coach for twenty-two years. He's known and respected. I drove home wondering if there was any chance. Any *possibility* that the scout was keeping an eye on me.

Roessler never said anything to me about it, so I just assumed that nothing was happening. I didn't want to ask. Well, that's not true. I did want to ask, but was afraid to. Roessler wouldn't have told me if I'd asked anyway. He's not the type to get kids' hopes up over what could be nothing. Oh well, I thought. I had two more years of eligibility left in college and had to decide which senior college to attend. Ithaca looked promising. They had a good baseball team, but one that I thought I would make and have a good opportunity to play. Who knows? Maybe I could finagle some scholarship money from them.

Our season ended May 17. We didn't get out of the first round of the Junior College qualifying round for a trip to the regional championships. We had to win to advance. We didn't win. School was coming to an end in early June and I would have my two-year degree. I had some decisions to make regarding continuation of school. I persevered with the Rockies in the spring and on into June. I wanted to keep in shape in case I had to go and work out for one of the colleges that I had applied for. Mark Mattera was his usual overbearing self. I think he's mentally disturbed. Most of us had learned to tune him out so it wasn't as bad as it was in the beginning. He's nobody. The contacts that he thinks that he has with the Major League scouts are nonexistent. Everybody knew it but him. He's just a big fat man in a tight uniform that wanders around Prospect Park screaming.

Maybe they should lock him up.

3

The Major League amateur draft is held every year in early June. All teams spend more than fifty rounds over three days drafting the best players they can find. Actually, they don't always draft the best *baseball* players. Often they draft the players with the best tools. Tools are the abilities to hit, run, field, throw and hit for power. A player who has all of these tools is called a "five tool player." Generally when a player is called a "tool guy" that means he can't play baseball.

Scout: "I've got a kid here with some great tools."

Translation: "I've got a kid here who can't play, but he runs like a rabbit."

Executive: "That sounds good. We'll take a flier on him and teach him all the other stuff later. Maybe he'll turn out to be a winner."

Translation: "Let's draft him. If he makes it we'll look like geniuses. If not, well, he *could* run, how were we supposed to know he wouldn't be able to play? Thus we'll keep our jobs."

The scouts and other executives think that it is easier to find a guy who has a gift, such as great speed, and teach him to play baseball. The theory is that you can't teach speed. Personally, I don't think that there's anything that can't be taught. Sure, you can't teach a guy to run like Rickey Henderson, but you can teach a guy to be a smart baserunner and to make the most out of the abilities that he does have. But these scouts are set in their ways and have a reason for taking the "tool guys." If there are two pitchers with identical abilities and one is 6'5" while the other is 5'11", the bigger guy is the one that they will take. He has the better "tools," they'll say. What they're really saying is, they're not confident enough in their abilities to judge intangibles like determination and courage. The bigger guy is the safer pick for them. If he makes it, they made the right choice. If they pick the smaller guy, well, he'd better make it. The scouts' jobs depend on making the right judgments in these cases. Only the bolder, more imaginative ones will take the chance on someone who hasn't got the obvious physical gifts.

Someone like me.

The Major League draft came and went without my name being called. No surprise there. For the record, junior college players can be drafted after their freshman or sophomore year. Senior college players have to wait until after their junior year. Some players who think they're going to get drafted leave their senior colleges after freshman year and go to a junior college just to get drafted. A couple of guys that I know got drafted, mostly in the later rounds. The big lefty from the Brooklyn Giants that the scouts were salivating over went to the Expos in the second round. That should be worth about a $500,000 bonus plus his contract. It could be more. I don't know the going rate. It would be a nice piece of change no matter what. Nobody from my school or the Brooklyn Rockies was drafted. Mattera wasn't committed, so it appeared as though everyone was staying put for the time being. Some big league teams hold open tryouts after the draft. I thought I might go to the ones in the New York City area. What did I have to lose?

4

A few days after the draft, I was sitting in my room trying to decide which four year college I was going to attend. I'd been accepted by Ithaca, Temple and Hofstra. I could also go to one of the city colleges. I didn't know if there were any scholarships available for 5'11" right handers with below average fastballs. I hadn't heard from any coaches. I wasn't expecting offers of room and board for my skills at playing baseball.

Staring up at the large Lou Gehrig poster I have in my room, I was having negative thoughts. A nine-to-five job would make me want to kill myself. What was I going to do? It wasn't like I wasn't intelligent enough. I could do many things. But I wanted a chance to play professional baseball.

Suddenly my phone rang.

I hate it when my phone rings because most of the time it's my mother calling from work asking me to do some repugnant task. It's not easy being the only child. Or it's my mother telling me to tell my father to do some repugnant task. That I don't mind. As long as *I* don't have to do anything.

"Yello?" That's how I answer the phone.

"Brett?" the voice on the other end asked.

"Yeah."

"This is Coach Roessler."

"Oh, hey. What's up?" I was surprised. I figured that he wanted me to help out at one of the summer clinics he runs for children.

"Listen, I just spoke with Juan Ramos, the scout from the Dodgers…"

"Yeah?" I broke in. Could it be that this time I would be glad that my phone rang?

"They're holding a private free-agent workout for a couple of guys that they may have some interest in," he continued. "They want you to go."

"You're kidding."

"No," he said.

Lou Roessler doesn't joke around too much.

"It's at Eisenhower Park in Long Island. Should I tell him you'll be there?" he asked.

"Yeah, absolutely," I said loudly. "Of course I'll be there."

My mind was racing a mile a minute.

"What time?"

"9:00 A.M., Saturday."

"Okay, Coach. Should I ask for anyone in particular?" I asked.

"There won't be that many players there. They'll have everything prepared," he replied. "Good luck."

"Okay. Thanks, Coach."

He hung up and I started running around my room trying to think.

My father, Phil, walked in the door at 4:30 P.M. He's a disgruntled postal clerk. We live in a two family house in Boro Park, Brooklyn, and you could always hear when someone was coming up the stairs. As he walked in, I was standing by the door waiting, grinning like a Cheshire cat. He gave me a look that said, "Whattayou want?" He's not nasty. He just prefers it when I'm seen and not heard and sometimes not even seen. He's sixty years old and likes his peace and quiet. My mother, Amy, works in Manhattan managing a law office. They don't hound me about getting a job, but they want me to do *something*. No lying around the house all day. So, here I am standing there looking at this short, bald man with a Tom Clancy novel and the newspaper under one arm and a cigarette in the other, wearing a postal shirt and navy slacks. I'm about to tell him something that he won't believe.

"You ready for this?" I asked.

"Ready for what?"

I had told my parents about the scout asking about me. But that was weeks ago. They didn't make it a habit to follow the intricacies

11

of Major League Baseball's drafting procedure. They had forgotten about it.

"I got invited to a private tryout with the Dodgers," I said.

He smiled and chuckled in a way that I knew he was impressed. "No kiddin'," he said. "When?"

"This weekend."

"What happens now?" he asked.

"Well," I began, "I hope that if they like what they see they'll offer me a contract. But, who knows?"

"Whattaya know?" he said loudly. He was impressed. I could tell, though he would never say it.

He added one thought. "Don't hit any scouts with the ball."

He knows of my tendency to hit things such as batters, teammates, umpires, and chain link fences seventy-five feet away.

My mother had much the same reaction as my father. Surprise and bemusement. And she was a little impressed too.

5

I called Traella the night before the tryout or workout or whatever they wanted to call it. I asked him if he knew about the procedure. I wanted to know what I should wear, how early to arrive, what to say, what not to say, etc. He sounded amazed. Should I have been insulted?

"Don't screw up and don't say anything unless they ask," he said.

I swore him to secrecy. If this didn't work out, I didn't want anyone to know about it. If it *did* work out, I would tell everybody and be real obnoxious about it to boot. He agreed.

I got to Eisenhower Park early. It's about a forty-five minute drive from my house. At 7:30 A.M. I pulled my car into the Eisenhower Park parking lot. A couple of guys were already there. I had no idea how many guys were coming or how many were going to be taken. I was wearing my college baseball pants and stirrups with sanitary socks. I had on a Kingsborough T-shirt and a long sleeved sweatshirt. I had my Kingsborough hat and jacket. In my bag, I had my gloves and spikes.

I don't wear a cup, so I had all the necessary equipment. (I don't wear the cup for two reasons: It's uncomfortable. And what are the odds of a ball connecting directly with the family jewels?) I nodded hello to the other guys there. There was nobody I know. That was good news.

Everything that I said previously about the sad condition of the Parade Grounds, the opposite is true for Eisenhower Park. They have real grass on the infield. There aren't pieces of broken glass everywhere. The fields are manicured. There are nice mounds with no holes. And there are even decent bathrooms and clean water fountains. It even smells like a baseball field. There weren't drunks staggering around or Jamaicans playing soccer and refusing to get off the fields so we could play.

At about a quarter to nine some official looking guys showed up wearing Dodgers jackets, and carrying what looked like video camera cases. Those were the radar guns. I didn't see the Spanish-looking scout and that disappointed me. They got themselves set up apparently waiting until the 9:00 A.M. start time. Some of the players were familiar with each other and chatted. A couple of guys from Connecticut struck up a conversation with me and we batted the breeze until the scouts gathered us together for the workout.

6

There were only eleven guys at the tryout, so I wasn't sure how this process was going to go. About nine of the ten guys were substantially bigger than me and the one that wasn't was a lefty. That didn't make me feel any better. The scouts gave us cards to fill out and had us stretch. Then they timed us in the forty-yard dash. Don't ask me why, because I haven't got an answer. I've never understood why it's important to know how fast a *pitcher* can run. I mean, who cares? I don't run real well, so that didn't go as well as I would have liked. I hoped that that wouldn't have a major effect on my chances.

They had a guy there, apparently one of their minor leaguers, with catcher's equipment. They had us warm up together throwing the ball back and forth between two guys and asked the first guy to get up on the mound to throw for them. They were going in alphabetical order, so I was one of the last ones to go. The first guy got up there and they let him loosen up on the mound and told him to tell them when he was ready. He warmed up and told them that he was ready to go. One of the scouts was behind the plate and had his radar gun at the ready. The pitcher, a 6'4", 200 pound right-hander, went into his motion and fired a fastball. It looked like he had some decent pop, but not greatly superior to mine. They had him throw five fastballs and asked him to throw his other pitches. They wanted five of each. He threw five curveballs, and then five change-ups. They asked him to throw two more fastballs and that was it. They had him sign their sheet and let him go. "That's it?" he asked. They told him that they would be in contact if there was an offer to be made. He went to sit in the stands to wait for the other player he rode in with.

7

One guy after another came and went. I wasn't going to be one of the last to go, I was going to be *the* last to go. The scout that appeared to be running the whole thing called my name. "Brett Samuels?"

"Here," I said.

"Come on up."

I got up on the mound and pawed at the dirt with my foot, making it more comfortable for myself. I have a ritual that I go through when I get to the mound. I pick up the ball with my glove and switch it to my bare hand. I take off the glove under my right arm and rub up the baseball with both hands as I dig a comfortable divot in front of the rubber. After that, I warmed up and told them that I was ready to go. They asked for five fastballs. I wound up and fired as hard as I could. I felt strong beforehand and my adrenaline was flowing, so the two things probably raised the velocity of my fastball by about five miles-per-hour. This is a common occurrence in the Majors too. The pitcher may not have great velocity warming up in the bullpen, but once they get into the game, the crowd and the pressure get their adrenaline to flow and that increases their speed.

They told me to throw five each of my other pitches. I wrapped my fingers around my curveball and fired one after another. They broke down hard, fast and late. That is extremely important. The closer to the hitting zone the ball moves, the harder it is to hit. I threw five fork-balls that moved well too. The spin is awkward and undefined so it is hard for the batter to judge what the pitch is by the rotation. It was going straight toward the plate and shooting down and away or down and in. I can control that to a certain extent depending on the amount of pressure I apply with my fingers. I didn't throw any more breaking pitches, even though there is one that I do use in a pinch. It is a violent pitch I call the twister. It's sort of like a slider, only more violent. It puts a strain on the whole arm so I throw it only four or five times in a game when I absolutely, positively need an out. But I don't think it's a good idea to throw a pitch in a tryout that shows the potential for arm strain. I also didn't throw my scuffball. I have an ingenious way to avoid detection. I've had umpires check the ball, my glove and borderline strip-search me with no payoff. There was no need for that pitch. I save that for games too. The scouts asked for two more fastballs and that was it. They told me the same thing they told all the other guys. They would contact me if there was any interest. I thanked them and drove home. I wasn't sure what they were thinking. You can never tell with scouts. I thought that I'd thrown well, but didn't get my hopes up.

8

"How'd it go?" Mother asked as soon as I walked in the house.
"I'm not sure," I said. "Who knows what they're gonna do?"
"Well, did they say anything?"
Maybe Amy should have been a lawyer instead of just managing the office. This was going to be a long interrogation. And I would have to repeat the whole treatment for my father when he got home.
"Mother," I said in frustration, "at this point, you know as much as I do. If they're interested in me or want to sign me, they'll contact me. I don't know any more about this than you do. Which isn't much."
I wasn't in the mood.
"What's your problem?" she said in a raised voice.

I just raised my hands and walked into my room without response. I didn't want to fight.

I was in no mood to delineate my whole big day with the Dodgers. She means well, but she can be a pest. My father got home from work and I gave them both a brief synopsis of what happened. "We threw about twenty pitches each. We ran. They timed us with stopwatches. There were only eleven guys there. They clocked our pitches with radar-guns. Blah, blah, blah."

Starting Monday I had to start looking for a summer job and there was also the tiny matter of which four-year college I was going to attend. I had much on my mind.

9

I didn't hear from the Dodgers or any other team for that matter. So, since it was Saturday, I decided to go and have a few drinks and look for women. I have a fake driver's license that states that I am twenty-three. It gets me in everywhere, except of course when there's a transvestite at the door deciding whether or not he likes the way I'm dressed. I prefer plain bars anyway. It's easier to pick up women. So, a couple of friends and I went to a '70s club with the posters from the '70s and the music from the '70s. People even try and dress the way they did, showing up in bell-bottoms and other god-awful get-ups. I had two Long Island Iced Teas, which got me hammered, and I didn't even meet any women. It wasn't my night. I consoled myself with the fact that I was going to have to deal with Mark Mattera in a few hours.

10

I'm a cheap drunk, but I never get hung over. Never. I'm always able to get through my day whether I've been out the night before. I wasn't scheduled to pitch anyway, although with Mark, you never know. I was getting my uniform ready to head for Narrows Field at noon. No Parade Grounds. We were playing the sandlot version of the Brooklyn Dodgers and they use the nicely manicured Narrows Field, which during the college season is used by St. Francis. The Dodgers always beat us. I looked forward to sitting in the nice bullpen that Narrows Field has. As I was putting on my shoes to leave the house, my phone rang.

"Yello?"

"Is Brett Samuels there please?" a voice with a Spanish-sounding accent asked.

"Who's calling?" I didn't feel like discussing my long-distance service carrier.

"This is Juan Ramos from the Los Angeles Dodgers," he said.

I dropped the receiver onto the carpet in my room and snatched it up quickly by the wire.

This wasn't happening. Was it?

"Um, yeah! This is Brett!" I said excitedly.

"How are you today, Brett? I was wondering if it might be possible to drop by your house to talk about a contract?"

"Umm, oh, yeah…" I stammered. I caught hold of myself. "Absolutely, you can come over. I'll come to you if you want."

He chuckled. "That won't be necessary."

I gave him my address (even though he already had it), and ran in to tell my parents. I had to repeat it three times before they seemed to comprehend what I was saying. Not only was I going to be a professional baseball player, but they wouldn't have to support me anymore. At least until the season ended.

11

I waited impatiently for Ramos to arrive. I didn't think the contract would be anything too complicated. I wasn't a draft choice and they weren't under any obligation to offer me any kind of bonus. I wasn't going to push my luck by asking for one. The last thing I needed was to say something stupid and for the guy to change his mind. When the draft is held, all of the players drafted get some kind of a bonus. The last player drafted gets a bonus. It's not much compared to what the top to middle rounders get, but it's *something*. An undrafted free agent, like me, gets whatever the team wants to offer. Occasionally there are free agents that are coveted by several teams. Those guys get a bonus. I am not one of those guys.

Juan Ramos rang the bell to our two-family house and as he was coming up the stairs I admonished my father not to say anything stupid. Samuels men have a genetic quirk where we engage our mouths before our brain is in gear. My mother has picked up a lot of legalese working in the law office and was going to look at the contract. I didn't need an agent as there wasn't much to negotiate. Ramos came in the door and shook hands all around. He told me what the deal was. I would receive no bonus. I would receive a plane ticket from New York to the Dodgers' rookie team in Great Falls, Montana.

Montana? Jeez.

I would be put up as a border with a family in Great Falls. The season started on June 16. It's not an easy life, traveling on buses, eating crappy food and playing baseball every night trying to learn to be a professional. He continued on for a few moments. My head was in the clouds. I probably would have agreed to anything. The guy was offering me something that, until now, was nothing more than a pipe dream. He handed me the contract and my mother looked at it with my father looking over her shoulder. At the top it said, "PLAYER'S CONTRACT." I would receive $900 a month from June through the first few days of September. If I were sent to any Fall or Instructional leagues, I would receive the same salary. Otherwise, I would go home and wait for another contract to stay with the organization or I would be released. I took the contract from my mother and laid it on the table. I took my father's lucky Parker pen, turned the top to extend the tip and signed the contract. I was now officially a professional baseball player. Property of the Los Angeles Dodgers.

12

I called Traella right afterwards to tell him that I would no longer be a member of the Brooklyn Rockies. Screw Mark, I thought to myself. Why should I call that idiot? Let Rob break the news. Rob was happy for me and imparted some friendly advice. "Remember how you managed to keep your mouth shut at the workout?"

"Yeah," I said.

"Well, keep doing that," he said.

I laughed. "I'll do the best I can."

"Good luck," he said.

Before he hung up, I had one more favor to ask of him.

"Rob, you have to do one thing for me."

"What?"

"Get Mark to say I stink. Not just that I stink. Get him to do the whole routine. 'Fuck 'im, he stinks.' The works."

"I doubt that'll be too hard," he said.

Mother seemed uptight about her nineteen-year-old son leaving home for the first time. I asked her what the difference would be if I was going into the military like she and my father had suggested numerous times. She thought that the military was a more regimented structure. She had no idea how the Los Angeles Dodgers' farm system was going to keep me in line. Like I was some kind of a wild-man or something. My father was happy. I wasn't sure if it was because I was going pro or because I was leaving. He said it was a little of both.

To tell the truth, *I* was a little nervous about leaving home. True, it would be the same thing if I were going to college. But, it's scarier when you finally get an opportunity to fulfill a dream and don't know if you can handle it. I didn't want to come home a failure after finally getting my opportunity. This was happening so fast. I was leaving in two days. *Two*.

I'm not the type to start drinking and smoking and doing drugs as soon as I'm out of my parents' sight. Women were another matter, but I could handle that with a smile. I was really going off on my own, though. I'd have to open a bank account and handle my finances. I'd have to feed myself and iron my own clothes. I'd have to do it all myself. I'd be living with strange people and using a strange bathroom. I have a thing about bathrooms.

I'd be going to places I'd never been. This was all so exhilarating and frightening. I forgot to mention that the odds of my making it to the Majors had to be astronomical, whether I was a professional or not. I didn't want to fall by the wayside, but the odds were not in my favor.

13

Opening day for the Pioneer League was June 16. I had a plane ticket reserved for me at John F. Kennedy International Airport to take me to Montana. There aren't any direct flights from New York to Montana. I was flying on Delta Airlines Flight 1429 to Salt Lake City, Utah, and from there I was taking Flight 473 to Great Falls, Montana. The layover between the two was about an hour.

I had much to do in the days before I left. My father would have to take care of my car. I had thought about having it shipped but decided against it. What did I really need it for out there? I would be on the road half the time anyway. I didn't think that there were many places to drive *to* in Great Falls, Montana.

I had a week to settle in before the opening of the season. There were lots of practices scheduled from what I understood. My mother was asking nine zillion questions about what's going to go on there.

"How do I know?" I screeched.

I have three decibel levels when I get annoyed. One is just a feminine squeal. Two is halfway between a squeal and a full-blown yell. Three is out and out screaming like a raving lunatic. Very rarely does that happen.

She just kept on. "What's the supervision like over there? Who's in charge? Where will you live?"

I felt like I was twelve and going away to camp. What would she have done if it was wartime and I was going to fight with grenades and guns instead of bats and balls?

She probably would have dealt with that better. My father is retired Air Force. He was in for twenty-two years and saw some combat action. He's killed people, even though he doesn't like to discuss it. He has trouble expressing his feelings.

"There's an Air Force base near where you're gonna be," he said simply. I still have my military ID, so I told him I'd check it out.

There weren't many people to share the news of my good fortune with. I wasn't tight with anyone on my college team. Friendly? Yes. Tight? No. My closest friend Tony Taglianetti was already in the minors. He went to Christ the King High School and was drafted in the thirtieth round by the Florida Marlins out of high school. An infielder that plays every day at a different position, he was in A ball — a level above where I was going. His versatility makes him very useful and he could make the Majors. When I called him to tell him the surprising news it took fifteen minutes to convince him that I was telling the truth. I had kept him appraised on my stellar improvement, but I think he thought I was making up stories.

"Yeah man, it's true," I insisted.

"Brett, who you bullshitting?"

"It's true."

This went on and on. I had to put my mother and father on the phone to finally convince him. He reacted much like my father. I think that they just want to make sure that I stay on an even keel. If I get too many congratulatory statements, my head might inflate to the point where I couldn't fit through the door of the clubhouse.

14

I packed my bags for my trip and I brought just about every article of clothing that I own. I made certain that I brought my spikes, glove and, yes, even my cup (they might force you to wear them). Coach Roessler called me the day before my flight.

"Brett, Lou Roessler here."

"Hey coach."

"I just called to wish you luck. Just do as you're told and no screwing around the night before you pitch." I *think* that was a joke.

"I'll try and control myself," I said laughingly.

"Just control your emotions and you'll do fine. You can call me if you need anything," he said.

"Thanks coach. I appreciate everything you've done for me."

What a great man and a great coach Lou Roessler is. The numbers of kids that he has helped in his twenty-two-year coaching career is countless.

Almost immediately after I hung up the phone, it rang again.

"Yello?"

The voice on the other end didn't even say hello.

"Why the fuck didn't you call me like a man and tell me you were leaving?" the voice demanded.

After speaking to Roessler, I now had the extreme displeasure of speaking to the exact opposite side of the coaching spectrum.

"Excuse me?" I said in a low voice.

"I deserve some respect. I'm the one that caused all of this to happen. Guys like you don't appreciate a fucking thing," Mark Mattera screamed.

"Listen Mark," I said calmly, "I don't have any obligation to you. You did nothing for me. You're a raving lunatic who's clueless. Don't you *dare* say that you caused this to happen. You did *nothing*." I was about to hang up, but then he said something else.

"You were nothing before I found you."

That was it. I started screaming.

"LET ME TELL YOU SOMETHING YOU FUCKIN' ASSHOLE. YOU'RE A LOSER AND NOBODY FUCKING RESPECTS YOU…"

"No one respects…" He sputtered trying to interrupt, but I plowed on.

"…THE WHOLE LEAGUE THINKS YOU'RE A JOKE, MARK! YOU'RE A LOW CLASS NOBODY, YOU FUCKING LOSER!"

"Why you…" He sounded like he was having a coronary and I slammed the phone down.

It took me a few minutes to calm down, but at least I told Mark what I thought of him. It felt very cleansing.

15

My parents drove me to Kennedy Airport for my scheduled 7:10 A.M. flight. They both took off from work to see me away. We found a cart in the parking lot and went into the Delta terminal and I checked in. I worried for some reason that the ticket wouldn't be there and the Dodgers had changed their minds. It was there though. I checked my bags in. I had two large bags in addition to my backpack. I packed almost every article of clothing that I owned and plenty of CDs. My parents were nervous. Mother was the obvious one and Dad was more outwardly cool. I'd be home in a couple of months. I bought a few magazines in the terminal shop and didn't eat anything. I hate eating that early in the morning. Boarding was beginning at 6:40 and I saw no reason to hang around. My mother hugged me before I walked to the gate. That was surprising for a Jewish family. It's very rare in fact.

"Be good," she said. I gave her a funny look.

"I'm an adult human being, Mother. You know you can trust me," I said with a smirk.

"Be good," she repeated.

"Yeah, yeah, yeah," I said as I walked through the gate.

I wanted to look back, but didn't.

16

I don't mind flying as long as the plane isn't packed, but of course it was. I'd never flown Delta before and the flight was surprisingly pleasant. It took three hours and we landed on time. I got off the plane in Salt Lake City and watched as people greeted their families and friends. Small airport, I thought. I was expecting there to be Mormons walking around like zombies waiting to try to convert the *Jew*. But there were none.

I had to head straight for my next flight. Delta Flight 473 from Salt Lake City to Great Falls. That flight was an hour and a half. We boarded the plane on the runway. It was a small plane. It wasn't as crowded as the first plane. I don't like crowds unless they're in the stands of a stadium and chanting my name.

I didn't know much about Great Falls, Montana, but I was sure that it was going to be less exciting than New York. That's not going out on too much of a limb. It's not a large town, but that meant there was less of an opportunity for me to get into trouble.

17

The general manager of the Great Falls Dodgers, Mason Standt, was at the airport to pick me up. It made me feel important until I realized that the coaches, manager, and front office types do *everything* no matter how repulsive the task. He talked to me a little bit. He knew a precious few things about a fascinating character such as myself. I thought it was his job to know the players. The only thing he said he heard about me was that I had a great curve. I just nodded. I didn't want to say anything stupid. My paranoia was increasing as the stakes grew higher. I didn't want to jeopardize my spot before I'd even started. Paranoia is a major part of my psyche. Standt mentioned some of the famous players that have passed through Great Falls. "You have an opportunity to be one someday," he said.

Everything was going to be explained at the first team meeting two days after my arrival. As we drove through Great Falls, it looked quiet and boring. Maybe it was better that way. He dropped my bags and me at the home of Karen and Bill Crane. They were the people I was to board with. The Cranes were, by my guess, in their mid-fifties. They were very polite and had sandwiches and milk waiting for me. I felt like I was coming home from school. I can't drink milk because I'm lactose intolerant, but I appreciated the gesture. Karen was short and slightly overweight with short blonde hair and glasses. Bill was bald with a cowboy hat and a paunch hanging over an oversized belt buckle with a steer on it. They seemed extremely nice and I hoped not to irritate them with my obsessive-compulsive habits. They had been boarding ballplayers since 1982 and had a spacious house. They told me that the other player that was living in the house was out, but should be home shortly.

18

I started to learn a bit about Great Falls. Great Falls is the second largest city in Montana with a population of around 55,000. That's small. It's even smaller when you consider that I'm from Brooklyn, New York. There are at least 55,000 morons in Bensonhurst alone. The move to the small town would be a big adjustment.

The famous thing about Great Falls is, of course, the Great Falls. There are five waterfalls on the Missouri River. Lewis and Clark spent a month trying to find their way around the falls during their expedition in 1805. Great Falls is almost all white and is a mostly agricultural town. Maelstrom Air Force Base is nearby just as Dad said.

There are events in Great Falls, but they're not the types of things to interest me. They have the pet and doll parade, the spring fling hoop thing (whatever that is), the Columbia sheep show and sale, the Cascade County 4-H livestock show, the altered classics car show, the miniature horse show and the big one: the Montana State Fair. This all sounded like stuff my parents would like. My mother loves doll shows and my dad would go for the cars and horses. Nothing much for me though. Good thing I figured to be pretty busy. Oh, I almost forgot about the Jesus Christ meeting. Everywhere I go people try and introduce me to Jesus. I've avoided the introductions so far. How much longer can I duck Jesus?

19

Great Falls of the Pioneer League has been an affiliate of the Los Angeles Dodgers since 1984 and in the Pioneer League since 1969. They've been in Legion Park since 1956.

The Pioneer League consists of eight teams in two divisions. They play 76 games from around mid–June to the first few days of September. After that there are two best of three playoff series. The winner of each division in the first half plays the winner of the division in the second half. That winner plays the other division's winner for the championship. The North Division has teams in Great Falls, Helena, Lethbridge, and Medicine Hat. The South Division has teams in Butte, Billings, Idaho Falls, and Ogden.

The teams are allowed to carry up to thirty active players on their roster. There are two rookie league teams in most organizations (the Dodgers have three). Generally one team is playing in the States and one in the Dominican Summer League (DSL). The Dodgers have two Dominican Summer League teams. A lot of great players come out of the Dominican Republic these days. From these teams, some players will be released, some will move up, and some will stay in rookie ball. Two years in rookie ball is not recommended. How many of these players might make it to the Majors? Not will, but *might*? About five or six in every organization. And that's being generous. It's harder with the Dodgers because there is that extra rookie team. My odds weren't real good, especially since I was probably there just to fill out the roster. But they were better than they were a month before.

20

At about 7:00 P.M. the evening of my arrival, I was unpacking and getting myself settled in my room. It was a nice room with a single bed, two brown dressers, a mirror and a small television. There were two flowery painted pictures on the walls to make things look pretty. I had my back to the slightly open door when I heard a knock. I turned around and was frightened at first. Standing in my doorway was what looked like a solar eclipse.

"Hi," he said extending a hand, "I'm Jon Duerson."

The guy was huge. A gigantic black man with a pleasant face and a crew cut. If I'd seen him walking along the nighttime streets of New York, I might have crossed the street. That's not politically correct, I know. I shook his immense paw and watched my hand disappear in his. He almost broke my hand with his grip.

"How big are you?" I asked without saying hello.

He gave me a puzzled half frown and said, "Six five, two forty."

"Jeez," I said.

He looked perplexed. Was I being obnoxious? I didn't think so.

"What are you, an infielder or something?" he asked in a deep voice with an ever so slight Southern drawl.

"I'm a pitcher, man." Everybody thinks I'm an infielder.

"Huh," he said without much interest.

It is true that I'm below average height for a pitcher, but for the population as a whole, I'm above average at 5'11".

We chatted for a moment. Jon was an 18-year-old catcher from Georgia taken in the second round. He'd arrived two days before I had.

26

Great Falls is much less exciting than Atlanta, he told me. I couldn't even begin to describe how dead it seemed compared to New York and I'd only been there for a few hours. Jon seemed to think all of the basic stereotypes about New York were true.

"What's with that mayor of yours over there?" he asked.

Everybody asks about good old Rudy.

"I hear he's an asshole," Jon said.

"Well," I responded, "asshole or not, he's cleaned up the city."

Jon had hit thirteen home runs in his senior year in a private high school in suburban Atlanta. I told him of my less conventional route to the pro ranks.

"Well, you never know," he said.

I didn't detect as deep a Southern accent as you might expect from a black guy from Georgia. I learned why when he told me that his father is a heart surgeon from San Diego and his mother is a French interior designer. So much for my stereotypes.

He had a girlfriend back in Georgia that he showed me a picture of. She looked like Michele Pfeiffer. My enlightened father would have said, "She's white, huh?" but I refrained from giving in to my genetic stupidity. I decided right then and there that if there was ever a bench clearing fight, here was the man I was going to hide behind. He told me about some of the prodigious homers he's hit. I told him about some of the prodigious homers I've *allowed*.

21

Duerson brought his car from Atlanta, a two-year-old white Acura, and he and I left the house two days later for the first team meeting. The meeting was scheduled for 9:00 A.M., but we left the house at 8:00 so we would definitely be on time. Walking into the locker-room at Legion Park I saw that there were only about five other guys there. Duerson had met them earlier. He introduced me around. One was an outfielder from Orlando, Florida, named David Christenson. He was 6'1" and 225 pounds and he was *built*. You could see through his baggy T-shirt and khaki shorts how ripped and huge his muscles were. I immediately thought that he was on steroids. I know the look. A couple of people I know have used them on and off for years. He was tan with dark hair, dark eyes and a sculpted menacing goatee. He looks like the type that women fall at the feet of.

There were names written on tape over the lockers. Guys were unpacking their stuff, so I found my locker and did the same.

The locker-room was up to the standard for many of the guys from the warmer weather states. For the minors it was first class. That's one thing about the Dodgers; they do things first class. The New York sand-lot locker-rooms, if there are any, are crap. The lockers were arranged in a large rectangle with two long tables in the middle of the room. There was a smaller round table off to the left with chairs around it and a couple of guys sat around it and played cards. There was a room off to the side with medicines, trainers' tools and a training table. Then there was a small manager's office near the back of the room. The lockers were alphabetically arranged. There was a shower in the back with a whirlpool. The showers weren't separated by partitions; there were just nozzles a few feet from each other. I wasn't too thrilled with the idea of showering with a group of men. It had nothing to do with homophobia, but I prefer to either shower alone or with a female. This would take some getting used to. All the guys seemed to be in the room as the appointed meeting time arrived. A tall, handsome black man with a neat afro flecked with gray walked into the clubhouse and to the front of the room. He was dressed casually in a collared sport shirt and slacks. I knew him from someplace.

22

Thirty guys were seated in the locker-room. All I could think of as I looked at our manager was I know this guy, I know this guy. I just couldn't put my finger on it.

"Good morning," he began. "My name is James Witherspoon."

That's it! James Witherspoon: former infielder for the Padres and Reds. I knew I knew him from someplace. He was a useful component on some good teams in the mid-to-late eighties and early nineties. He got traded from the Reds the year before they won the World Series in 1990. He'd never appeared in the postseason. As I recall, he was a pretty good player who played lots of positions. He was now forty-two and trying his hand at managing. He looked like he could still play.

He proceeded to tell us the rules of conduct for the Great Falls Dodgers.

"First of all, be on time. If the bus is scheduled to leave at eight A.M., it leaves at eight A.M. No excuses. No exceptions. Secondly, on the road there will be no, I repeat, no women in the motel rooms. If you get caught with a woman in your room you will be suspended or released. We do check. Hair must be neatly trimmed and not one inch over the collar. Mustaches must be neatly trimmed and no beards or goatees."

A number of guys had goatees. They looked around the room at the announcement of that rule.

"As for the ears, noses, tongues, eyebrows or whatever else you guys have pierced," he said, eliciting a slight laugh as he waved his hand back and forth, "they're out during games, practices, team functions, and road trips."

This was going to be a slight problem for me. Unlike some other guys, all I have is an earring. No tattoos or anything. Just an earring. The thing about my earring, though, is that it is a thing called a ball hoop. A ball hoop has a metal ball with two small notches where the hoop connects to the ball. They're very difficult to insert. The ball is small and the hoop part doesn't give way and you have to force it in. It hurts and takes a long time if you're clumsy and I have a tendency to be clumsy. Now I had to take it in and out almost daily. I wouldn't wear it at all, but I didn't want the hole to close. How inconvenient. I'd have to buy a new earring that wouldn't look as good. I like my ball hoop though. This is man stuff.

"And regarding tobacco," Witherspoon went on noticing several guys in the room with either dip or chew in their mouths, "there is no tobacco allowed on the field in any of the minor leagues. None."

The guys really groaned about that one.

Witherspoon shrugged. "Personally, I don't care if you want to dip or not, but rules are rules. No dip on the field or in the dugouts or bullpens."

Dip is sold in small circular canisters and guys put it between their lower lip and gums. It's flavored in cherry or wintergreen and other flavors. When you first try it, it gets you hammered. I was stumbling around the bullpen the first time I tried it with the Rockies. But, it's like any other drug. You never get the same feeling each subsequent time as you did the first time. But, you keep doing it because it becomes wired into you. If you quit you get the same type of withdrawal symptoms as with harder drugs only to a lesser degree. Also, you can't swallow any of the juices or you'll get sick. A few rare exceptions are the guys who use it only at the ballpark. Others are constantly walking around with a cup or bottle filled with brown spit. They carry them everywhere. I knew one guy in college who had dip in his mouth every time I saw him. *Every time.* It could be morning, noon or night. There was always a brown puddle in front of him. Guys chewing tobacco are easy to spot. They're the ones with one of their cheeks puffed out like a chipmunk. The guys with dip are harder to spot. If you see someone with their lower lip over their bottom teeth as if they're trying to get a closer shave on their chin and they let out a little spit once in a while, then you've found a player dipping. Kids were doing it to emulate their heroes, so baseball was trying to wean the minor leaguers right from the start. I don't know if it has worked. One approach that is working is the former Major Leaguer Bill Tuttle talking to the players. Tuttle chewed tobacco for years until he got mouth cancer and had to get his jaw amputated. If that doesn't scare kids straight, I don't know what will.

Finally, Witherspoon said, "The main thing is for you guys to behave in a professional manner on and off the field. The last thing I need or want is aggravation. I'm a patient man. I'm here to teach you how to play professional baseball and how to act like a professional. I'm easy to deal with. Just do your job." Sounded fair to me.

Discipline generally loosens as you climb the minor league ladder. Occasionally, you run into a drill-sergeant type who says, "Baseball is war." And nonsense like that. Down here in rookie ball, a certain amount of discipline is necessary with the seventeen to twenty-one year olds. Many of us were away from home for the first time. The temptation to go wild was rampant and readily available.

We went in alphabetical order to get our uniforms, practice jerseys, caps and jackets. I wound up with number fifteen. I wore twelve in high school and sixteen in college. Most ballplayers are particular about their uniform number. There are good and bad pitchers' numbers. Fifteen is a good pitcher's number. Duerson had to take the biggest uniform available and wound up with number three. The uniforms had Dodgers in script across the front just like in the big leagues. The jackets were the same. They were royal blue with Dodgers in white lettering scripted across the front. The hats had a G over an F signifying Great Falls. I tried on my hat, size 7⅛. It fit, but my hair fanned out to the sides of my head. It's really thick and curly and without getting it cut regularly I start to look like Krusty the Clown.

The first practice was at 9:00 A.M. the next day.

23

There were thirteen pitchers and seventeen position players on the team. Six of the guys were on their second tour of duty with Great Falls. Watching them in practice made me wonder what goes through a scout's mind when he recommends a player. Some of these guys wouldn't have made my college team. It couldn't have been that they weren't in shape; they'd been playing and working out for at least the last four months. They just weren't any good.

We had a light workout. The pitching coach had us throwing in the bullpen and was watching our mechanics. I immediately didn't like this guy. Standing about 5'10" with a greasy mustache and greasy hair and about three spare tires around his middle, he looked like an aging porno star. Real sleazy. He had a feminine way of speaking and walking and laughed at his own jokes in guttural sounds. It sounded like, "Guuuhhhh huhhh."

The first thing he told me when I threw my curve was, "You can't hold a ball that way."

"Ugh," I said under my breath trying to remind myself to keep my mouth shut.

I hold my curveball in a very unusual way. My middle finger is resting against the seam and my index finger is on top of the middle finger as if I have my fingers crossed. I'm applying intense pressure to the middle finger with my index finger. That pressure carries through to the ball. My thumb is on the bottom of the ball lined up with my middle finger. I let my forearm apply the force on the side of the ball and pull down at the end as I throw. This causes a sharp, nasty break. This coach, Jeff Finestra, whom I'd never heard of, failed to see the break. He focused on my grip. Everyone's got something to say. I didn't argue with him, but I asked politely, "What difference does it make how I hold the ball as long as it does what it's supposed to do?" He immediately ran to get Witherspoon like a child.

I'm gone.

That's all I could think of. The first practice and I'm gone. The other guys were watching to see what was going to happen. One pitcher, Matt Bradley whispered, "Cool it, dude. They're gonna toss you out." It was too late.

Witherspoon had been behind the batting cage watching the hitters hit when he came to the bullpen with Finestra.

"What's the problem?" he asked me.

"No problem," I said. "This is the way I hold my curve. He's telling me it's wrong." I said gesturing at Finestra with my head.

"Throw it," Witherspoon said.

I wound up and threw my curve.

"Another one."

I threw another one.

Witherspoon looked at Finestra and pulled him to the side. "I don't need this baby shit," he said in an annoyed tone. "The kid has a good curveball. Leave him be."

"Yeah, but..." Finestra started to protest.

"Yeah, but what? It does what it's supposed to do. Let the kid hold it any way he wants."

Witherspoon walked off. Even though he'd pulled Finestra off to the side, we heard the whole exchange. This was not a good relationship. I didn't think that this was James Witherspoon's hand-picked pitching coach.

Finestra basically threw a tantrum for the rest of the day. He was stomping around and making faces. Very mature. We were looking at each other as if to say, "This is our pitching coach?"

Baseball practices are, by nature, tedious. Everyone runs at some point, but running is about all we pitchers have to do. We stretch, run, get our throwing in, run, work on our location, run. Running consists of basic sprints called poles. Running from one foul line to another to build up leg strength. I never had much of a taste for that. Distance running is a little more palatable for me. One thing I *cannot* stand is the repetitive drills that we have to run over and over again.

Ground ball to the right side, pitcher covers first. Ground ball to the right side, pitcher covers first. Ground ball to the right side, pitcher covers first.

Over and over and over again. It's the worst. I don't even think it does that much good because half the guys on this level screw it up anyway. Either they drop the ball, or the runner beats them to the base. Guys in the Majors screw it up. What do they expect from us?

Practice lasted four hours and Witherspoon let us go. On the ride home, Duerson was raving about Witherspoon and coach Billy Hanson. He asked me how Finestra was.

I scrunched up my face.

"Yeesh. I have no idea where they found this guy. I was there for two minutes and he was telling me how my curveball grip is wrong. The curve is the only reason I'm here. I'm no high draft choice like you. I make do with what I got."

"What happened?" Jon asked. I related the story.

"Don't worry about it. Witherspoon doesn't look like the type to put up with much crap. Finestra won't last here if he keeps that stuff up. Watch," Duerson said.

"A guy can dream I guess," I said.

24

Practices were becoming more slow and redundant as opening day rapidly approached. Witherspoon seemed to be deciding who his starting pitchers and relief pitchers would be. The ones drafted as starters would start and the ones drafted as relievers would relieve. I'd probably be the mop-up man, I thought. I wasn't complaining, mind you. I was just happy to be there.

I wasn't happy about Finestra the "pitching coach." I never thought anyone would make me miss Mark Mattera, but Finestra somehow managed it. All this guy seemed to do was stalk around the pitchers as they did their work, laugh his disgusting laugh, "guuuuhhh huhhhh," and talk about how honest he was and that he was a pitcher.

"Iiiiii'm a pitcherr. Iiiiii'm being ohhhnest," he said with his head tilted.

He was vile. None of the pitchers could stand him and Witherspoon knew it. We thought he might be trying to dump him, but was meeting with resistance from the front office. There had to be some strange reason Finestra was kept around. I actually saw Finestra drop a glob of spit out of his mouth and catch it with the back of his hand and suck it back into his mouth. I almost passed out. The previous year's manager, Stan Cox, kept Finestra around all year. It didn't look like that was going to happen again. At least that's what everybody hoped.

25

One day, after practice, a company representative from Rawlings named Michael Shaw was in the locker-room to talk to us. Everyone who gets signed to play in the minors signs with a major glove company. Most every guy gets the same basic deal regardless of which company he signs with. Once in a while a hotshot will be coming out of college as a sure-fire Major Leaguer and he'll be able to make his own deal. But schleps like me sign with Rawlings or Louisville Slugger or whoever. I've always used Rawlings gloves. They seem to have the best leather. The basic deal that Rawlings gives to 99.9 percent of the players is a four-year contract with two free gloves per year. You get the fielding glove of your choice. No batting gloves or bats. Just the fielding glove. That was fine with me. I have no use for bats or batting gloves since they use the designated hitter in the Pioneer League.

I picked two nice gloves. One was the Pro-24TL. It has a tan shell and is called a Trap-eze model. It doesn't have the usual webbing. It has five stubby fingers and there are laces going up where the webbing would usually be. It makes you catch the ball in the pocket where you're supposed to catch it. Ozzie Smith and Ken Griffey, Jr., use the Trapeze model.

The other was a Pro 504TL model. That was a regular glove with customary webbing that you see in a sporting goods store. Infielders and outfielders sometimes use gloves with open webbing. I've seen pitchers use gloves with an open webbing. How are they supposed to hide the ball that way? I've always used closed webbing gloves. Retail, these gloves would cost about $200 a pop. We get them for free. I like the perks that come with playing pro baseball. I'd break them in slowly while using my black Rawlings Pro-8 that I'd had for a couple of years.

Everyone has a different method of breaking in their gloves. Some guys run over them with their cars. Some put them in the microwave. Some beat the glove with a special hammer that shapes and loosens the leather. I've always soaked the glove in warm water, then stuffed two baseballs in the pocket and tied the glove closed. Once it's dry, I rub shaving cream in the palm and shape it the way I want. Then I play catch with it until it's loose. Then I can use it in a game. Some guys stick their index fingers out the back of the glove to cushion the blow of catching the ball. I just don't catch the ball effectively that way. I don't know why.

26

Opening day was two days away. Workouts were becoming more intense and Witherspoon looked about ready to kill Finestra. Now Finestra was snatching the ball out of guys' hands to show off his horrendous knuckleball. Why? I have no idea. A knuckleball is supposed to be thrown with the fingertips and have no spin. The wind and air currents make it do crazy things. I can't explain the physics. Our second baseman, Don Bosetti, throws a good one. I've told him that if he doesn't make it as an infielder, he could make it as a pitcher. He's 5'10" from Huntington Beach, California. Very intense. A man of few words. He mostly grunts.

After practice the general manager of the big club came down to check out the new recruits, see how we were progressing and talk to us. After practice we gathered in the clubhouse for a pep talk from Dodgers GM Stephen Jones. He gives this talk every year apparently. Jones is 6'2" and has perfectly coifed, gelled, styled hair and dresses immaculately. He looks like Gordon Gekko from *Wall Street*. He never played in the majors; he played several years in the minors with the Mets and Dodgers. After he retired he became a scout and worked his way up to his current position. I'll never forget that meeting.

The following is his multi-syllabic speech verbatim:

"Good morning, gentlemen. Presented to you at this moment is a befalling. An abundance of aptitude has dropped anchor. Without exception, an individual in association with the Los Angeles Dodgers baseball club has witnessed a capability in each and every one of you. I won't prevaricate. This vocation is non-yielding. Only a smattering of you shall receive the ultimate accolade of becoming a member of the Los Angeles Dodgers. The thoroughfare is lofty. Those of you who attain the highest honor will be requited for your intrepidity."

There was silence. Guys were sneaking bewildered glances at each other.

"Any questions?"

Silence.

"I shall be observant of your development."

Silence.

"Godspeed, gentlemen."

Then he turned and disappeared with Witherspoon into the manager's office and closed the door.

"Brett," Mike Strock, a pitcher from San Diego called to me, "you're smart. What the fuck did he just say?"

"Hey man, I stopped listening after we dropped anchor," I whispered.

27

Our season finally opened on June 16. The Medicine Hat Blue Jays were in for four games. The Blue Jays organization doesn't worry about winning in rookie ball. They draft kids with the intention of teaching them how to play. Perennially the team is not very good. The players are talented, but as a team they're too young and inexperienced to win. Some teams send twenty- and twenty-one-year-old veterans down to the rookie leagues to try and win. That makes no sense whatsoever. The point of this league is to *teach*. Winning is secondary. There's no real point in padding an organization's record down in the bushes. Developing players should be the number one priority.

The lineup was posted before the game. Mostly the higher draft picks and better prospects were starting for us. Our starting pitcher was a twenty-one-year-old lefty from Denver named Wade Mills. He's 6'4" and 220 pounds with dreadlocks and tattoos all over his body. He had a pierced tongue, but took it out because of team rules. He hadn't been pitching all that long, but the Dodgers drafted him in the eighth round from Arizona State as an outfielder who would pitch occasionally. The organization decided that he would be nothing more than a pitcher and he groused about it. He seemed to be a minor attitude problem. He threw very hard, but was wild. He could bring it up into the midnineties and he had no clue as to where the ball was going. They were trying him as a starter, but his future looked to be in the pen.

Things were tense in the clubhouse before the game. Guys prepare in different ways. Some smoke, some play cards, others listen to music to pump themselves up. Witherspoon had to let the pitchers know what their roles were. That's usually the pitching coach's job, but our pitching coach was clueless and Witherspoon ignored him as much as possible.

How odd is this little nugget? Finestra has a male roommate that has lived with him in-season and off-season for ten years. Did I hear someone say longtime companion? Just a hunch.

There was much pomp and circumstance for opening day. There seemed to be around 2,500 people in the stands, by my best guess. There was red, white and blue bunting around the stands and the team executives spoke to the crowd before the game, celebrating another season of Great Falls Dodgers baseball. I was wearing my jacket because it gets chilly at night in Montana. The early mornings and nights are cold. Even in June. I started to get discouraged because I didn't see any way in which I was going to get much of a chance to play. I was the last pitcher on the staff as best I could tell. There were too many guys who were high draft picks. Those guys were given big bonuses and were going to play. My only hope was to perform well when the opportunity arose. *If* the opportunity arose. Would I get an opportunity?

The game started and Mills opened by walking the bases loaded. It didn't matter that he was throwing bullets. None of them were over the plate. Duerson went out to calm Mills. Mills then struck out the side on ten pitches. The guy has good stuff.

There isn't much to do in games that you're not playing in. You have to find ways to amuse yourself. The bullpen is the place to be for goofing around. Just don't let the manager catch you. They let you play around within reason, but you can't be too crazy. They keep a tight rein in rookie ball.

Mills started walking the ballpark again in the third inning. He walked two and gave up a two run double. Then in the fifth he gave up a three run home run. The Medicine Hat Blue Jays were looking better than their reputation. Mills got hooked after allowing six runs in six innings. Jaime Robles and Mike Strock finished the game for us. We were shut out until Christenson, looking uncomfortable without his goatee, hit a towering homer over the centerfield fence with two outs in the ninth. That elicited the only cheers we received since the start of the game. Duerson struck out to end the game. We lost 6–1.

I didn't get to pitch in games two or three either. Was I ever going to get into a game? We lost both of those games. We were 0–3. Not a good start. I know we were there to learn, but I'd like to win once in a while. Duerson homered in game two. As soon as he hit it I thought it was going to Mars. It still hasn't landed. I have never seen a homer go that far. It went completely *over* the center field fence and disappeared into the Montana night. It didn't help us win.

Two things happened in the fourth game of the series: We won and I got into my first professional game.

Our starter was Miles White. He's an eighteen-year-old lefty from Indiana. He got pounded, giving up a grand slam in the second and a three run homer in the fourth before he got yanked.

When Witherspoon told me to warm up, I almost tripped running to the bullpen mound to get ready. I'm always nervous before I come into a game. My stomach was tossing and turning worse than usual. I was so pumped up that it only took me about ten pitches to warm up. I'm lucky I didn't hurt my arm. It was cold that night.

I came in to pitch with none out in the fourth. I heard the announcer say in a high, whiny voice, "Now pitching, number fifteen, Brett Samuels. Samuels." I got chills. Witherspoon handed me the ball and told me to throw strikes. I nodded. Duerson told me the same thing, plus the signs. One was for the fastball, two the curve, three the forkball, four for the twister. If he put four fingers down and fluttered them, he wanted the scuffball. Everybody tries to figure out how I scuff the ball and I won't tell. I haven't told anyone. Well, I told my cat back home. But she's sworn to secrecy. You never know when some present teammate might be an opponent in the future. It's better safe than sorry. Never share potentially damaging information.

If there were a runner on second base, the second sign would be the indicator. That meant that if he put down two fingers, the second sign after that was active. So, if he put down one, two, two, three, four, two, one, the forkball is the pitch. I know it's confusing. I've been in the stretch position and looked at the runner for a second and forgotten what pitch I was supposed to throw. If you see a pitcher step off the rubber with a slow runner on base, it's probably because he too has forgotten what pitch he was supposed to throw.

I threw my eight warm-up pitches and toed the rubber. The umpire called the batter into the box. His name was Steve Drews. You never forget the first guy you pitched to in your first professional game. He's a righty and the plate looked close. It's an optical illusion, but the plate looks a lot closer when there's grass on the infield. It helps you throw harder.

I stared in for the sign with my hat pulled low in front of my eyes to look intimidating. It probably didn't work. That stuff works for Roger Clemens. Not me.

Duerson put down the sign. One. Fastball. I reached into my glove and gripped the ball. I stepped back with my left foot. I pivoted with my right foot and lifted my leg high in front of my face. I brought the ball out of my glove, rocked back and launched myself toward the plate. I released the ball. The ball moved toward the plate. The next thing I heard was a sickening "whap!" My first professional pitch and I … hit … the … guy … right … in … the … ribs.

39

I grimaced. I hadn't done it on purpose. Drews glared at me as he made his way toward first. He didn't rub it although it had to have hurt. I wasn't throwing at him. For real.

I pitched two innings, giving up one double and one walk in addition to the hit batsman. Not bad for a debut. We were down 8–0 when I came in. It was 8–3 when I left and we scored seven runs in the final two innings with Christenson hitting two more homers for a come-from-behind 10–8 victory. I didn't get the win, but I contributed by holding them down for two innings. Witherspoon patted me on the back after the game for a job well done.

There was a reporter from *Baseball America* in the locker-room talking to a couple of guys. *Baseball America* keeps track of the minor leaguers. He wasn't interested in talking to a charming, witty guy like me.

Duerson and I went home and the Cranes congratulated us. They listen to the games on the radio. KEIN 92.9 FM carries the games. Hey, I was famous.

I called Mom and Dad when I got home. My father answered the phone and when I told him that I finally got to pitch, the first question he asked was, "How many did you walk?"

Such confidence.

"One," I replied.

"How many did you hit?"

"One. I gave up no runs, one hit, walked one and hit one. Not bad, huh?"

He grunted.

28

Having heard and read about the dreaded minor league bus rides, I wasn't looking forward to the next day's trip to Helena, Montana. We'd been informed that it wasn't that long a ride; so how bad could it be? I did my usual paranoid once-over of the bus before I got on, and it seemed okay. It was your standard everyday travel bus with fabric seats in a disgusting, splashy, loud color and semi-tinted windows. There was extra room in the back where guys could presumably play cards and get down to some serious male bonding. From the looks of this group I didn't figure that too many of them would be reading on road trips.

I was sitting by a window waiting to leave. My mind was wandering about nothing in particular when I felt someone sit in the seat beside me. I turned my head to see who it was and saw Chris Purton, a twenty-year-old outfielder from Boston staring at me with his face approximately two inches from mine, if that far. Purton has a pasty white pallor, receding blonde hair and his eyes are perpetually widened as if something has just surprised him. (I have a pasty white pallor too, but Purton is whiter than I am. He's almost translucent.) I stared back at him waiting for him to say something.

"Hi, Brett," he finally said in a breathy voice.

Is this guy coming onto me?

"What's going on?" were the only words I could come up with. I looked around the bus for someone to save me from an unwanted sexual advance. No help was forthcoming.

"Brett, can I ask you something?"

"I guess so," I said warily. My eyes were open about as wide as Purton's by now.

"Have you accepted Jesus Christ as your savior?" he asked in complete sincerity.

Here we go.

I had a number of ways to respond to this. I could have pulled out the Jewish star that I wear on a chain around my neck. (Not for religious purposes mind you. Just for luck.) I could have made a smart-ass remark and pissed him off royally, or I could've said yes and appeased him in hopes that he would go away.

"Um, well, um, no," I stammered. I hadn't accepted Jesus Christ as my savior.

He smiled a smile that said I wasn't one of the intelligent few who had repented their sins through Jesus and would be allowed into heaven.

"Have you ever thought about it?"

"Um, well, um, no."

He nodded like he knew something I didn't and then pressed a pamphlet into my hand. It was entitled "Jesus Loves You."

"If you have any questions or just want to talk, let me know. Jesus saves. *He* loves you."

I raised the corners of my lips in a slight smile and narrowed my eyes. "That's ... great, Chris. Just ... great," I said.

He got up and looked at me for a long moment, smiled and trudged off with his Bible and pamphlets in hand.

No, Jesus and I have yet to find common ground. One thing that I didn't mention to Purton is that I do enjoy one aspect of religious fanaticism: televangelists!

My favorite is a guy by the name of Peter Popoff. The Peter Popoff show looks like a *Saturday Night Live* skit, except it is really happening. The first time I saw it I thought it was a joke. They have the organ music playing in the background as Popoff "heals" people. I've seen him heal tumors, blindness, paralysis and other assorted ailments. He also advertises special gifts. One is a booklet (written by him, anointed by God, of course) that promises divine wealth along with a bigger house, a better house, blah, blah, blah. It promises divine wealth all right ... for him! My personal favorite is the "Miracle spring water from the Chernobyl nucular accident." Nucular. Not nuclear. Nucular.

He never asks for money. It's all yours for free. I'm curious as to whether they send you their stuff if you *don't* send a tax-deductible donation.

Actually, the more I think about it the more I think that I ought to pay Popoff a visit. Do you think that he could heal my lack of arm speed and anoint me a dominating fastball?

29

Rick James, a tall, thin third baseman and outfielder from Detroit, sat next to me for the bus ride. He's twenty years old, 6'4" and 190 pounds. His name is really Rick James. I'm sure everyone is familiar with the musician Rick James, otherwise known as the "Superfreak." The first time I met the Great Falls Dodgers version of Rick James days before, I had to resist the urge to laugh because I didn't want him to beat the hell out of me. Once I realized that he was a good guy, I started singing the song "Superfreak." "Wowww, she's Superfreaky, owwwww."

He looked down at me as I was doing a silly dance. I can sing but am not much of a dancer. I was waving my arms and hopping around.

"Ber ner ner ner, nerner, nerner. Ber ner ner ner, nerner, nerner." I sang the beat of the song and then the words. "She's a very special gii-iirl. The kind you don't bring home to muthaaaaa." I can be so obnoxious when the mood strikes me. The other guys were laughing hysterically. They laughed even harder when Rick picked me up and dumped me ass first into the clubhouse garbage can. All in good fun of course. I must admit, it was pretty funny. And he acquired the nickname that he didn't seem to mind: The Superfreak.

Finally, everyone was on the bus and ready to go to Helena. The bags and equipment were safely packed in the compartments underneath. I couldn't tell how much English the bus driver spoke or didn't speak because all he did was smile and nod a lot. James Witherspoon took a seat in the front of the bus and as Jeff Finestra looked for a place to sit, Witherspoon quickly dropped his notebooks and scouting reports on the seat next to him so Finestra couldn't sit next to him. A cool move, I thought. Finestra wound up sitting next to the only guy sitting by himself: Chris Purton. Finestra was going to have Jesus crammed down his throat for the hour and twenty minute ride to Helena. Right after we left, the Superfreak turned to me and asked me what Purton was talking to me about.

"What d'you think?" I asked. "He's recruiting people for the Rapture."

"Yeah? You gonna become a man of the Lowuuuud?" he asked in his best southern evangelist voice.

"Oh, yeah. That's exactly what I need to do is call my mother and tell her that I was born again." I handed him the pamphlet that Purton had given me and he promptly threw it out the window.

The Superfreak is one of those guys who needs lots of attention. I was trying to read *Rolling Stone* magazine and he kept interrupting me by poking me, talking to me and reading over my shoulder. I was reading a blurb about Lauryn Hill when Rick asked me if I liked her music. I told him no.

"So why are you reading about her?" he asked.

"What, I have to like to the music to read the article? Do *you* like her music?"

"Aww, man," he said in a frustrated voice. "I'll only listen to that bitch while she's suckin' mah dick." His head bobbed left and right as he said "suckin' mah dick."

The way he said it made me laugh.

"I can't argue with that logic," I said.

The driver got us there in one piece, but the fact is the trip was only eighty-six miles. There wasn't much of an opportunity for him to drive us into a ravine.

The ride wasn't long enough for interteam tensions to cause problems. When you travel with thirty guys, several coaches, an athletic trainer and a creepy pitching coach, fights can and do happen. All went smoothly, though, so I started to think that nightmarish stories of minor league travel are overblown.

30

The Helena Brewers are affiliated, obviously, with the Milwaukee Brewers. Helena didn't seem to be my kind of place. Lots of guys with cowboy hats and people who hunt. I'm not into guns or hunting. The town was apparently a gold-mining town years and years ago. There's a casino too. I enjoy gambling except that I'm a conservative gambler who doesn't know when to quit, which is a recipe for losing small amounts of money and getting aggravated. I was sure to wind up in a casino sooner rather than later. We had four fun filled days in Helena and after the second I wanted to hang myself I was so bored. The guys spent their time after the games trying to get laid. I didn't see anyone that piqued my interest. I'm a rarity: a picky baseball player. The other guys (Christenson especially) aren't very discriminating. I have one iron clad rule: a woman that I'm going to fool around with must, *must* have teeth. I don't think that's asking for much.

As far as the games go, we won three out of four. Duerson hit another bomb in the first game. I told him that if he cut the shots he hits into little pieces he'd hit around .750. He said he'd take it under advisement. I pitched in the only game we lost and did even better than in my first appearance. I had four strikeouts in the two innings I worked and didn't even hit anybody. I hoped that soon I could get into a closer game where my performance would have more of an impact. After the game, Witherspoon pulled me to the side and asked me how I scuff the ball. Being in baseball for a long time allows you to pick up certain movements on both players and balls. He's been around the game all his life and is very perceptive. I denied all and he didn't press me.

Some of the guys were bragging about their conquests in Helena. I saw some of those conquests. I have but one comment: Bleccchh! Aren't there supposed to be women that look like Susan Sarandon walking around teaching us how to play the game and read poetry?

We piled on the bus after the final game for the trek back to Great Falls to host Lethbridge. It was quite an eventful ride. As we were driving along the barren interstate back to Great Falls, most of the guys were trying to sleep. Some were tired and others were hung over. I was trying to read. The Superfreak had his head on my shoulder and was sleeping. I didn't have the heart to wake him.

As the bus motored along the highway, we were startled by a sudden commotion in the back. Guys stood up or craned their necks to see what was happening. I turned around in time to see several guys holding Wade Mills back and lying on the floor of the bus was … Jeff Finestra. Whoa!

How the guys kept from cheering, I don't know. Did you ever see a bug lying on its back and flailing its arms trying to turn over? Well, that's what Jeff Finestra looked like. Witherspoon ran to the back to see what was going on. There was lots of screaming, yelling and cursing with Mills trying desperately to get to Finestra and Christenson holding him in a bear hug. Finestra was on the floor in a heap holding his jaw. I had a look of complete amazement on my face as I watched this unfold. I stayed out of it, of course. Mills could have killed Finestra for all I cared. Witherspoon started yelling. I'd never heard the man raise his voice.

"Knock that shit off, Wade! What the fuck is going on?"

Finestra got up and tried to get to Mills. It was convenient that there were about ten guys separating the two by now. Mills would have given Finestra the beating of a lifetime if there weren't.

45

Once Witherspoon and the guys got Mills calmed down, Finestra was escorted to the front of the bus. Guys were wide awake and whispering about what happened. Witherspoon stood in front and addressed the whole team.

"All right you guys, shut up." Guys kept whispering. "SHUT UP!" Everyone shut up.

"We're going straight to the ballpark now to have a meeting. I am not going to put up with this kind of crap on my team. Now shut up until we get there. The next person that opens his mouth is gonna have me to deal with," Witherspoon said and sat down.

Nobody said a word for the rest of the ride back to Great Falls. That's leadership.

31

Finestra is a creep as I documented before, but then again, so is Mills. They could both have gotten tossed from the vicinity of this team for all I cared. About three other players had had problems with Mills and would dearly have loved to crack him. Me included. While watching him throw between starts I noticed that he was moving his upper body down to meet his lower body during his leg lift. I also noted that he was looping his curveball. It had no snap and looked like it was rolling in the air toward the plate. That type of curve might as well have a sign attached to it that says, "hit me." He wasn't getting any help from Finestra and Witherspoon wasn't around. When Mills was done throwing I told him about what I saw. He expressed his appreciation immediately.

"What the fuck do you know?" he demanded.

I stared in response.

Then he said, "You think I'm gonna listen to some fuckin' free agent punk from New York? Fuck off."

To compound matters, he did this in front of five other guys and some fans.

My eyes widened and my jaw set. My mouth opened slightly and then I clenched my teeth. According to the other guys I turned purple. Not red. Purple.

Mills is a lot bigger than I am, but at that point, I didn't care.

"Well," I growled, "I didn't realize his Holiness had been reduced to playing rookie ball in Montana with a worthless slug like me. You're welcome, you fucking prick."

I stalked off before I got angry enough to get a piano wire from the Cranes' piano to strangle Mills with it.

Never again, I decided, will I provide unsolicited advice.

Forget the rudeness, but if there's one thing I know, it's pitching mechanics. I was just trying to help the guy. It taught me an important lesson about minor league baseball. Every man for himself. Winning is fun, but the bottom line is career advancement.

Did your team win a championship? Yes? Okay. Did you have a successful season? No? Here's your ring. Now beat it. Worry about yourself first and foremost.

More importantly than any of this was Mills' blatant disobedience towards Witherspoon by reinserting his forbidden tongue ring. You wouldn't find me defying Witherspoon's rules, but Mills seems to be trying to be baseball's answer to Dennis Rodman. If he won twenty in the bigs it would be tolerated, but he wasn't in the bigs. He was in the Pioneer League.

We got back to the ballpark late in the evening and trudged tired-legged into the clubhouse. Finestra had a puffy lip and an ice bag on his jaw. He was swollen and looked ridiculous. We all sat in the chairs and couches. Witherspoon went to the front of the room and looked around for a moment. He was outwardly angry. I'd seen him get slightly annoyed during the first few weeks of the season, but never like this. He had a ritual he would follow when something happened during a game to anger him. He would sit in his corner of the dugout and raise his hand slightly above his hairline with his hand and hold it there for a second like he was checking himself for a fever. Then, he would slowly move his hand downward the length of his face like he was wiping away any urge to yell at the youngsters. It must have worked because I'd never seen the man yell.

Now, though, it looked like he needed a Valium.

"Under no circumstances," Witherspoon began, "does anyone on this team put his hands up to any coach. *Ever!*" He seemed to want to say "even him" referring to Finestra, but didn't.

Nobody said a word. He looked mad enough to kill both Mills and Finestra. Without saying anything else, he told us all to go home. We would deal with the situation the following day. In the car home I asked Duerson what had happened. He knew as much as I did. That didn't stop him from expressing a heartfelt opinion.

"Fuck 'em both," he said.

32

We walked into the clubhouse the next day and looked at Mills' locker or at what used to be Mills' locker. He was gone. Released.

Apparently you really can't raise your hands to the coaches. Even a relatively high draft pick like Mills has to face the consequences. Somebody would pick him up, but punching coaches is a black mark that you'd probably prefer not to have on your resume.

Finestra wasn't around either, thankfully.

The story began to circulate around the clubhouse about why Mills attacked Finestra. It seems that Finestra had made some disparaging comments about Mills. Mills had the flu for a few days and it looked like he might miss a start. Finestra made the comment that he had been a better pitcher at 50 percent than Mills was at 100 percent, so having the flu would mean some serious trouble.

I didn't think that it was that big of a deal. Who cared what Finestra said? But Mills heard about the comment and confronted Finestra on the bus. Finestra came up with a smart-ass answer. And of course, Mills nailed him. When you're dealing with two imbeciles these things happen. Such is the life in a baseball clubhouse. It's worse than junior high school sometimes. So, Mills was gone.

Guys were sitting around the clubhouse playing cards and watching TV when Witherspoon poked his head out of his office and started calling pitchers in alphabetically. One by one they marched in and out after around five minutes apiece. Nobody would say what it was about. When Matt Bradley came out though, he whispered to me, "You're gonna love this."

Witherspoon called my name and in I went.

Witherspoon, seated behind his desk, asked me to sit down.

"I'm going to make this quick Brett. Have you learned anything from Jeff Finestra since you've been here?"

I thought that this was some kind of trick question for a moment.

"Is this a trick question?"

Witherspoon frowned. "No," he said.

"Well," I began cautiously, "I'll be honest with you Skip, I learned more from my last sandlot coach back in Brooklyn and he was a complete psychopath."

Witherspoon's fingers were steepled in front of his face and he had his head tilted down slightly and his lips pursed.

"I don't like to bad-mouth people behind their backs," I continued, "but I thought there would be more of a teaching aspect in professional baseball and I just haven't seen it."

Witherspoon scratched the side of his face.

"Okay, Brett. Thank you."

I left the office and sat down next to Bradley.

"What was that all about?" I asked.

"I guess they're finally thinking of getting rid of him," he replied.

Nothing more was mentioned of it for the time being.

Finestra was walking around like he owned the place for the next few days. A "nobody fucks with me" attitude. I couldn't blame Mills for hitting him, but it was a stupid thing to do. It cost him his job.

33

Lethbridge was in for three games. The second game of the series was a truly happy day for me. I got my first professional win.

I entered the scoreless tie in the tenth inning. Tommy Gianelli and Billy Jones had shut Lethbridge out for nine innings. I came in and held them for three and in the bottom of the twelfth with two out and two on, Duerson hit one over the right-centerfield fence to get me my first win. He's a great friend.

Everyone was waiting at home plate as he trotted in and was slapping him on the back. I got a few back slaps of my own in recognition of my victory. It was a joyous trip back to the clubhouse as a huge grin enveloped my face. A kid retrieved the game ball and traded it to me for two new balls. He didn't want my autograph though, the punk. After a few celebratory drinks I asked Duerson if he wanted the ball since it was his game-winning homer. He wrapped one of his long arms around my neck.

"Naaahh," he said. "Let's just say you owe me one, motherfucker."

I did indeed owe him one.

34

I made a specific effort to stay out of the many casinos in Great Falls. Sometimes I'm lucky, but I never know when to stop. Probably better to save my money.

Helena came to town two games ahead of us in the standings. It didn't really matter very much though. There is a first half division winner and a second half division winner in the Pioneer League. As long as you win one of the halves, you make the playoffs. The first round is a best two of three series between the division winners of each half and then the winners play the opposite division winner best two of three. I was confident that we would make the playoffs.

The first game was rained out, so we sat in the clubhouse staring at each other until they decided to call it. We played a doubleheader the next day, losing the first but winning the second. We remained two games back of Helena. And yes, Finestra was still around.

We had to go to Lethbridge for two games and then to Medicine Hat for three games. The rule was when the customs officers came on the bus as we entered Canada, we were to keep our mouths shut and say that we had no criminal records if asked. Whether that was true or not, I don't know. I didn't know the criminal histories of some of this crew, but I'm quite sure there were some misdemeanors at the very least.

Before we left I told Christenson that if he had any juice (steroids) he's better leave it behind. He continued to deny, deny, and deny. Maybe even he believes that he's not juicing. I knew better. I think that the stuff is legal in Canada, but am not too sure. I don't know if you're supposed to be transporting it from one country to the next.

We boarded the bus for the approximately three-hour ride to Lethbridge. As we sat on the bus waiting for Witherspoon to board for departure we saw Finestra put his stuff in the equipment compartment underneath the bus. Then as he went to board the bus, Witherspoon put his hand up and stopped him. They started talking but we couldn't hear what they were saying because we couldn't get any of the windows open. The door was open but it was hard to hear. We all watched. Guys sitting on the left side of the bus crowded on the right side to get a good view of the action.

Bradley, seated to my left, said, "I hope *he* hits the prick too."

Witherspoon and Finestra started jawing back and forth with more intensity. Things were getting pretty heated. Finally, Finestra tried to push his way past Witherspoon and get on the bus. Witherspoon placed the palm of his hand in the center of Finestra's chest and shook his head no. Witherspoon gestured at the luggage compartment and seemed to be telling Finestra to get his stuff. Finestra folded his arms and pouted like a whiny child.

Witherspoon's mouth closed tightly and he calmly walked over to the luggage and grabbed Finestra's stuff. He then proceeded to fling the luggage halfway across the street. Finestra started waving his arms and screaming incoherently. This was like rubbernecking during a car accident. You just *have* to look.

Finestra grabbed his bag and ran toward the bus. Witherspoon grabbed Finestra's shirt collar and slammed him back first into the side of the bus and he made a loud thud. We could see Witherspoon's teeth clenched and his face an inch from Finestra's face. He was firing him. Finestra was being left behind.

After it was over, Witherspoon climbed aboard the bus and the guys started cheering.

He looked at us and said slowly and evenly, "Knock it off. That was not pleasant. Don't cheer like it was. Act like professionals."

Everyone shut up. The pitchers were quietly ecstatic. I had to hide under a seat because I was laughing so hard and didn't want to have Witherspoon toss me around too. If you had seen the look on Finestra's face you would be laughing too.

A new pitching coach was joining us in Lethbridge.

35

Our new pitching coach arrived just before game time. We were all introduced to him in a brief dugout meeting. Wes McCormack was a former Major Leaguer. A two time twenty game winner with Minnesota and Philadelphia, he had some credentials. He also had a reputation for being an iconoclast. He did things his way or no way. (My kinda guy.) That's probably why he moved around so much pitching for four teams in his thirteen-year big league career. He ran into trouble almost everywhere he went because he had no patience with the usual baseball nonsense. The 6'2", dark haired, bespectacled, mustachioed man looked like he could still pitch at his current age of fifty.

He commanded immediate respect from me and I think from the other guys too. Here was a guy who had the balls to ask "Why?" if a manager asked him to stop lifting weights in fear he might bulk up too much. Major League managers hate to be questioned. And woe to any pitching coach who tried to tell McCormack what pitches to throw. He lasted in the big leagues because he won. He also didn't *make* the big leagues until he was twenty-six, despite some huge seasons in the minors, because he was too much of a rebel. (That may be a lesson for the Brooklyn boy.) This man could teach us how to pitch and along with Witherspoon would teach us how to win.

McCormack may have wondered what he had gotten himself into after the first game at Lethbridge. We fell behind 10–0 before scoring five runs in the last two innings to lose 10–5. We got to the ballpark for the second game and I had a nice surprise waiting for me during batting practice. As I was loitering in the outfield shagging flies during batting practice, I saw Witherspoon and McCormack talking by the bullpen with disgusted looks on their faces. They looked very aggravated. Just then the Superfreak ripped a shot into the corner past the bullpen. As I ran to give chase, Witherspoon called my name. I hoped that I wasn't the cause of the aggravation, which is always a possibility.

"What's up?" I asked.

"Listen," Witherspoon began, "Gianelli might not be able to go tonight. He's got the runs. If he can't pitch, you're starting."

"Great!" I exclaimed.

McCormack, a psychologist type, looked at me sideways and said in a sarcastic tone, "Think you can handle it?"

"There's only one way to find out," I answered.

"Stay loose and relax. We'll let you know in a little while," Witherspoon said.

I continued to hang around in the outfield shagging flies and selfishly hoping that Tommy Gianelli's diarrhea would continue. Apparently he'd had some Mexican food that afternoon and Montezuma was taking his revenge. For me, eating Mexican food is asking for trouble. I have a really sensitive stomach. One of my main concerns when I go anywhere is whether or not there's a clean bathroom. If the bathroom isn't clean I can't use it. I cannot describe the looks I got the first time the other guys saw me trudging off to the bathroom with a magazine under one arm and a package of baby wipes under the other. Cleanliness is important. Especially for a fanatic like me. I also have a variety of antidiarrhea and stomach settling medicines that I carry with me everywhere. Imodium AD, Pepto Bismol, Mylanta and Tums. It depends on the situation as to which one I'll use. I don't use them every day, just once in a while. I didn't share any with Gianelli either. Why cut off my nose to spite my face? Team is one thing, opportunity is another.

Shortly before game time, McCormack told me to head for the bullpen because I was starting. When I got to the bullpen, Duerson, unaware of Gianelli's gastrointestinal distress, asked ever so politely, "What the fuck are you doing here?"

"Hey man, I'm starting."

"Oh. Well, don't make me have to hop around too much," he pleaded.

Why does everybody tell me something like that?

36

Lethbridge can hit. I had to make sure not to walk a bunch of guys and give up a bunch of homers with men on base. If I did that, this would be my first *and* last start.

Gianelli's spot in the rotation was tenuous as it was, and if I did well the spot could become mine. We didn't score in the first half inning and in the home half I strode purposefully to the mound. It was chilly so I was wearing a turtleneck. There was a decent crowd at Henderson Park, Lethbridge's home field. They seemed indifferent when I was announced as the replacement starter. I had to concentrate and make sure not to overthrow. That means you're trying too hard and the ball usually sails high or doesn't have any liveliness or movement. I followed my usual routine as I got to the mound:

I picked up the ball with my glove and flipped it to my bare hand.

I removed my glove by placing it under my right arm and rubbed up the baseball while digging a comfortable hole for myself with my right foot. (Incidentally, the minor league mounds have all been brilliantly manicured in my eyes, but you must remember what I'm used to back home.)

I made sure there was a nice landing spot and slipped my glove on. I adjusted my cap. I looked in at Duerson squatting behind the plate and began my warm-ups.

When warming up a pitcher signals to the catcher what pitches he is throwing by making certain gestures with his glove. The accepted number of warm-up pitches at the start of an inning is eight. A flip upward with the back of the glove is a fastball. I threw two. A turn of the glove is a curve. Two of those. A drop motion is the forkball. Two of those. I threw a fastball and a curve from the stretch position as if there were runners on base and was ready to go. I made a flipping motion with my glove towards second base indicating to Duerson that he should make his practice throw to second. An eerie calm had settled over me as if I were taking a test that I had thoroughly prepared for. The infielders threw the ball around the infield. For some reason, Bosetti threw the ball directly to me instead of throwing it to the Superfreak playing third. Superfreak looked around with a funny look on his face and asked, "What am I, wood?"

I managed a smile and flipped him the ball. He flipped it back.

Fasten your seat belt, I thought to myself.

I stepped onto the mound with both feet and started in for the sign. The Lethbridge leadoff hitter, Bobby Smith, stood in. Duerson put down one finger. I wound up and ripped a fastball right down the chute for strike one. Then I threw four straight balls, all high, to put the leadoff man on. So much for my eerie calm. Then I conserved pitches by hitting the next guy in the back. First and second. Uh oh. I went three and oh on the third place hitter and was on the verge of real trouble when he did me a huge, possibly career-saving favor. I threw a high fastball and he swung at it and popped it directly behind home plate. Duerson went back and squeezed it for the first out. I started to breathe a little easier. Their cleanup man was batting and I threw him a great curve, which he grounded to the Superfreak at third. Stepping on third and firing to first, the Superfreak turned a double play to get me out of the inning. Into and out of trouble just like that. Lucky, lucky, lucky.

Duerson led off the second and hit one to Mars to give us a 1–0 lead. I had a lead and started rolling along. I was throwing strikes and getting ground balls. I gave up a single in the third and a double in the fourth. Then I retired ten in a row. We loaded the bases in the seventh with one out, clinging to that 1–0 lead. Christenson whiffed after ripping two vicious shots foul. Duerson was batting with two outs. Lethbridge changed pitchers to have a lefty pitch to the lefty swinging Duerson. The new pitcher, Stan Alvarez, warmed up. He looked like he was a fastball pitcher. Jon Duerson is a dead fastball hitter, lefty or righty. Alvarez was bringing it at around 90. As Duerson stepped in, I had a premonition.

"He's gonna hit another one," I announced to no one in particular.

The first pitch was a fastball that ran high. The second pitch was another fastball, slightly inside, but not too far in for Duerson to swing at it. As he turned his hips, his bat whipped around and creamed a line shot down the right field line. It was hit so hard, we wondered whether it had the height to make it over the wall as we jumped from the dugout to watch it. Mystically, though, it started to rise and crashed into the right field foul pole right over the 330 sign on the right field fence. Grand slam. I had a cushion now. It was 5–0. We pushed across another run in the eighth. Six nothing. I wanted the shutout desperately. The bottom of the ninth came around. Our bullpen was quiet. I had told Witherspoon and McCormack that I wanted to finish the game.

McCormack said, "Don't just say you want to finish it, get out there and do it."

The first batter popped to Christenson. The second singled to center. I struck out the third batter for my fifth strikeout and the second out in the ninth. Their cleanup hitter, Mark Bell, was up again. He was the only thing standing between me and my shutout. And possibly my place in the rotation and with that my career as a viable prospect. I threw a 1–0 curve. It hung. Bell smacked a long drive deep into the alley in left-center. I smacked my glove against my hip in disgust as I ran to backup third. There goes the shutout. But, as I watched the play unfold, I saw that Rod Woods, the centerfielder, had taken off like a shot at the crack of the bat. He was running as fast as I'd ever seen a human being run and seemed to be gaining on the ball. I squinted and raised my hands in front of me, hoping. Rod reached the ball at the fence and grabbed it running full speed into the ad-laden wall. Bouncing off the wall, he regained his balance and held the ball up in his bare hand. Game over. I shook both fists in the air as a huge smile came across my face. Everyone was shaking my hand and smacking me on the ass. McCormack told me it looked like I *could* handle it after all. Witherspoon just winked. I'd seized my opportunity with the jaws of a pit bull. In a time of put up or shut up, I put up. And it was all because of a guy getting the shits.

After the game I did my first star of the game interview with radio announcer Stu Ornstein. All twenty listeners back in Great Falls now knew what my lovely voice sounded like. I was giddy and probably very annoying during the three-hour ride into Medicine Hat. Duerson and Christenson told me that they would take me to celebrate in Medicine Hat.

"It looks like the Jew-boy owes us niggers some shit," Woods said.

Typical baseball clubhouse humor. And it was true indeed.

37

When I was in college I had a radio-announcing class. One of the guys in the class was always talking about having to leave class to get laid. "I had to go and get *laid*. And it was worth it. Smoke is still coming out of my ears." That kind of stuff. I heard this about five times. One day I said to another guy leaving class, "Hey man, that guy don't get no pussy."

"I know he talks so much," he responded quickly.

It has been my experience that guys who talk like that don't get laid at all whatsoever. That being said, I must tell you that if you hear that stuff from a baseball player, it is more than likely true. Duerson, Christenson, Bosetti and Superfreak James took me out and got me smashed after the first game in Medicine Hat. Christenson picked up not *one*, not *two*, but *three* women. THREE! I was amazed. He rehashed the whole story the next day. It was the most unbelievable thing I'd ever seen. And they weren't bad looking either. As far as minor league groupies from Medicine Hat go, that is.

After winning two of three in Medicine Hat our record was 10–8 after eighteen games. Good enough for second place in the standings.

My name was in both *Baseball America* and *USA Today Baseball Weekly* telling about my five hit shutout. I bought three copies of each. I kept one and sent one each to my parents and Coach Roessler. I considered sending one to Mark Mattera to cause him another heart seizure, but I thought, "Fuck 'im. He stinks."

38

Aside from sex, the things that baseball players do to amuse themselves hold no appeal to me. I hate playing meaningless card games. I despise chewing sunflower seeds (I can never get the seed out of the shell correctly and wind up spitting all over the place). And I don't like chewing tobacco. There's not much else to do other that tease each other about physical imperfections or whatever else we can think of, and bitch about playing time. I don't bitch about playing time, but I'm world class at bitching about everything else. If there's really crappy food on the bus trips, I bitch. If there's no clean bathroom, I bitch. If there aren't any good-looking women around, I bitch. You get the idea. It's a better habit than smoking.

Days before, McCormack had given me a useful tip. He noticed that I concentrated on pushing off the rubber with my back leg to generate power. He suggested that I adjust my way of thinking. That's a cool thing about McCormack. He doesn't tell people what to do. He makes suggestions. Instead of concentrating on pushing, I should concentrate on *exploding*. The mere word felt more powerful and it felt better the moment I tried it. McCormack is a great man. I wasn't too far removed from coaches who barked out orders that you were supposed to mindlessly follow. And if you didn't you weren't going to play. What choice was there?

I had to chart pitches for the next game against Helena at our field. Some teams have the pitcher from the day before chart pitches; some have the next game's starter do it. There is a chart with the other team's lineup and boxes next to their names. In the boxes are balls, strikes and the like. I had to chart what the pitcher threw, whether it was a ball or a strike and what the batter did. I also had to keep a running tally of how many pitches were thrown. It isn't as bad as it sounds. If nothing else, it keeps your head in the game. I did that for almost every game in high school. But for now, every fifth day is plenty.

39

I got my next start against Helena at Great Falls. I wasn't as good in that one. I gave up a two run homer in the first and trailed 2–0 when Christenson and Anthony Lee hit back-to-back homers and we took a 5–2 lead. With two outs in the eighth I walked a guy and then gave up a single. Witherspoon came out and yanked me. Mike Strock closed it out for me and saved my third win. I was 3–0 and believed that I was rooted in the starting rotation. I started to think that maybe I had found my niche in life. Hopefully career advancement was in my future.

Tommy Gianelli wasn't as lucky. Getting diarrhea wasn't as much a transgression as pitching like crap. He was released. There's not much to say to a guy when he gets released. Some of the other guys hid in the trainer's room or the bathroom until Gianelli had left. It's called avoidance, something many baseball players are great at. I can't do that though. I watched Gianelli toss his stuff into a bag. He had been crying. He tried to hide it but it wasn't hard to tell. Just before he left I shook his hand and wished him luck. He gave some advice.

"Don't eat any bad Mexican food," he said.

He managed a wry smile and struggled with his heavy equipment bags as he walked out the clubhouse door, glancing back just once.

That could have been any one of us.

40

We hopped on the bus for an eight game road trip. First it was off to Butte for four games. That's a two and a half hour ride. And then we would head to Billings. The duration for that trip was widely disputed. Some guys said four hours and others said five and a half. Either way wasn't as bad as it could have been. A couple of guys from the Medicine Hat Blue Jays said that some of their road trips took over twenty hours. One of their guys, Jay Collins, who went to Harvard said, "It's like a concentration camp without the comforting prospect of death on the horizon. Except these guys smell worse."

I couldn't decide whether that was an insulting metaphor to use when talking to a Jewish guy. I think it was. No wonder teams get into fights on buses. I'm surprised that we'd had only one up to that point. A form of cabin fever takes over after a while.

We won two of the first three games over Butte and it was my turn to pitch the fourth game. I won my third straight start. Duerson homered again and it was an all around good night. I gave up one run and three hits in seven innings. I was a little wild, walking five, but I struck out seven. I think the ump was missing some calls. In his defense my pitches break so late that it's easy to miss them sometimes. Besides, the umps in rookie ball are learning their craft just as the players are. You find that most of them are just regular people. Some good, some bad, some ugly. If you don't mess with them, they don't mess with you for the most part.

41

For the record, the ride to Billings took four hours and fifty-five minutes. Sitting in the seats behind me, Matt Bradley and Rick Abner were talking about baseball history. Presumably they want to have knowledge of their craft. They were looking at *The Great American All Time Baseball Record Book*. All I heard about was how "Rogers Hornsby hit .424 and George Sisler hit .420. Jack Chesboro won 41 games. Cy Young won 511 games. Imagine how they would do today. Yak, yak, yak." They went on and on until I just couldn't take it anymore. I jerked around in my seat.

"THOSE GUYS WOULDN'T DO THAT TODAY GODDAMMIT! THEY'D BE LUCKY TO HIT .300!" I yelled.

They looked at me.

"What are you talking about? And why are you yelling?" Abner calmly asked.

"Because you're making me nuts. Those guys were hitting in the .420s, right?"

"Yeah," Abner said.

"How good do you think the pitching was then? Are you telling me that those guys were better hitters than Tony Gwynn? Better hitters than George Brett? Come on."

"Why were their averages so high then? And what about Cy Young and Jack Chesboro?" Bradley asked.

"How hard could they have been throwing for Chrissakes? They were pitching every other day! The only guy to hit .400 back then that might hit .400 today is Ted Williams. That's it. And *nobody's* gonna win 500 games and *nobody's* gonna win 41 games in a season or hit .420 again. Nobody!" I said.

Everybody seems to think that it's funny when I get all worked up and agitated, so they were pretty much laughing by then. The argument went on for a few more minutes. They kept insisting that I was wrong. The bottom line is that players now are better than ever. Those averages from the twenties are an aberration and will never ever be duplicated. The best analogy I can come up with is if players today used aluminum bats. *Then* you'd see averages as high as they were in the twenties. You'd also see pitchers and infielders wearing hockey goalie's equipment or getting killed on a regular basis. Case closed.

That was an eventful bus ride. I made a career decision then too. No longer would my scuffball be called a scuffball. It would heretofore be referred to as a "cutter." Cutter is short for cut fastball. I cut the fastball all right ... literally. If anybody asks it's the "cutter." Scuffball was eliminated from my vocabulary on the bus from Butte to Billings. I left it somewhere on the interstate never to be found again.

42

Standing around in the bullpen the guys started riffing on me and decided that I needed a nickname. I hate being called "Sammy." They started bouncing ideas off of one another. I had no say in the matter. They started in about my hairdo and tried to choose between "Krusty" and "Chia-pet" as my new nickname. For those of you unfamiliar with the "Chia-pet" products, they are little ceramic animals that you put seeds into and it grows what looks like green fur. There are other products including a "Chia-head." So it wasn't long before calling me "Chia-pet" degenerated into calling me "Chia-head." Naturally that's the one they chose. I'd prefer "Krusty."

During that same bullpen session I must have had a target on my back. They started trying to drag my scuffing secret out of me. I refused to acknowledge the implication. As I left the bullpen I gave them a tantalizing comment.

"You guys just better remember one thing. Everything I do is plotted by a mastermind."

As I said "mastermind" I tapped my right temple with my right index finger. Then I turned to walk away ... and tripped over the ballbag and fell flat on my face.

"Hey mastermind," Strock yelled, "watch out for the ballbag."

Christenson met two girls at the ballpark and he brought me along to have drinks. I finally found a groupie that I wanted to have sex with after twenty-six games. She was a pretty brunette with short hair and a tight body. I do have taste. Unlike many athletes I used a condom. I'm paranoid. Dave Christenson lives on the edge and has no such qualms. She must have enjoyed my company because I saw her after every game of the four game series. I wasn't pitching during the series, so it was okay. I didn't see any deficiency in my leg strength afterwards. The guys made me share all the lurid details. A staple of a healthy baseball clubhouse is much sex talk due to all the testosterone.

43

Speaking of testosterone, Christenson finally decided that he trusted me enough to let me in on his not-so-well-kept secret. He admitted his steroid use and agreed to let me watch him shoot the stuff into himself. I don't make judgments about it. I just find it interesting. He had a scheduled shot after the second day after we returned from the road.

I pitched the first game back in Great Falls against the Ogden Raptors. They are an affiliate of the Milwaukee Brewers. For some strange reason the Brewers have two affiliates in this league. Why have two teams on the same level?

At any rate their team wasn't very good. I gave up three runs in eight innings along with six hits. None were hit very hard. The Super-freak and Christenson hit back-to-back homers in the fifth inning. I was 5–0 and rolling.

Sex didn't weaken my legs.

Witherspoon pulled me off to the side after the game and finally asked me straight out about my "cutter."

"Are you loading up the ball?" he asked.

"Hell, no Skip. That's a 'cutter.'" I said.

"A cutter," he said skeptically, his head tilted down and his arms folded.

"Yes. A 'cutter.' That's my story and I'm sticking to it."

"Well, don't get caught throwing your cutter," he advised, winking.

"Okay, Skip."

Smart man, that Witherspoon.

McCormack walked by during this exchange and added, "Cutter my ass."

I went to Christenson's house the next day at 11:00 A.M. It was raining lightly and Duerson wasn't around so I had to take the bus.

"This better be worth it," I said.

Christenson looked at me. "*You're* the one who wanted to see this," he said.

I need to be entertained regularly to keep my mind occupied.

It was truly interesting. There were the preloaded syringes filled with 200 mg of Deca-Durabolin. He was taking one shot a week along with four tablets of Dianabol a day. Dave was built, but it wasn't entirely obvious that he was using. I have a pretty good eye for genetics when it comes to bodies and his body and genetics didn't match. His wrists and hands are relatively small. His natural body size didn't fit his bulging extremities.

He shot the Deca into his ass.

He then asked me if I wanted to try some stuff. It would probably raise my velocity. He thought that because I was so interested I wanted to try it. I declined.

He persisted and I said I'd think about it.

I wasn't really going to think about it. I have no inclination to shoot needles into my own ass or to have anyone else do it either.

44

We swept the Raptors out of Great Falls and won the first game against the Idaho Falls Braves. They are an affiliate of the San Diego Padres but are named the Braves. Why? I have no idea.

We had won five in a row when it was my turn to bring my sparkling, spotless record to the mound. It was spotless before the game and not so spotless after the game. I lost.

I went seven innings and gave up four runs on four hits. Two of them were homers. Major League bombs is a better term. I threw two high forkballs and they both got crushed. I didn't throw a tantrum or anything like that, but I was disgusted with myself. It had gotten to the point where I felt like I was the legitimate ace of the staff and now this. I hate losing. The guys were cracking jokes and doing things like mooning me to try and lift my spirits. It didn't help. I was still de-pressed. I had to start a new streak.

During the last game against Idaho Falls I was seated on the bench when Rod Woods got thrown out trying to steal third. Don Bosetti had just struck out and was cursing as he sat next to me, removing his bat-ting gloves.

"That's a bad play," I announced.

Bosetti, leaning over and fixing his socks looked up at me from the side and asked, "What's a bad play?"

"Getting thrown out stealing third. You should never make the first or the third out at third base. It's an old baseball axiom."

Sitting up, Bosetti said, "That was the *second* out, dickhead."

Pondering that revelation, I came up with a new axiom.

"Well," I said, "you should never make *any* out at third base."

45

Helena came to town for two games and then the first half of the season was over. After that it was like a new season. We had to go straight to … Helena. Sort of a home-and-home series. Five straight games against the same team is a great way for tensions to run way high.

We lost the two games at home to Helena. We got mauled in the second game 13–1. Miguel Santana was brutal for us and a few of the guys didn't appear to be hustling. Jogging to first on groundouts and not having their heads in the game. Mental mistakes were running ram-pant. Guys weren't tagging up on long flies or advancing on passed balls and wild pitches. Witherspoon can deal with physical mistakes, as they are part of the game and help us learn. Mental mistakes are another matter. He watched as we flopped around on the field for two days and had had enough. There was a team meeting at the conclusion of the 13–1 massacre. We all sat in wraparound towels and shower shoes and Witherspoon laid it on the line. As he spoke, he stood completely still: "If you guys do not want to be here, I'm quite sure we can find another group of guys from the same towns you came from who would be will-ing to come here and play a game hard for three hours every night and get paid for it. I'm not the kind of guy to make threats. You should all know me by now. One thing I will not tolerate is being made to look bad. You guys don't hustle; you don't play the game the fundamental way in which I have tried to teach you to play; it makes *me* look bad. *I will not tolerate being made to look bad.* If you don't play hard, if you don't run balls out, if you don't hustle, you can forget about the fines, you just won't play. I do not accept guys being laxadasical."

He paused.

"Do I make myself clear?"

Some guys nodded. Most said nothing.

"Do I make myself clear?"

Everyone said yes in unison. He can be pretty intimidating when he wants to be. That explains why I got so nervous when he called me into his office a few minutes after he dressed us down.

I shot Duerson a look that said, "What did I do?"

He shook his head indicating that he didn't know.

Witherspoon was seated at his desk when I walked in. He didn't ask me to sit. "What is wrong with you?" he asked.

I didn't know what to say. I just stood there looking puzzled.

"You make me sick," he said.

For a second I thought he was joking.

"I make everybody sick, Skip," I smiled. He didn't return the smile.

"What'd I do?" I asked. I didn't know what he was so mad at me about.

"I don't tolerate disrespect any more than I tolerate not hustling."

"Skip, I honestly don't know what you're talking about. I'd never disrespect you."

I thought I might start to cry.

"Why were you making faces during the meeting?" he asked.

"Faces?"

"Yes, faces."

"When?"

"Don't play stupid," he said.

"Believe me, I'm not playing. I really don't know…"

"It was near the end of the meeting when you made a face."

I thought for a second and realized what he was talking about.

"Oh!" I exclaimed, making a sour face of realization.

"I wasn't making faces at what you were saying Skip," I said.

"Well, what then?"

"Laxadasical," I said.

I'd inadvertently made a face when he mispronounced a word.

"What?"

"Laxadasical," I repeated.

"What about it?"

"It's not a word."

"What are you talking about? Of course it's a word," he insisted.

"No it's not. It's either lax or lackadaisical. They both mean the same thing, basically. But they're two different words. I'll bring in my dictionary to show you."

He looked at me for a long moment.

"Okay," he said. "Bring in the dictionary. If you're wrong I'm fining you $50."

"What do I get if I'm right?"

"I'll tell you what, if you're right you don't get fined $50."

That sounded fair to me.

46

Helena won the North Division in the first half. We came in second with a record of 23–15. Idaho Falls won the South Division first half. In order to make the playoffs we had to win the second half. There's no break between the halves like in the Majors or even the higher minors. Since we play such an abbreviated schedule I guess that means we don't need a break. We opened the second half at Helena. I pitched the second game and won, allowing two runs on six hits, walking three and striking out nine. Nine! My career high. I was six and one. One thing that helped me raise my strikeout total while reducing my walks was a tip McCormack gave me. He told me to lower my gigantic leg lift slightly. I didn't throw like Nolan Ryan, so there was no reason to have a leg lift like his. All my high kick was doing was knocking me off balance. I lowered it slightly and it did wonders. Everything the guy says seems to work. And he's got a great attitude. If you listened to him, fine. If not, well, it's your career, do whatever you want. He also seems of the opinion that I will gain some velocity as I grow and fill out. We'll see.

Mike Strock is a piece of work. Get this episode: There is a type of change-up where you curl your index finger and it makes a circle on the side of the ball touching the thumb. You use the three remaining fingers to take some speed off the ball. It looks like the "okay" sign. Some call it the circle change and others call it the "okay" change. McCormack was watching Strock throw the other day. In between pitches he turned to him and said, "Mike, do you throw the 'okay' change?"

Strock looked at him with complete sincerity and said, "Ehhh, it's not bad."

47

Sitting in the bullpen for the next game with Helena we were trying to outdo each other with stories about growing up playing this game. The sleazy coaches, little league parents, and money under the table were some things discussed. I had one that topped them all though. I told them about Harry the Buttslammer. When I mentioned the creep's nickname everybody looked at me like I was some kind of lunatic. I then told them the story.

When I was seventeen, I played for a police precinct youth team in Brooklyn. A few years before I got there, there was a guy named Harry who was the president of the Precinct Youth Council. It seems that Harry was revered by one-and-all as a kind, benevolent family man dedicated to the area youths and the Youth Council. There was one problem though: Harry had been selecting boys from the Youth Council and providing individual private instruction. That instruction consisted of Harry molesting the young boys. I only heard the story third hand, but one kid came forward at the age of fifteen after suffering six years of this torture. Two others came forward shortly after that. It was a huge scandal and Harry wound up being dragged into that very same precinct in handcuffs with a jacket over his head. He went to jail for a year and a half and, get this, when he was released he wanted to become *involved with the Youth Council again.* And, this is even worse, there were *some organizers of the council that wanted to allow him to become involved again.*

The guys were staring at me as I related this story.

"You're making that up," Matt Bradley said.

"It's a hundred percent true, man. I wouldn't make up a story like that," I said.

"If you weren't there, how do you know?" Juan Robles asked.

"I didn't believe it myself. I didn't join the team until I was seventeen and Harry was already locked up. But, I was pitching a game when our coach started yelling at some old guy sitting in the stands. The guy refused to leave. *He* was one of the guys who wanted Harry the Buttslammer reinstated. *Harry* was there. He was off to the side of the field watching from an entrance."

I went on, "It really distracted me. I couldn't concentrate and started walking guys. As if I ever needed any help to start walking guys. When I finally got off the field I asked one of the other guys what was going on. He told me the story. The Buttslammer was there."

"He only went to jail for a year and a half?" Bradley exclaimed.

"I think it was a plea bargain," I shrugged.

"They should've chopped his nuts off," Strock said.

"What happened to the kids he fucked with?" Wayne Grace asked.

"I don't know. I know they all sued. I think they settled out of court to put it to rest. If I had known about this, I might not have joined the team."

"How much did they get?" Bradley asked.

I didn't know, but before I could answer, Robles said, "It could never be enough."

48

On the bus ride to Ogden, Utah, the usual things were going on. Card games, sleeping, several guys reading the Bible and guys teasing each other. On any team one of the major pastimes is guys abusing each

68

other until one feels about the size of a peanut. Some guys can't take it and things erupt into violence. On the buses and in the clubhouse, everyone was fair game. Our shortstop, Mike Queen, was always teasing other guys. The thing is, he only went after guys who didn't have the ability or willingness to fight back — like the Bible guys or the ones whose English wasn't that strong. On this particular trip he was teeing off on twenty-year-old pitcher Miguel Santana. Santana is skinny, doesn't speak English very well and throws *extremely* hard, albeit erratically. Queen was getting on him about everything. Santana didn't respond, because he wasn't sure how. He was smiling uncomfortably but I could tell he was really getting upset. After a few minutes of this, I'd had enough.

Queen was one of those guys who was always making homosexual jokes. Around a sports team, there is lots of that. Guys asking other guys to suck their dicks and stuff of that nature. There are homosexual athletes in real life, of course, but I haven't seen any. (So far.) Queen once said that once the lights are out, a guy sucking his cock is the same thing as a girl sucking his cock.

Maybe he's really gay. Maybe he's not. It can get pretty wild in his home state of Louisiana from what I understand, so who knows? I did know that I'd heard enough. So I started giving Queen a taste of his own medicine.

"Hey, Queen," I called from the other side of the bus, "you're always talking about guys sucking your cock. Are you a fag or what?"

He responded in his backwoods, trailer park drawl, "I'm not lahk yew. Ah prefuh wummen."

"You prefer women? You guys hear that? Does that mean that you've sampled men and decided that you prefer women? Or does it mean that you like both and go with whatever's convenient at the moment?"

The guys started laughing … at Queen.

Queen tried to respond, "Ah kin git layud iny tahm ah waunt."

"Of course you can, with that attitude and orientation. You're a friggin' bisexual."

"Wha' don' you suck mah diuck."

"Now, now Mike. I don't swing that way. But I'm sure you'll find someone. It's okay. I'm not judging you. I'm a liberal. You can do whoever and *what*ever you want."

"Whauh's that s'posda meaun?" he asked. He was getting *mad*.

"Nothing. I just mean, well, you *are* trailer trash from the back-woods. I've heard about the inbreeding and bestiality that is a part of your culture. I saw *Deliverance*. I'm just impressed that you still have teeth."

He glared at me and I could sense what was coming.

"No offense," I said and smirked.

Everyone was laughing at him. He looked around and flew from his seat and charged at me. He's only 6'1" and 185, so it would've been an even fight.

"Ah'm gonna kill yew mutha fucka!" he bellowed.

A bunch of guys were between us and grabbed him before he got within two feet of me. They were all yelling, "Hey, hey, hey." And "Whoa, whoa." And, "Calm down."

I was standing as Queen was pushed back to his seat.

Witherspoon was in the back by now. He doesn't usually interfere with clubhouse stuff.

"All right you guys, cut that shit out. If you can't take this shit don't dish it out. Knock it off!" Witherspoon said.

Everyone calmed down. I tried to smooth things over with Queen by sticking my tongue out at him. He lunged at me again.

"Yowuh deahd!"

Witherspoon came running back with a pissed off look on his face.

"If you guys don't knock this shit off i'm gonna stop this god-damned bus and kick both your asses. Both at once or one at a time. It makes no fuckin' difference to me."

Everyone was quiet for the rest of the ride.

49

I had thought that Utah was going to be a really uptight state. You know, Mormons, Orrin Hatch and the like, but there were a few girls hanging around as our bus pulled up to the hotel. Many of them were even pretty! Which is a change of pace from many of the groupies we ran into. We got in early, so there would be a few hours to kill before we had to be at the ballpark. If guys wanted to get in a little nooky before the game it was there for the taking.

We won the first three games of the four game set from Ogden. They looked like crap and we were playing remarkably well. The highlight of the first three games was watching James Witherspoon get his first ejection of the season in game two. It was pretty funny to watch. He looked like he was about to lose it in the first inning when the ump blew a call at the plate costing us a run, but he held it together. He wasn't so restrained in the seventh when Duerson blasted a shot that skimmed off the right field foul pole. It should have been a home run, but the first base ump called it foul. Everyone on our side of the field saw that it was fair since we had a completely unobstructed view. The ball was going on a completely straight line and then shot urgently to the right. What else could it have hit? A raindrop? Duerson was standing between home and first holding his helmet with his right hand and slapping it with his left. Witherspoon came running out. Apparently he didn't see the logic in the umps' explanation because he started screaming louder and louder and cursing more and more. I wouldn't have believed a black man's face could turn beet red if I hadn't been there and seen it. I'd never seen the man go berserk like that. It was a plethora of "FUCKIN' THIS, THAT AND THE OTHER THING!" and "MOTHERFUCKIN', COCKSUCKIN', BLEEPITY, BLEEPITY, BLANKETY, BLEEPITY, BLANK."

He said things that I wouldn't say. He said things that I wasn't even sure I'd heard. And I'm from New York!

The call stood as called. There were no appeals and no opinions received from the other umps. Witherspoon spent the rest of the game in the clubhouse. We won anyway.

I pitched the last game of the series and lost. I pitched seven innings and gave up seven hits, walking three and striking out five. I gave up two runs, but we didn't score any. The runs came on back-to-back home runs in the second inning. I couldn't tell which one had gone farther. After the game, Bosetti dutifully informed me that the first homer went 413 feet and the second went 418.

Thanks a lot. That information should be passed along on a need to know basis. And I did not need to know.

71

50

Back home for four games with Billings and then four with Butte, I wandered into the clubhouse to find that Christenson decided that having loaded biceps wasn't enough. He had to load up his bats too. I heard a sawing sound from the area of the equipment room and roamed back there to see what was going on.

"What are you up to now?" I asked.

"Giving myself an advantage," Christenson replied.

"How?"

"Cork, my man. Cork."

He had sawed off the top of one of his bats and drilled a hole in the barrel. Inside the hole, he stuffed cork. Then he replaced the top of the bat. This is supposed to do two things: One, the bat is made lighter by the removal of part of the barrel and that improves bat speed. Bat speed in addition to the cork allegedly lengthens the distance the ball travels. Physicists say this is impossible. But they also say that it is impossible to make a ball curve. I *know* they're wrong about that. Two, the quicker you are with the bat, the longer you can wait before swinging at a pitch. That gives you more time to make a decision.

After all that, he took another bat and imperceptibly flattened one side of the barrel. Hitting with a flat bat makes it a lot easier to hit. Hitting a round ball with a round bat is the hardest thing to do in sports. Hitting a round ball with a flat bat is like hitting with a tennis racket.

I warned Dave that if he got caught, it's suspension time. That would either teach him not to get caught the next time or not to cheat at all. Like most players, he'd take the former.

51

The conversations around the team were getting stupider and stupider. I walked out to the bullpen to throw between starts and caught Mike Strock and Matt Bradley in the middle of a heated discussion.

"You're wrong," Strock said in a slightly raised voice.

"You're outta your mind," Bradley responded.

This went back and forth with similar dialogue for a few minutes. I wasn't about to get involved, but then got dragged in.

"Brett, you know stuff. Maybe you can settle this," Bradley said.

"Who decided that he should be the arbiter?" Strock asked in a demanding tone.

"Because he's smart."

"Who says?"

I wasn't going to get in the middle of the argument about whether I was qualified to settle the first argument any more than I was planning to get involved in the first argument.

"He's Jewish. All Jews are smart," Bradley said.

I looked at them with my face scrunched up after I heard that one. (One quick question: If a stereotype is a compliment, is it okay to use the stereotype?)

"All right, all right. We can ask him," Strock reluctantly agreed.

"Brett," Bradley said.

"What? WHAT?"

"Can you settle this for us?" Bradley asked.

"Settle *what*?"

"Which do you like better, *The Addams Family* or *The Munsters*?"

I looked at the both of them as if they'd just escaped from the local asylum.

"Do you mean to tell me that you've spent at least the last ten minutes that I've been here, and God knows how long before that, arguing the merits of *The Addams Family* and *The Munsters*?"

"Yeah. So? Whaddaya think?" Strock asked.

"That," I said, "is without a doubt the stupidest question I've ever heard, bar none."

"Excuse us, Mr. Ace, we didn't mean to waste your time," Strock said in a derisive tone.

Mr. Ace? I like that.

"I didn't mean it that way," I said.

They looked at me.

"*The Munsters*, man. *The Munsters*," I said and walked away.

Imagine anyone comparing *The Addams Family* to *The Munsters*.

52

It didn't take long for Christenson to get busted with his doctored bats. In the second inning of the game against Billings, he hit a shot with the flattened bat that moved like a whiffle ball. It curved about twenty feet after he hit it and went into the corner for a double. The Billings manager asked the umpire to check the bat and they found the flattened surface. Dave Christenson had been caught with the evidence barely out of his hand. The jury has found him guilty of using a loaded bat. He was ejected of course and would soon be hearing from the Pioneer League office. A suspension was likely. How long it would be was anybody's guess.

Witherspoon was incensed ... at Christenson. He didn't know that he was loading his bats and if he had he would, at the very least, have shown him a smarter way to do it. At the most he would have stopped it. The sickest part of the whole thing is that Christenson didn't need to use loaded bats. Maybe the insecurity that leads him to use steroids also led him to try and gain an advantage against the opposing pitchers.

53

We lost three out of four to Billings and our record stood at 29–21 when Butte came in for four games. Christenson got word from the league office just before the first game with Butte. An eight game suspension and a $150 fine. That's a lot of money considering what we're making. He felt like an idiot.

I pitched the opener and won 5–2 to raise my record to 7–2. Seven innings, one run, four hits, four walks and five strikeouts. I threw a few more twisters than usual and my arm was very stiff afterwards. McCormack told me to be careful with that pitch due to the violent arm action. He was right.

Duerson hit the longest home run I've ever seen. 517 feet! That one landed on Jupiter. I still think if he cut the bombs he hits into little pieces he'd hit .750.

Nobody was sure what Christenson was going to do with his unscheduled vacation. Witherspoon wanted him to keep his mind on baseball. For his part, Christenson said, "I'm gonna pound the weights like a maniac during the day and bang every girl I can get my hands on at night." At least he was going to keep busy.

I have a friend like him back in Brooklyn. I told the story in the clubhouse. My friend's name is Stone and he is the consummate pick-up artist. I've never seen anything like it. He could pick up any girl in any nightclub if he wanted. He had been with some of the best looking women I'd ever seen. On the other hand, I've also seen him go with some of the most repulsive women I'd ever seen. He would just go for whatever passed in front of him no matter what they looked like or where they'd been. I remember one Tuesday night three of us went to a nightclub called "Wedge's" in Manhattan. Naturally it was empty. We were hanging around when another friend named Rich went over and tried his luck with a girl on the other end of the room. Stone saw a female walk by. He followed her and started talking to her, trying to pick her up. She was Asian and didn't appear to understand a word he was saying. There was a good reason for that: She barely spoke English. When I moved in for a closer look I thought that she was an escaped Viet Cong. She had on a black skirt, a black shirt and a black hat. (Maybe she was a burglar now that I think about it.) She wasn't ugly, but she was short with a scary look about her. She could blow at any moment and not in a good way. She may have been on a kamikaze mission. A few minutes passed and Rich came back.

"Where's Stone?"

"Don't ask," I replied.

A second later, Stone reappeared.

"No luck?" I asked.

"Brett, gimme the keys," he said excitedly.

"What for?"

"Come on, man. She wants to fuck!"

I rolled my eyes.

"You gotta be kidding," I said.

"No. Gimme the keys."

"Stone," I said, "I give you my keys and I never see my car again. I'm not insured for suicidal explosions."

75

"Stop fucking around. Gimme the keys," he demanded.

I thought about it for a second and gave in. I gave him the keys. What's the difference?

Fifteen minutes passed and Rich and I went into the lobby of the club. I looked to my left and what did I see? Seated on a bench I saw Stone and the Kamikaze still in the club. He was still trying to convince her to go to the car with him. She looked bewildered.

Rich and I went over.

"Stone, let's get outta here."

He grudgingly agreed.

The Kamikaze seemed to be following us as we got outside. Stone kept on trying. She showed him a pass that she had for another night-club. He took one final shot.

"We drive you here," he said to her, "you give us blowjobs?"

She looked up at him and nodded urgently making what sounded like affirmative grunts and whimpers that puppies make. "Mmm mmm mmmm mmm."

"Guys! She's gonna blow us."

Rich and I were about fifteen feet ahead, laughing hysterically and shaking our heads no. A second later the Kamikaze looked at Stone and asked with total sincerity, "What's a blowjob?"

Stone, not missing a beat said, "You mmmm mmm" pointing to her lips, "on us mmmmm mmmm." Pointing to his cock.

She was taken aback.

"Ooooh. You *bad*. You *baaaaad* boy."

She started walking across the street and Stone removed his cock from his pants. He was walking along the East Side of Manhattan with his cock in his hand as she looked back and shook her hand up and down at him with her middle finger extended.

"Sucky wucky fucky wucky sucky!" Stone yelled.

By then Rich and I were doubled over with laughter. The funniest part was when we got in the car. Sitting in the back seat, his cock still out, Stone exclaimed, "The worst part is that we used all the money we had to get into that place. We got no money left to eat!"

Christenson is the same type of guy.

54

We won three out of four against Butte and then traveled to Idaho Falls. Idaho Falls had a good team. They'd won the first half of the Southern Division and had the hardest thrower in the league. Closer Jed Curdish was from Iowa and looked like Zeek who just escaped from the barn. He was 6'4" and 185 pounds, with an overbite that extended so far in front of his face that it would provide shelter for a small family. He was long and gangly and kind of looked like the Disney character "Goofy." There was nothing goofy about him when he got out on the mound. He went into his motion and it was so free, easy and smooth that I'm amazed that he generates the power that he does. He lifts his leg, turns his hips and *rips* the ball. Duerson can get around on most anyone's fastball, but he had no chance against Curdish. No one did. No one touched him. Sitting in the bullpen with Mike Strock when Curdish came in to pitch, Strock turned to me after Curdish's second pitch and said, "That one *sounded* low." We couldn't tell by watching. You can't judge what you can't see. Thankfully the designated hitter is used in the Pioneer League so we wouldn't have to hit against him.

If you're wondering why we use the DH when we are an affiliate of the National League's Dodgers, I have a simple explanation for you. If you have seventeen position players on a Rookie League team there aren't many at bats to go around in only 76 games. There are only eight fielding positions to fill. So, to waste at least four valuable plate appearances with a pitcher disrupts the teaching process. Why have a pitcher batting down here when his hitting is not going to improve that much anyway? It's better to let a position player get the valuable experience hitting against professional pitching and to become acclimated to it than to have the pitcher hit. We're down here to learn.

Even though they had the flamethrower Jed Curdish, we swept Idaho Falls anyway. I pitched the greatest game of my life in the second game. A complete game four hit shutout with one walk and seven strikeouts. I had everything working from the first pitch on. Everything was going exactly where I wanted it to go and the exploding technique that McCormack suggested was really paying dividends. I didn't give up a hit until the fifth inning and the ones that I did give up were dunkers. Usually Witherspoon and McCormack will find some mistake to focus on after they tell us about the good things we've done. This time, they had no complaints.

There were two strange things about this game: One, I had absolutely nothing warming up in the bullpen. I wasn't sure if I'd get out of the first inning. Two, Duerson was the DH for this game. Rico Etchesteria, a twenty-year-old defensive whiz from Houston, was behind the plate and called a great game. He also homered.

Later, I asked Duerson if he was jealous. "What are we, lovers for Chrissakes?" he asked.

After the four game sweep in Idaho Falls, our record was 36–22. That was good enough for first place in the Northern Division. The searing fastballs from Jed Curdish didn't give us any trouble this series because he never had a chance to close any games.

55

Some of you may be wondering why I never mention any sightseeing during any of these road trips or homestands. I have a legitimate answer for you. But first, I must pose a question: How many of you out there can say you've traveled to Idaho Falls, Idaho; Billings, Montana; Butte, Montana; Helena, Montana; Lethbridge, Alberta; Medicine Hat, Alberta; and Ogden, Utah?

Those of you who have know what I'm about to say. Those of you who haven't better believe what I'm about to say. *There are no sights to see!* Traveling around these towns is just plain boring and we have to do it over and over and over again.

I'm not trying to say that I'm Mr. Big Time New Yorker complaining about small towns. I'm easily amused. There's plenty of time before night games and after afternoon games to find entertainment. And it's not as if we didn't go looking for things to do. Other than the casinos, what is there? There is a zoo in Idaho Falls that Duerson, Christenson and I went to see. They have a penguin cove exhibit and a petting zoo. I had to remind Christenson not to try to have sex with any of the goats, male or female. "Fuck you, Brett," he responded. I like zoos, so that was fun. But that was it for Idaho Falls.

In Billings there's the Yellowstone River where we went looking for girls but had no luck. Also, there was a turn of the century train depot that no one wanted to bother looking for.

Butte, a mining town for gold, silver, and copper, wasn't any more exciting than Billings. We found out that Evel Knievel, the daredevil motorcyclist was born there. Nobody seemed to care. There was something that piqued our interests in Butte. There used to be a famous brothel in town. Unfortunately it closed in the early eighties. Oh, well.

Helena had some interesting old buildings. The marble constructed state capital was a sight that we enjoyed for about a minute and thirty-seven seconds. There was the Cathedral of Saint Helena where Strock and I ran into team evangelist Chris Purton. (Isn't a cathedral Catholic? What was the born again Christian doing there?)

"Have you come looking for answers to the questions of life?" he asked.

"I have the answers to the questions of life," Strock said. I was afraid to ask what he meant by that.

We were told that Lethbridge had many lovely parks but we found it more interesting to stay in the area of the hotel and stare at sidewalk cracks. Medicine Hat has a hockey team in the Western Hockey League but they weren't playing while we were there. There wasn't much else to see.

My favorite stop was by far Ogden, Utah. They have a sizable Evangelical Christian Community. Those people are wild. We went to the Ogden Nature Center. It was a frigging forest. I think you're allowed to hunt there if that is to your taste. Not my deal. I can get through my road trips without killing animals. I went looking for the Aerospace Museum but couldn't find it.

Now maybe it's clearer as to why guys drink until they can't stand up and have as much sex as possible. There's nothing else to do!

56

It is better for a manager to be feared by his players than it is to be loved. Fear inspires players to go above and beyond the call of duty.

Fear forces players to do things that they might not want to do, but do it regardless because they are afraid. Love is different. Players have loved managers and gotten them fired anyway. You always hurt the ones you love. They have been indifferent and disrespectful to the managers that they supposedly loved because they felt that someone else might have been better suited to the job. Once a manager loses the fear, he loses their respect. After that he loses games. After that, he loses his job. A manager doesn't have to be a martinet to have that fear. He just has to react in certain ways to situations that arise over a long season. The way James Witherspoon dealt with the Wade Mills and Jeff Finestra situations let everyone know that certain behaviors were not going to be tolerated. That instilled the fear that allowed him to be laid back and still command respect. Some guys were physically afraid of Witherspoon. It wasn't because he was physically imposing. He stood 6'1" and weighed 190 pounds—the same as his playing days. I told a story that I remembered from the time that Witherspoon played for the Reds. I remember weird things, things that no one else would remember the day after they happened, let alone nine years later. I remembered this vividly. The Reds were playing the Pirates on a scorching hot day in Cincinnati. It was a Sunday and they were playing a doubleheader. This was the fifth game in the series because there were rained out games to be made up. Tempers were short because of the heat and the fact that tensions develop between teams the more they play each other. Witherspoon was playing first base when the Reds pitcher hit Pirates outfielder Dave Davis with a pitch. Davis was the biggest and most intimidating player in the league. Standing 6'6" and weighing 235 pounds, he was enigmatic and moody. The word around the league was that nobody messed with Dave Davis. Davis, his mood rainbow one of the darker colors, was none too pleased with getting hit. As he strolled slowly toward first base, he glared at the Reds pitcher. He got to first and suddenly decided to visit the mound and hit the pitcher back. Witherspoon stood between Davis and the mound.

"You're not going over there, Dave," he said.

Davis looked down at the smaller man and growled, "Oh, no?"

"No, Dave," Witherspoon said. The two had known each other for years.

"What the fuck are you gonna do to stop me, motherfucker?" Davis replied, pushing Witherspoon for emphasis.

With that, Witherspoon brought his hand back as quick as a flash and punched Dave Davis right in the jaw and knocked him cold. Both benches emptied, touching off a fifteen minute fight. The only thing that anyone could talk about later was James Witherspoon knocking out a man five inches taller and forty-five pounds heavier with one shot. The story followed him around.

The fear that Witherspoon inspired instilled the discipline that was needed to teach us how to play and win. And it helped that the players liked him. That's what made him a good manager.

57

Duerson and I got back to the Cranes' house from the trip and Karen Crane informed me that my mother had called. I called her back and she had some sobering news.

"We're coming," she said.

"Coming where?" I asked.

"To Montana."

Terrific.

"When?" I asked.

"In two days."

"Two days? Where are you staying?"

"We were hoping that you could find us someplace."

What a pain in my ass. I had no time to plan my parents' vacation.

"I'll look around and call you back," I muttered.

I went to the phone book and looked up several hotels and motels in the area. I found four within two miles of the ballpark and called mother back.

"All right, there are four places that seem okay near the ballpark," I said. "How long are you going to stay?"

"A week."

"Well, there're three hotels and a bed and breakfast."

"Ooooh, a bed and breakfast," she cooed. "What's that like?"

"I don't know, mother, I haven't seen it. If I were you, I'd stay at the Holiday Inn or Comfort Inn."

"Can't you go and see what the bed and breakfast is like?"

I got annoyed. "No mother, I can't go and see what the bed and breakfast is like. I have some responsibilities here, you know. I'll give you the number if you want to call."

With that, I gave her the phone number of the bed and breakfast and the other hotels I found.

They decided on the bed and breakfast. Or, I should say that mother decided on the bed and breakfast. Phil Samuels keeps his mind clear of such matters. They gave me the flight information and I borrowed Duerson's car to pick them up. Of course, on the way back from the airport, I got lost. I saw it coming. I get lost in New York and I've lived there my whole life; what chance did I have of finding my way around Montana? I had called Great Falls GM Mason Standt for directions. I later told him that his directions sucked. I was actually happy to see my parents again.

"Whose car?" Dad asked.

"My roommate's."

"What year is it?"

"I don't know, Dad."

"How much did he pay for it?"

"How do I know?"

This went on for ten minutes.

"When's your next game?" mother asked.

"Tomorrow against Lethbridge," I said.

"When are you pitching?" Dad asked.

"In three days."

"Do you know where you're going?" Mother asked.

"Yes, Mother."

"You still haven't gotten a haircut?" she said.

My hair was rapidly looking like an unkempt bush in need of pruning. I think Witherspoon was going to tell me to cut it, but then I started winning, so he left me alone. I'm not going to cut it until I have a terrible outing. It could look like Dr. J's hair during his Afro laden heyday and I still wouldn't cut it if I were on a hot streak.

I was about to throw my parents from the car or jump out myself when we finally arrived at the Chalet Bed and Breakfast about a half mile from the ballpark.

58

Mom and Dad came to the ballpark after spending the day looking around the town with me. Somehow they managed to find things to look at for more than a half hour. I was amazed. They've always been able to amuse themselves with boring crap in small towns. They met the Cranes. My father managed not to say anything stupid and Karen Crane made my mother tea. Thankfully, my mother was informed that I had been behaving myself. My father got all of Duerson's car information, registration and VIN number included. At the ballpark, they had seats right behind home plate courtesy of the Great Falls Dodgers and watched as I did all the boring things that I had to do every non-pitching day. They watched me run then work on my pitch location. I brought Witherspoon over and everyone shook hands.

"You're son's quite the character," he said.

"Is that good or bad?" Mother asked.

Witherspoon thought about that for a second, smiled and repeated, "Your son's quite the character." He patted my shoulder and walked away.

As for the game, Miguel Santana pitched a five-hit shutout and we won 1–0. Afterward, that moron Mike Queen walked by my locker and said, "Yowuh parents ahr heah? Do they know that yowuh an ayuss-hole?"

"No," I quickly piped up, "but I did tell them that you're a fag."

I pitched the third game of the series. My parents' presence didn't affect my good groove. I was slightly more nervous than usual. I didn't remember the last game I participated in that my parents witnessed. I was masterful. I snapped off some of the most vicious twisters I'd ever thrown and some great "cutters." My fastball got clocked at 87. My best yet. Maybe I was starting to fill out or Wes McCormack's suggestions were starting to work. Maybe both. This was my second straight shutout. I walked none and struck out six. A beautiful five-hitter showed my parents that I was doing well indeed. Duerson hit one of his bombs that looked like a Titleist hit by Tiger Woods. That was all my dad was talking about, still reluctant to praise his son. That was okay.

My parents enjoyed Great Falls. They hit the casinos and won $1,500. My father used to be (and apparently still is) an excellent gambler. Mother let him play and he won enough to pay for the whole trip. There were plenty of restaurants and Dairy Queens for them to eat in, and they managed to find some sights for us to look at. They never embarrassed me either. As much as I hate to admit it, I missed my parents.

59

I had barely noticed but the season was almost over. We'd played so well that the second half division championship was ours. We were coasting with a record of 40–24 as the bus rolled along S-3 East toward Medicine Hat. I got a no decision in the third game of the series. I gave up only one run but we scored only one, until Christenson, returned from his suspension and using a legal bat, homered to give us the lead. Mike Strock got the win in relief.

Next, we went to Lethbridge and had a chance to clinch a playoff spot. We had to sweep four straight to do it, but the opportunity was there. Witherspoon emphasized the need to get the job done when the opportunity was there. Keep the killer instinct.

Jack Kray pitched a shutout in the opener and we won the second game 8–5 after falling behind 5–0. Chris Purton must have prayed extra hard before the game because he hit one out of the park. Jesus saves *and* he helps you hit home runs. (I don't have any problem with guys being religious, but when they start thanking Jesus Christ for them being successful in an athletic contest it makes me cringe. Why don't they blame Christ when they fail? That would be fair.)

The third game was rained out, so if we swept the doubleheader, we would clinch the division. Rain delays are sooooo boring. I went to sleep on the trainer's table for the entire delay. After the game was called, I asked Witherspoon if I could move up in the rotation to pitch the second game. That way I would have the opportunity to be on the mound when we clinched and be at the bottom of the dog pile on the mound in the victory celebration. It's one of my biggest nonsexual fantasies.

He said no and it's probably for the best, because I might have ruined the Jon Duerson show. He homered in his first three at bats in the first game. One to left, one to center and one to right. The fourth time up he walked. We won 10–0. In the second game he hit two more! Bosetti also homered and Christenson tripled home two runs. Five home runs in a doubleheader is an amazing achievement and I'm glad I had a front row seat for it. We were ahead 7–2 when Witherspoon brought Strock in to close it even though it was a nonsave situation. Everyone was on the top step of the dugout as Lethbridge batted in the bottom of the ninth. My stomach was churning. I couldn't hold in my excitement. Strock got two quick outs. Then he got two quick strikes. He wound up. We were ready to run to the mound. He fired … ball one. We stopped ourselves as we were charging to the mound and went back to the dugout. Strock rocked and fired again. Curve. Strike three swinging! Strock jumped in the air and Duerson ran to the mound and lifted him up. Everyone charged from the dugout and piled up on the mound. Guys were hugging and slapping each other on the back. James Witherspoon and his coaches sat in the dugout watching us kids celebrate our first professional championship. They smiled to themselves and didn't let us get too crazy. They were hoping for more celebrations in the future for this group of kids.

60

We had three meaningless games at home against Medicine Hat before the playoffs. They were meaningless in the standings, but I wanted to head into the playoffs on a high note. It turned out to be a very high note as I pitched another shutout. A 6–0 win gave me a record of 10–2. In my mind I was, without a doubt, ready for the playoffs. We ended the season with a record of 48–25, best in the league. We were hoping that a championship was on the horizon.

61

The way the playoffs are structured in the Pioneer League meant that we, the second half Northern Division champions, had to play Helena, the first half Northern Division champions. In the Southern Division Idaho Falls had to play Billings.

In a playoff series the manager generally likes to start the series with his ace and get a quick lead in the series. Most of the time I think they do it so they won't be second-guessed for not doing it. If the concept of second-guessing is new to you, I can explain it in simple terms. You know how after a game talk-radio hosts, fans, sportscasters, owners, newspaper writers, and anyone else with a pulse criticizes the manager for the things that he did? And then they say what *they* would have done? That's second-guessing.

We went to Helena to play the first game of the playoffs and received a wonderful send-off from the hometown fans in Great Falls as we climbed onto the buses. The first game was in Helena and then we had to come back to Great Falls for game two and if necessary game three. We arrived in Helena and dismounted the buses. Witherspoon reminded us to keep focused on the task at hand and not get distracted by outside influences. There was a larger contingent of media types around to cover the playoffs. The championships are important to the periodicals. *The Sporting News, USA Today,* and *Baseball America* were there in addition to the local papers and news stations. Witherspoon gathered us in the clubhouse before the game because he could see that we were tight. Witherspoon hated team meetings. He hated them as a player and he hates them as a manager. But he could tell how uptight the young team was and wanted to calm us down: "Okay, guys. Now listen, I know you're feeling a whole lot of pressure right now and that's good. It means you care. I played with guys whose main concern was the postseason share and where they were going on vacation after the season. I don't see any guys in here thinking that way. I've been in big games before and know how you're feeling. Let me be straight with you and this is not bullshit. Once the game starts, it is the same as any other game. The nervousness is going to magically go away for the guys on the field and the guys in the dugout should feel the nervousness evaporate as the game gets going. Playing good, solid fundamental baseball is the way to win. It's the way we've played all season and I know that if we keep our cool and focus on our jobs, we will win this game. I don't want you thinking about the rest of the series. One game at a time. This is not a big league cliché. One game at a time."

He looked at all of us sitting in front of him. Satisfied that his words had sunk in, he clapped his hands.

"Let's have a good game, guys."

We went on the field ready for action.

62

My arm felt good warming up and I think I was throwing harder than I ever had before. My heart was pounding and my adrenaline was flowing. Duerson and McCormack had to tell me to take it easy as I was warming up because I looked like I was trying to throw too hard. If I do that during a game my pitches will be up in the strike zone and that's when I get pounded.

We didn't score in the top of the first and we took the field. I got to the mound and threw my eight warm-ups. Their leadoff batter stepped in and I fired the first pitch for a strike. After that it was surreal. All of my pregame nervousness went away. I was doing, wittingly or unwittingly, exactly what Witherspoon told us before the game. One pitch at a time may sound like a cliché, but it's true. If you start thinking five pitches ahead, you get into trouble. Focusing on the moment is an important aspect in this game.

Christenson homered with two on to give me a lead. Nine innings after I climbed onto the mound nervous and shaky, I threw the last pitch of the game. A vicious curveball. The batter swung and missed. Duerson squeezed the ball in his glove and shook his bare hand balled in a fist and ran out to the mound. He wrapped his huge arm around my neck and screamed, "YOU ... ARE ... THE ... MAN!"

I don't think he realized that he was strangling me and my feet were dangling five inches off the ground as we walked around the mound. He finally let me go and I was able to breathe again.

A smile crossed my lips and I shook my glove and my right hand in front of me. All my teammates came charging to the mound and were slapping me on the ass and patting me on my unruly head of hair. We had a joyous trip back to the clubhouse and floated onto the bus all the way back to Great Falls. My record was 11–2. Our lead was one game to none. One more win and we were going to play for the championship.

63

The next day, as I read the newspaper reports of the game and listened to the recorded interviews I had done, I decided that I needed to work on my interview technique. I used the phrases, "I mean" and "y'know" way too much. Athletes in every sport do that and sound ridiculous. I had to concentrate on what I was saying.

Game two was never in doubt. We were back at home in front of a capacity crowd. Miguel Santana was on the mound for us and had been great for most of the season. Rod Woods led off the game with a home run and we never looked back. Leading 2–1 in the bottom of the eighth, Duerson put the game just about out of reach with a two-run shot. Mike Strock came in for the ninth and, just as he'd done all season, got the save. We mobbed each other on the mound, celebrating another clinching. We were heading to the championship series of the Pioneer League against the Idaho Falls Braves.

Witherspoon set up the rotation for the championship series. I was pitching the second game if we lost the first and the third game if we won the first. I was really feeling like the ace.

We won the opening game on a grand slam by the Superfreak, so I would pitch the third game ... if it were necessary. It turned out to be necessary as Idaho Falls shut us out in game two. The season came down to one game. Win and we get a ring. Lose and ... well, lose and we *don't* get a ring. I started thinking that if we won I might win the Pioneer League Player of the Year. I would definitely get the playoff MVP if we won.

What am I saying? If we won? When is the operative word. I'm unhittable.

I was getting full of myself. Not outwardly, but in my own mind I thought that I could do nothing wrong. I was ready.

I thought.

64

There was more coverage than ever at the championship game and a huge crowd. Everyone was eager to see the Great Falls Dodgers join the list of champions that the Dodgers organization is always talking about. Many front office types from the big club were at the game. I wasn't nervous on the outside, but on the inside I could barely control my bladder. I went out there for the start of the game, nervously waited through the national anthem, and the game began. I got through the first inning with no trouble. In the bottom of the first, Duerson hit a two-run homer to give me a lead. I went out for the second inning swelled with confidence. I got the first batter. Then my mind started wandering.

I thought about how I would react when the final out was recorded in the bottom of the ninth. I was thinking this in the *second inning*.

I thought about what I was going to say to the media as I collected the playoff MVP.

I thought about being Player of the Year.

I thought about all the women that would be chasing the big star of the Pioneer League champion Great Falls Dodgers.

I thought that maybe the *Los Angeles* Dodgers would want to bring the nineteen-year-old phenom up to the big leagues for a look.

I walked the second batter in the second inning. Then I gave up a double to score a run. I started reverting to my old Brooklyn Rockies behavior when I would struggle back home. I didn't keep an eye on the baserunner and used the same cadence as I checked him three times. He stole third. I gave up a single to tie the game.

What's happening?

I saw Witherspoon out of the corner of my eye giving Duerson the "yak yak" sign with his hand signifying that I needed a pep talk. Duerson came out and talked. Unfortunately, I didn't hear a word he said. I wanted to go home and hide under the covers of my bed. Not my home in Great Falls. My home in Brooklyn. I felt like I was starting to hyperventilate. I was overthrowing. I walked the next batter on four pitches. Wes McCormack ambled to the mound and tried to straighten me out. The next batter missed a bad twister and then luckily grounded into a double play.

When I got back to the dugout, Witherspoon came over to make sure I was all right. I convinced him that I was fine. I *was* fine. The game was only tied. Things would be okay. I started to compose myself. Our half of the inning ended and I went back out for the top of the third. Before I could blink, the bases were loaded. There was action in our bullpen. The Idaho Falls third place hitter Jalen Lester was at the plate. I threw him a curve for strike one. Then I threw a low inside fastball to the left-handed hitter. That is exactly where left-handed batters like it. He dropped his bat head. The ball started rising in an arc toward the right field corner. I watched in horror as the Superfreak ran toward the wall. I bent at the hips and put my hands on my knees as it cleared the 335 sign in right field for a grand slam. I kept repeating the mantra, "This isn't happening. This isn't happening. This isn't happening. This isn't happening." But it was happening. Like a snowball becoming an avalanche, I couldn't stop it. We were now down 6-2 in the third inning. The infielders were in shock. I was in shock. I glanced at the dugout and nobody was coming to get me. I had to pitch to the next guy. I pitched to the cleanup hitter and he hit one over the centerfield fence. Seven to two. Witherspoon slowly came out to the mound. I had my head down as he arrived. I must have looked like a deer in the headlights. I wanted to cry as I handed him the ball. He looked into my eyes.

"Brett," he said, "keep your head up. You have nothing to be ashamed of. You're one of the main reasons we're here."

My ass. I have plenty to be ashamed of. I choked.

I nodded and walked off the field. I actually heard some boos. I got to the dugout and didn't know how to react. A couple of guys came over and smacked my knee or patted my head and said, "Hang in there."

Some guys throw equipment around when they get shelled. I've done it myself. But not this time. It wasn't my pitches that failed me. It was my head that failed me. I choked plain and simple. My dream season had turned into a nightmare at the worst possible time. We lost. *I* lost. Nobody specifically blamed me, but who else was there to blame?

65

Sitting in the dugout watching the Idaho Falls Braves celebrate the Pioneer League championship it occurred to me that I may not be ready for A ball let alone the Major Leagues as I had arrogantly thought before the game. I didn't handle the pressure even passably. I didn't handle it at all. The other guys were nice to me. Patting my back and ass and telling me that I got them there. That was little consolation, though. I wanted to win and be the hero. I wanted to dominate and raise my hands in victory on the mound. I wanted a ring.

Witherspoon pulled me aside in the clubhouse and hit everything right on the head. He told me that he knew that I was thinking about the celebration after the game rather than thinking about making quality pitches. I wasn't focused on the task at hand.

"You have to have an even greater ability to concentrate in big games than you do in regular season games. When things get hot, you have to keep your cool."

My eyes reddened trying to hold back tears. I don't like to cry. I managed to hold them in. I listened and nodded. After he'd finished, he told me to keep the press clippings from this beating more prominently displayed than the clippings for my shutouts. They're more important.

After the reporters enjoyed the thrill of victory in Idaho Falls' locker-room, they came to our side to witness the agony of defeat. I understand why major athletes get annoyed with the media from time to time. They ask the same stupid questions over and over again. And then they misquote you.

They picked at my carcass for a while as I sat at my locker with my legs akimbo. I answered the stupidest of the stupid questions. I didn't say that I choked even though they asked. That was all the big club had to hear.

After most everyone had cleared out I was still sitting at my locker feeling sorry for myself. Duerson came over. He hadn't said much to me up to that point regarding this debacle. I figured that he was disgusted with me.

"Hey man," he said, "at least now you can get a haircut."

That made me laugh a little.

"Let's get outta here, Chia-head." He said.

And that's what we did.

66

My first professional season was over. It had to be termed as successful despite my awful showing to end the season. I was an afterthought free agent signee and ended up as the ace of the staff. I wound up 11–3 in sixteen games with thirteen starts. I pitched 102.1 innings, gave up seventy-five hits, walked thirty-one and struck out eighty-five. I gave up too many homers with twelve and ended with an ERA of 2.56.

I wondered if the last game screwed up my shot at Player of the Year. I'm not sure whether they vote before or after the playoffs. So, who knows? It turned out okay because Duerson won it. If it couldn't be me, I'm glad it was him. We had a final team meeting and cleaned out our lockers. Witherspoon told us that we'd hear from the club in a couple of days regarding fall and winter work. Some guys would have to wait to find out whether they would be invited back at all. I was safe from that. I think. Even James Witherspoon didn't know where he was going to end up. You never know what the big club is going to do. He shook everyone's hand as they left the locker-room. Everyone went their separate ways for the winter. There are no real good-byes among the players. It's pretty much shake hands and say, "See ya next year ... hopefully."

In most cases the friendships are not really friendships. They're more like in-season associations. Although I like to think that I made some real friends in Great Falls. Duerson and I went back to the Cranes' house to say goodbye. They gave us gifts as we were leaving. We must not have been that bad to live with after all. The gifts were small-encased models of the great falls of Great Falls. Karen Crane hugged us goodbye. Duerson dropped me at the airport before his long drive back to Georgia. I hoped to see him at one of the fall leagues.

"If not, I'll see you next year," I said. I didn't add "hopefully."

"Cool," he said.

He drove off.

I found a luggage cart and strolled into the terminal and headed back to New York City.

I headed home.

◆ PART II ◆

67

I wasn't given many instructions from the Dodgers for the fall and started to worry about getting released. My friend Tony Taglianetti was back in Brooklyn too and looked at me the way he usually does, like I'm an asshole.

"You just went 11–3, didn't you?" he asked.

That straightened me out.

Dad was thrilled with my baseball card. I had about twelve of them. We only get two packs each from Topps so we had to trade with the other guys to get our own cards. None of the guys were cashing the Topps contract checks that we received when we signed, but I suspected Christenson of cashing his. I thought about cashing mine, but didn't.

Mother put my individual team picture up on the wall in the dining room. I always look good in pictures. I'm very photogenic.

With no instructions from the Dodgers for the off-season other than to gain some weight, whatever that means, I went about my business as usual. Taglianetti got me a job in a batting cage on Long Island running children's sports classes. I had some minor disagreements with another guy who worked there. He was always interfering with the way

I ran my classes even though he had the same job as I did. He was in no position of authority over me. He was around forty years old too. He seemed odd to me. Why was he spending his time running children's sports classes?

By now, you may have gotten the idea that I view men involved in youth programs with a jaundiced eye. Whether it's justified or not, I always think that these men are pedophiles trying to get close to children. Where are most pedophiles going to go? To the Boy Scouts, to the little leagues, and anywhere to be near children. All I know is that I wouldn't have left my kid (if I had one) alone with that weirdo at the batting cage.

When I wasn't working, I was lifting weights. I had thought that most players are asked to play in the fall leagues, but that isn't the case. It all depends on what the organization feels that a player needs. I had pitched about twice the amount of innings I had previously pitched for one season. My arm was tired at the end. The team wanted me to, if nothing else, increase my stamina. The Dodgers strength coach gave me a workout program to use. I had to report to Dodgertown in Vero Beach, Florida, at or around the end of January. As always, during my time off I managed to find time to amuse myself. Telling girls that you're a minor league baseball player and showing them your baseball card is an excellent way to get laid.

Taglianetti and I took a few days off in October and visited Los Angeles for a mini-vacation. I called the team office and they let me have a look around Dodger Stadium and the locker-room and weight room. The way the Major Leaguers have it is unreal. Everything is first class. There was the tarpaulin on the field, but I went on the mound enjoying my own private fantasy. I looked into the empty seats and imagined a person filling every one of them and cheering for me. I went into my pitching motion a couple of times. Taglianetti came up behind me and made a clicking noise with his mouth simulating someone hitting the ball.

"I'm surprised you didn't automatically jerk your head around toward the seats. It should be a stimulus response thing by now, like Pavlov's dog," he said.

One thing about Los Angeles: If you grow up in New York you're used to everyone looking at you like they want to kill you. Nobody says hello. People barely say hello if they *know* you. Forget about strangers. But in LA people smile at you and say hello. They're friendly. It takes some getting used to. Also, you don't know whether a woman is smiling to be friendly or because she wants to have sex with you. In New York if a woman smiles at you and starts a conversation you automatically assume she wants to have sex.

On the way home we almost got thrown off the Avis bus. Hard to believe, isn't it? When you drop your rental off, Avis has a shuttle bus to the terminals. While you're on the bus the driver asks you to call out the name of your airline for you to be let off. We were flying Tower Air and every time she asked which terminals the passengers needed, we would yell out "Tower." By about the fourth time, everyone on the bus started cracking up ... except the driver. She got on her little microphone.

"For those people who keep calling out 'Tower,' somebody else might miss their terminal because of you," she scolded.

When she started asking for terminals as we got to the Tower terminal, we yelled in unison, "Did you get Tower?"

We started laughing and ran off. Tony decided later that it would have been a perfect ending if we *did* get thrown off the bus.

He was right.

On a brighter note, I met a twenty-eight-year-old blonde on the flight home. I hung around with her a couple of times when we got back to New York. It was an all-around good trip.

68

It's common for minor leaguers who go home during the fall and early winter to work out with local college teams when they start to prepare for the season. I went to work out with Kingsborough starting in early January. I wanted to be in some semblance of baseball shape when I went to Vero Beach. There's a difference between being in "shape" and being in "baseball shape." The summer before I joined Kingsborough I worked out like a maniac. I was lifting weights for an hour and a half a day in addition to doing aerobics. I thought I was ready for anything that Roessler threw at me. I learned my lesson after the first day of camp in late August. I couldn't walk normally for a week after the hell we went through. It was Roessler's style to work our asses off in camp to weed out the guys who didn't really want to play. It worked because about fifteen guys quit.

It wouldn't look good for the Dodgers to see me laboring during wind sprints. Coach Roessler had kept track of my progress during my rookie ball season and was impressed. His telling me that meant a lot because he doesn't like to show much emotion. He's quite the stoic. A few of the kids I played with in college were still around. There's a large turnover on junior college athletic teams. Those that had been my teammates seemed to be giving me more respect than I remembered. I guess that's what going 11–3 does for you.

In early December came some sobering news. The Dodgers made a blockbuster trade with the Yankees, getting superstar third baseman Jared Kemerrer. They sent catcher Rich Simpson and infielder Jaime Lopez along with two minor leaguers. One minor leaguer was a moderate prospect from Triple A. There was a low minor league prospect sent away too. No, it wasn't me. And it wasn't Duerson, Christenson, or Strock. They traded Rick "Superfreak" James.

I was saddened by the news. I enjoyed the laid-back attitude of the Superfreak and I liked hanging around with him. Such a shame. I was upset for days after that. It made me feel like a piece of cattle even though I wasn't the one traded.

The good news was the trade of Simpson. It signaled to me that the Dodgers were planning on the arrival of Jon Duerson within the next two years. They signed defensive specialist Patrick Olson to a three-year contract to hold the job until Duerson was deemed ready. He probably would have hit eighteen homers up there when he *was* eighteen. This is all my own speculation, mind you.

Right before the New Year, Taglianetti and I went to a nightclub called "Webster Hall" on Manhattan's Lower East Side. It's called the largest nightclub in the world, but I don't know that it really is. It's hard to pick up girls there, but we had complimentary passes for reduced admission plus a free drink each. Sometimes you have to decide what's important. So, I was standing in the club by one of the speakers on the main dance floor on the second floor when my attention was grabbed by something to my right. I looked and saw a guy. But this was no ordinary guy. He was wearing a baby bonnet, baby booties and a diaper. This guy was dressed up as *baby New Year*. When I saw this I opened my big, fat mouth.

"What the fuck is he supposed to be?" I asked Taglianetti.

He looked and laughed. The next thing I saw was a large black man glaring in my direction. He was around 6'7" and 315 pounds, and looked *pissed*. He was bigger than Jon Duerson, and that's pretty big. I started mentally making out my will.

"Tony, Tony…," I fairly whispered to Taglianetti, grabbing at his arm and hoping for either some protection or someone to accompany me to the great beyond.

The man-mountain walked toward me and looked down. I managed a faint smile. *This guy is gonna kill me.* In a flash, he … extended his hand!

"Good fuckin' question, man!" he said, engulfing my hand in his. "Good fuckin' question."

"Yeah!" I exclaimed, breathing again.

Taglianetti turned to me. "When are you gonna learn to keep your mouth shut, Brett?"

"Someday, Tags." I said, "Someday."

69

It was late January and I was preparing to report to Vero Beach, Florida, for my first real spring training. Vero Beach is affectionately called Dodgertown. Everything Dodgers.

I had spent the whole winter working out and drinking Met-Rx trying to follow team orders and gain some muscular bodyweight. I purposely didn't step on a scale throughout the winter so I would be surprised at how well I'd done.

Boy, was I surprised. I jumped on the scale and saw that my weight had made a miraculous jump from 170 to … 172.

I gained *two* pounds.

All the Met-Rx did was make my stomach worse. If that was indeed possible. I was so disgusted. But what could I do? I have an ultra-fast metabolism. I suppose it's better than being fat.

I had received a letter from the Dodgers telling me that I was due in camp by February 2. It was a form letter. I was insulted until I discovered that they sent the same letter to everyone. I had to set up my own flight. I checked out the flight schedules to Vero Beach, Florida. There are no direct flights from New York to Vero Beach. I had to fly into Melbourne, Florida. That's only an hour drive into Vero Beach, give or take. Also, the flights from New York stop off in Atlanta to change planes. Learning this, I called Duerson and asked when he was reporting.

"I'm not sure yet," he replied.

"Well, I'm booking my flight today and have to stop in Atlanta. Why don't you get the same flight with me into Melbourne and we can drive in together."

He said okay.

I booked my flight for January 31. I wanted to make sure and get there early to make a good impression on whoever my new manager was going to be.

70

"What the fuck did you do to your *head*?" were the first words out of Jon's mouth when he saw me.

"Whatever happened to 'good to see you and how was your winter'?" I asked.

Just before leaving for Florida I cut my hair. Short. Extremely short.

My father called it a GI. I looked like I was ready to sign up to bomb Baghdad.

"What'd you do that for?" Duerson asked.

"Why not?"

"We can't call you 'Chia-head' anymore," he complained. He seemed disappointed.

To be honest, I don't know why I do certain things. I grow my hair long or cut it short because they seem like things to do at the time. It gets oppressively hot in Florida, from what I understand, so I thought that short hair would make things more bearable.

"Can you tell I gained weight?" I asked, flexing my arms.

"Oh, yeah. Let's see." He grabbed one of my biceps with his immense paws. "You don't look like you gained more than maybe ... hmmm ... two pounds."

"Awwww, shuddup," I said, turning away.

On the plane the talk turned to baseball.

"Where do you think they're gonna send us?" I asked.

"Us?" he asked with eyebrows raised. "*I'm* going to the show. You? I got you pegged for another year in Great Falls."

"Ha!" I said. "You're probably unaware of this, but I had it written into our contracts that we go as a tandem. Wherever you go, I go."

"Lucky me," he said. "I'm the only nigger in the world with a Hebe for a caddy."

We took Delta Flight 1095 from Hartsfield International Airport into Melbourne, Florida, landing at ten minutes to noon. We went to Avis Rental Car and rented a Chevy Lumina for the short ride to Vero Beach. Luckily Avis didn't have a picture of me with a line through it because of the California bus incident. It's a short ride. That's if I don't get lost. I got good directions into Vero Beach from Avis. Duerson read them and I followed them implicitly. They worked perfectly until I almost went the wrong way at the fork in the ramp. I was supposed to turn left onto SR-60E. I almost went right and made several illegal moves to get back on the right track. No cops were around to witness the infractions. The forty-three mile drive took forty-five minutes. I spied the lovely view of the water and palm trees as I pulled into the peaceful spring training site of the Los Angeles Dodgers.

"Probably lots of girls here," I commented.

"Helluva lotta good that does me," he groaned. A rarity among baseball players, Jon Duerson is faithful to his girlfriend.

I pulled into the Dodgers complex. It was time to go to work.

71

Duerson and I were rooming together along with another guy who hadn't arrived yet. We didn't know who the guy would be. After we dropped our stuff off we went and looked around the complex. There were a few guys working out in the weight room and a couple of guys in the batting cages, but we didn't see anyone we knew. Vero Beach was peaceful and quiet. I was sure that would change as more and more players arrived.

The next day, we reported to the complex for the first workout of the spring. We arrived early and were amazed at how many players there were. They don't separate the minor leaguers in the minor league complex. Everyone is lumped together. There must have been over a hundred pitchers. It's a good thing that I didn't see that when I first signed. I might have packed my stuff and gone home. We found Witherspoon the second day there. They were sending him to the class A team in Vero Beach. If we were sent to a high A team we had a 50-50 chance of playing on his team again. The Dodgers have advanced A ball teams in Vero Beach and San Bernardino, California.

We found out that some of our teammates from Great Falls had not received contracts for the new season. They'd been released. Matt Bradley and John Stynes were two of them. Don Bosetti shot off two toes on his left foot while hunting so they released him too. I spoke to him shortly after I arrived and he told me he was going to use the education clause in the contract to go back to school. (Minor league contracts have a clause that allows a player to go back to school and the team has to pay for it.) Organizations release players for lots of reasons, good and bad. I knew a kid who signed with San Francisco out of college. He had had elbow problems in the past. The scout who signed him knew this and told him that if he had any problems to let the scout know and he'd take care of everything. If that sounds kind of cryptic that's only because it is. The kid's elbow started flaring up and he called his friend the scout. The next day the kid was called into his manager's office and released.

The only difference between rookie ball and high A ball is that high A's season is twice as long. Spring training is horrible. The tedium makes guys want to kill themselves or others. The endless rundowns and covering first base. Aaaaaagh!

The running is by far the worst. John McGraw decided that pitchers had to run, so they run. Nobody keeps in mind that times were slightly different then. There were no weight machines or advanced equipment to keep the legs in shape. Running was all there was. The main reason that I don't like to run is that it makes me tired. I mention this to other players and they look at me like I'm some kind of a lunatic. Nobody agrees with advanced thinkers like me.

Dave Christenson arrived in camp and no one recognized him. I was lying on the training table reading the newspaper when I saw him.

"Dave," I exclaimed, "what the fuck happened to you?"

He was enormous. He'd gained fifteen pounds, all muscle.

"I bulked up," he said.

Can everyone say growth hormone?

"Bulked up?" I said.

He's also gotten two new tattoos. One was Jesus on the cross and the other said "MOM." I had to ask about the Jesus tattoo. "Are you *that* religious Dave?"

"I didn't know what else to get," he said.

And that explains that.

People who are ignorant about performance enhancing drugs think that everyone who takes them goes bald and has acne covering their body. That is not the case. It depends on many factors. The specific drugs and the metabolic disposition of the user determine what side effects there will be, if any. Other than some slight facial puffiness there were no visible side effects on Christenson. Of course no one knew what was going on underneath.

One final spring surprise and it's a doozy. Rod Woods walked into camp. Previously known as "Hot" Rod Woods, he looked like Rod Woods but was no longer Rod Woods, we discovered. He had taken to wearing a skullcap and had become a Muslim.

"My name is no longer Rod Woods. I have taken a Muslim name. I will now be known as Kareem Akeem," he announced.

"Oh, you're kidding," I said.

"No. And I do not appreciate you denigrating my new beliefs."

"Come off it, Rod."

"My name is Kareem Akeem."

"Yeah? You gonna be selling meat pies by the exit of the Brooklyn Bridge?" I asked. (There are always Muslims from the Nation of Islam standing by the Brooklyn Bridge exit in downtown Brooklyn selling meat pies.)

"If my Muslim duty requires it, yes," he said.

I raised my hands in a resigned fashion and said, "Ho-kay." And walked off.

Kareem Akeem huh? I considered calling him Cassius Clay but thought better of it.

The Dodgers are a melting pot. Nobody spends more money in foreign lands looking for talent than the Dodgers. Japan, Korea, Taiwan, Mexico, Venezuela, Puerto Rico, the Dominican Republic — they were all represented. I have a working knowledge of Spanish so I can communicate with many of the foreign players. My Japanese, however, is severely lacking. I do speak some Ebonics, though.

72

Florida is the place where ballplayers get laid more than anywhere else. There are two spring training leagues. The East Coast and Central U.S. all play in Florida in the Grapefruit League. The West Coast teams play in Arizona in the Cactus League. The Dodgers are a West Coast team that plays in Florida as they have since their days in Brooklyn. Women interested in meeting and laying ballplayers congregate in Florida and are never disappointed. There are always beautiful, willing women available. And ballplayers are not very choosy. I succumbed myself numerous times. The team rules were looser in Florida than they had been in Great Falls so we were able to cut loose a little more.

Players are sent to different complexes for games. There are numerous games during the day, and as guys are cut from the big league camp, the numbers in the minor league complex balloon. Mostly it's mix and match. The caliber doesn't really matter. The coaches, scouts and front office people have an idea of where a player is going to wind up right after the last season ends. Opinions don't change unless you tear up the league completely.

We were playing the Yankees' minor leaguers in Tampa and I ran into Rick "Superfreak" James.

"Hey, hey," I yelled. "The Superfreak!"

"Shut up!" he said in a raised whisper. "They don't call me that here."

How no one caught onto that name is beyond me.

A side note: The Superfreak wanted to know why I chopped off all my golden locks. What is the big deal? I wonder.

I pitched relatively well during the spring. As camp broke in late March I was sent to the Dodgers' high A affiliate in San Bernardino, California. That meant I was considered "advanced," whatever that means. Also being sent to San Bernardino were Duerson, Christenson, Woods (Akeem?) Strock, Jack Kray, that idiot Mike Queen and Miguel Santana.

73

As we prepared to start the season for the San Bernardino Stampede, we learned that we had to find our own apartments. There was much more freedom afforded to us in A ball. We weren't treated like children as much as in Great Falls even though most of us hadn't matured much, if at all. Duerson and I decided to room together. We found a nice furnished two-bedroom place on 27th Street not too far from the home park, The Ranch. It cost only $650 a month and we were making $1,250 a month. Along with the meal money we were to receive we'd have lots of money to find trouble if we chose. Jon had his car shipped, so transportation wasn't a problem.

Christenson also upped and bought himself a car. He got a late model Ford Explorer with all the features. There was one problem: Dave Christenson is the worst driver I've ever seen. Combine basic road rage with steroids and growth hormone and you have a motorized assassin. Mailboxes beware. According to Christenson's way of driving, red lights don't mean stop. They are merely a suggestion that you may want to *consider* stopping. I rode with him once. When I exited the vehicle I crawled along the sidewalk kissing the concrete. Never again!

Thankfully San Bernardino is a hundred times livelier than Great Falls. A county of 1.8 million with lots of colleges around which means lots of college girls. There were several local newspapers and a newly built stadium. The temperature goes from the 50s in the night to the 90s during the hotter days.

The California League has two divisions: the Freeway and the Valley. There are ten teams in the league and five teams in each division. Six teams go to the playoffs in a similar split division format to the Pioneer League. Teams with the best full-season record in each division get a first round playoff bye. The other split-season division winners meet a wild card team with the next best record in a two out of three quarterfinals. The winners of that meet the teams with the byes in the semifinals in a best three of five. The winners of that meet for the championship. If all of that is confusing, that's only because it is. There's also an all-star game in mid–June broadcast on ESPN 2. That would be cool to go there, I thought.

Our manager was a psychopath. Mickey Martin was thirty-one and never played in the Majors. He seemed to have adopted the mannerisms of Crash Davis, the character from *Bull Durham*, with some Norman Bates sprinkled in. He would be calm one minute, chatting with you casually, and then he would see something like a guy with the bill of his cap curved wrong and he'd start screaming like a raving maniac. If you wore your socks wrong, he'd start screaming. If a sea gull landed on the field, he'd start screaming. You get the idea. He'd been managing for three years. He had a gorgeous wife. How he got her was a mystery because Mickey's face looked like someone had been using it for a pincushion. He has greasy, receding black hair and a personality like a tetanus shot. The rumor was that the aforementioned wife, a sensuous brunette with short hair and huge tits, would select one player a year and carry on a torrid affair. I wouldn't mind, but Mickey's personality seemed tailor made for a murder-suicide.

74

Stephen Jones, the GM of the big club, came down right before the start of the season for his annual speech to the minor leaguers. I remembered the one from the previous season and came prepared with my dictionary and thesaurus. He walked into the clubhouse and I turned to Duerson, grinned and rubbed my hands together with glee.

"Here we go," I whispered.

Jones stood in front of the assembled San Bernardino Stampede. He had on a Hugo Boss suit and his hair was perfectly gelled and styled as usual. The new guys sat around waiting for the speech in rapt attention. Jones made his speech.

"Gentlemen, a multitudinous totality of you were fragments of the schematization during the antecedent continuum of days."

Huh?

Seemingly the closer one gets to the bigs, the larger the words become.

"You are cognizant of what I am on the verge of propounding. For those of you who are unseasoned, this will be enthralling and stimulating."

He made a dramatic pause, looking for some reaction. Did he consider the open-mouthed stares accompanied by drool a reaction?

"This is the apical portion of A ball for the Los Angeles Dodgers. In the abstract, you are merely three strides from the zenith."

I looked at Duerson who couldn't keep a straight face. Christenson was chewing his nails. I hadn't much of a clue as to what Jones was saying and I consider myself reasonably intelligent. I couldn't turn my thesaurus pages fast enough.

"However, things are scrutinized in greater proportion as your opportunity aggrandizes. The premium is commodious also."

"Attainment metamorphoses into something more imperative as the contests increase. The period of acclimation is concluded."

I was left to imagine how Jones speaks to the guys in the Majors, but then they probably don't listen anyway.

"This endeavor shall be managed as a means of livelihood. Prior achievements do not relate to a forthcoming accomplishment."

"Complete daily commitments and elevation will ensue."

He appeared to be wrapping up.

"Godspeed gentlemen."

"Any questions?"

I was tempted to make a smart-ass remark. After going 11–3, I could have gotten away with it. But, I kept my mouth shut. The next thing I knew Jones was pointing in my direction.

"Yes?"

I craned my neck scanning the room. Behind me was pitcher Jeff

Durst, the first round draft pick from Florida State. He had raised his hand.

"Uh, yes," Durst said, "can I ask you something?"

"Certainly."

"What the hell are you talking about?"

Jones looked annoyed. I turned toward my locker and bit my tongue trying not to laugh. Most of the others were doing similar things, including Mickey Martin. Jones left and everyone started laughing. Durst won admiration from many of the guys because what he did took some balls. But it wasn't that much of a gamble considering that he was the Dodgers' number one pick in the draft and they had a huge amount of money invested in him. He could probably have walked up to Jones and called him a cunt and nothing would have happened.

Despite Jones' interminable speeches, I'll say this for him: He's an effective general manager. He's made some solid, gutsy moves regarding personnel and staff at both the major and minor league levels. The big club contends consistently every year and draws three million fans annually. The minor leagues are well stocked with young talent to collect and trade just like life-sized bubble gum cards. He just has to lose some of the verbal gymnastics. Or at least speak so we know what he's saying. Who knows? He might even be saying something worthwhile. But we'll never know as long as he sounds like Webster's New World Thesaurus.

75

Mickey Martin's pitching coach was his brother Marky Martin. Marky has the same skin problems as Mickey and with those names maybe they should have been in a boy band like the Backstreet Boys. I even have a name picked out. How about "Acne"? Marky seemed okay though. He even had all the dugout chatter down pat. And he second-guessed just like a sports talk radio host.

"You gotta throw that breaking ball when we're behind these hitters."

"Bring the gas. Gotta throw some strikes now."

"Attababy, attababy, way ta be."

It's a good thing we had such responsible teachers down in the bushes. A guy's liable to get confused. We quickly discovered that the best thing to do with Marky was to ignore him. Word spread quickly that if he told you to do something, you should just nod absently at whatever he says and he'll leave you alone.

On the Stampede there were representatives from around the globe. Guys had come from Australia, Japan, Puerto Rico, Venezuela, the Dominican Republic, Mexico and of course Brooklyn. There was another Brooklyn player on the team. A stereotypical Brooklyn Guido named Frankie Scarsi. Or in his own words "Frangie Scarzee."

If you don't know what a Brooklyn Guido is, I suggest you rent the unintentionally funny movie *Out for Justice* starring Steven Seagal. Any character is appropriate to define a stereotypical Brooklyn Guido. Spike Lee also does a dead-on characterization of them in his movies.

I tried to play a hilarious joke on Japanese outfielder Makatoshi Hakatoshi. I walked up to him in the clubhouse and starting cursing him out in a friendly tone.

"Hey. How ya doing? You're a real fucking asshole. If you have a sister or maybe a girlfriend or wife that you'd like me to fuck, just let me know."

I went on like this for a few moments. He was smiling and nodding as if he had no clue what I was talking about. The problem was that Makatoshi had grown up in Southern California and was a third degree black belt in tae kwon do. Luckily he didn't beat my face in.

We opened the season in Lake Elsinore, California, against the Lake Elsinore Storm. They're an affiliate of the Anaheim Angels. An interesting point about them is their hitting coach Ricky Lopes. He was a light hitting shortstop for whom it was a yearly struggle to keep his batting average above .200. The better hitters in the league would compare their averages against Lopes' to make sure that they hadn't descended to the netherworld of Ricky Lopes. Naturally some front office genius decided that Lopes was qualified to be a hitting coach.

Do medical schools take surgeons who botch seventy-five percent of their diagnoses and make them into professors? That's the equivalent of what baseball does.

Who needs Ted Williams?

The bus trip to Lake Elsinore was a short one of forty-five miles in forty-five minutes. I was halfway expecting to start the opener based on my previous year's performance and the fact that I had had a strong spring. The joke was on me. Number one pick Jeff Durst got the start.

"This is a friggin' caste system," I muttered to myself.

I don't think that was the fair way to go about things. Why is it that just because Durst was the number one pick in the draft he got the opening day start? It may not sound like a big deal, but it was. I was penciled (?) in for the third game.

If it's any consolation, Durst got knocked around and lost 6–2. I don't like losing, but any player who tells you that jealousy and pettiness don't exist on any team in any team sport is a liar. It happens subconsciously and often consciously that you want the other guys to do more poorly than you. It's nothing against Durst personally. He's a nice guy and he has great stuff. The difference between him and me is money. If Durst goes 0–10 he's not going anywhere because of the amount of money invested in him. If I go 0–10 I'm back in Brooklyn applying for the post office.

76

In my first start in the third game of the season, I lost. We started the season 0–3. I didn't pitch all that badly, but I didn't pitch all that well either. Six innings, six hits, three walks, and four strikeouts. I took the loss and was cranky afterwards.

We won the fourth game as Miguel Santana pitched brilliantly in a 2–1 win.

On the short ride back to San Bernardino I started talking with the other Brooklynite on the team, Frankie Scarsi. He was telling me all about his "mint Olds Delta 88" and his "slammin'" girlfriend. As with many Brooklyn Guidos when not in the vicinity of black people he called them "niggers." He'd been stuck in A ball for three years and I started to believe that they were keeping him around as roster filler. I was roster filler once.

Duerson and I were arguing as to whether Mickey Martin would be more aptly described as psychopath or a schizophrenic and were unable to agree on a diagnosis.

77

Jack Kray won our home opener against the Bakersfield Blaze in front of 1,800 people. The Blaze is an affiliate of the San Francisco Giants so there is a natural rivalry between the two teams. It comes from the Giants-Dodgers rivalries of years past. What that has to do with us has yet to be explained.

There are lots of girls running around San Bernardino. I'd heard stories of the great looking women running around in California, and thankfully they appeared to be true. Duerson hit his second homer of the season right over the center field wall. The San Bernardino Stampede was chugging along at 2–3.

In the next game Durst got pummeled again. What a shame. We lost 8–3 and Mickey Martin was upset with the four errors we made. I know that he was upset because he charged into the clubhouse and threw the table with our postgame food spread halfway across the clubhouse. Cold cuts were flying all over the place. He was trying to get our attention and he succeeded. We were all attentive to the fact that he's a nut. It also gave me a question to ponder: If you have to lose, does that mean you have to starve too?

I asked Mike Strock that very question.

"Yes," he said. "If you lose you must starve."

78

Lake Elsinore came into town and I got my first win of the season. I was all over the place warming up, but once I got into the game I was fine. I threw some great curves and some sharp moving "cutters." I had gotten stronger over the winter despite not gaining any weight.

Lake Elsinore's manager Ryan Brooks had the umpires check the ball on me because he thought I was scuffing it. The ump came out lazily and checked my glove and my hat and didn't find anything.

You'll have to look harder than that.

The ump then told me that if I was scuffing the ball I had a great way of doing it because they couldn't find anything.

I stood there looking innocent. As Brooks trudged back to his dugout I hollered at him that he should spend his time finding a qualified hitting coach instead of hassling me. After that episode, Brooks and Mickey Martin started yelling at each other from the dugouts. No fisticuffs resulted. For the record I wouldn't mess with Mickey Martin. He's not a big guy, but he just looks like he's crazy. Don't fight with crazy people is my motto.

I wound up going seven innings and giving up six hits and two runs. Duerson homered again and my record was evened at 1–1.

79

Christenson had a new thing that he was doing before every game. He called it his pregame psych-up. He drank two cups of black coffee. After that he mixed up a double dose of a preworkout thermogenic called "Ultimate Orange." He then started banging his head into the runway wall leading to the field and then proclaimed himself ready for action. His eyes, never too steady to begin with, looked wired and ready to explode from their sockets. Everyone decidedly stayed out of his way. Sometimes he appeared to have trouble holding in his pent-up aggression. I started to become afraid of him hurting himself or someone else. What his stomach is made of, I don't know. One cup of black coffee and I'm bouncing off the walls. Two and I'm sitting in the toilet for an hour. Maybe Christenson should have stuck to his high school sport of football. Or hockey. The qualities that he has are quite beneficial in hockey.

We were taking another short bus ride to Adelanto to play the High Desert Mavericks. Football was the topic of discussion and I started talking about something interesting. There are so many NFL players who have handicapped or ill children. Off the top of my head I named Jim Kelly, Dan Marino, Boomer Esiason and Doug Flutie. And those are just quarterbacks. I wondered aloud if the cortisone shots and the painkillers that they have to take to be able to compete are a factor. I've never heard anyone discuss it before. Nobody seemed interested.

"Oh, the difficulty of being such an intelligent soul," I said to Duerson.

"Yeah, real intelligent. But you got no common sense," he replied, making a face.

80

Durst finally pitched well in a 10–2 win over High Desert. Third baseman Carlton Gray and Christenson both homered. Mickey Martin tightened up worse in a blowout. His blood pressure must be in the stratosphere and if the rumor of the ever-present bottle of whiskey in his desk is true, well, that can't help matters either.

We lost the second game of the series when Christenson, playing first base, let a grounder roll through his legs to let the winning run score. That led me to start thinking about Bill Buckner and his taking the blame for the Red Sox failure to win the 1986 World Series. Bill Buckner has been crucified in Boston ever since Mookie Wilson's grounder rolled through his legs to let Ray Knight score the winning run in a game and series the Red Sox were one strike from winning. I never really understood why the blame was put squarely on the shoulders of Bill Buckner. First of all, the Red Sox had a two run lead with two outs in the bottom of the tenth inning. They had their best reliever on the mound. Buckner wasn't the one who gave up three straight singles. Calvin Schiraldi was. Buckner didn't throw the wild pitch allowing the tying run to score. Bob Stanley did. And let's say that Buckner fields that grounder cleanly and gets Wilson out. The game was *tied*. There was no guarantee that the Red Sox were going to win the game. And after they lost, they still had game seven to get the job done. Granted, John McNamara made a mistake leaving Buckner in to play first when he had defensive specialist Dave Stapleton sitting on the bench. But I understand where he was coming from. Buckner had been playing for fourteen years and was about to win his first championship. They had a two run lead. McNamara wanted his loyal veteran to enjoy the moment out on the field with his teammates as they won the World Series. It was a mistake. They happen. But to blame Buckner and Buckner alone is totally unfair. The man had around 2,700 hits for his career. And knowing the Red Sox, they would have found another way to lose the game and the series. Simply because they're losers.

81

I started the last game of the series against High Desert and pitched beautifully … but lost. Eight innings plus, two runs, three hits, no walks and six strikeouts should be good enough to get a win. But we couldn't score against their short left-handed junkball pitcher. I was livid after the game because Mickey yanked me in a tie game in the ninth inning after I had given up a single. Not only did that take the game out of my hands, but he didn't even bring in Strock, our best reliever. He brought in Jose Alvarez. I was standing on the mound after giving up the single getting ready to work to the next batter when I saw Duerson standing behind home plate and looking at the dugout. I looked too and saw Mickey Martin striding toward me. I thought he wanted to tell me something, but then I saw his arm motion toward the bullpen.

"Is he taking me *out*?" I asked Duerson, on the mound now.

"Looks that way," he said.

I was incredulous. I had my mouth open and was squinting at Mickey trying to comprehend this move. I couldn't figure it out, so I asked.

"What are you doing?"

"I'm bringing in the lefty," he replied, refusing to look at me. He had his hand out and was waiting for me to give him the ball. I had it behind my back.

"You're what?" I asked calmly.

114

"Bringing in the lefty," he said. Then suddenly, without provocation he started screaming at me right there on the mound.

"I DON'T HAVE TO EXPLAIN STRATEGY TO YOU! I'M THE FUCKING MANAGER. YOU'RE THE PLAYER! GIMME THE GODDAMNED BALL!"

I wanted to strangle him right then and there. He wanted the ball? I was about to give it to him by jamming it down his throat. I clenched my teeth and was about to respond when Duerson got between us slightly and told me to go to the dugout. I decided that he was right. Killing the manager is not conducive to making the Majors. I angrily flipped the ball to Mickey and stormed off.

I got to the dugout and threw my hat and glove on the bench. I was enraged. When Mickey started walking back to the dugout I got up from my seat on the bench and started walking toward his corner of the dugout. Marky Martin intercepted me.

"Listen kid," Marky said, "my brother overreacts sometimes. Don't do anything stupid."

"Bullshit Marky," I replied. "I wouldn't have been as pissed if he hadn't just fucking embarrassed me out there. I don't give a fuck who he is, I'm not putting up with that crap."

Mickey got back to the bench and I walked over. I moved next to him and got close enough so that no one else would hear.

"Mickey, manager or not, you ever fucking embarrass me like that again and I'll jam the fucking ball down your throat and pull it outta your ass," I said in an angry whisper.

I didn't look back as I stormed down the runway into the clubhouse.

Alvarez gave up a double and the runner scored, giving me the loss. Mickey didn't say anything to me after the game and I didn't say anything to him.

82

Still enraged on the ride home to Bakersfield, I sat staring out the window at the trees passing along on the interstate. I had time to calm down since it's a three-hour ride. I started to think that this job isn't all it's cracked up to be. Sure there are all the girls you want and you can potentially make a ton of money, but there are some drawbacks. Traveling with a group of men for instance. People think it's great fun to travel with a team, but there is no limit to the crassness of men. And baseball players are worse. Jerking off and spilling the results onto unsuspecting teammates is popular. Regular bodily functions and snot rockets are used as weapons of comedy. Then there are the farts. You have to spend at least 90 percent of your time with these people. Try doing that for eight months and see how great *you* think it is.

As we rolled into Bakersfield, Mickey came over to me and said, "Sometimes things get fucked up, kid." Then he walked back to his seat. I took it as an apologetic gesture. Maybe next time he'll leave me in the game.

83

I was glad that the towns of the California League are more cosmopolitan than the towns of the Pioneer League. There were some sights to see. There were the horseshoe shaped mountains to take pictures of. And there were the inevitable things that Mother would like, such as farmers' produce stands on the sides of the highways. My dad has a great move; he'll be driving along the highways knowing that Mother likes to stop at roadside flea markets and fruit stands and he'll just drive right by them. Then when she starts yelling at him about it he'll either play stupid and say, "I didn't know you wanted to stop there." Or he'll ignore her entirely.

We lost the first game against Bakersfield and won the next two to return home at 8–8. It wasn't a very eventful series. Duerson continued his hot hitting by homering again. That made it six homers in sixteen games. He might have been right with his prediction on the plane to Florida. He might be going to the Show. Before the game there was a woman called the "Dynamite Lady" who climbed into a box of explosives as it blew up. She travels from one minor league park to another doing this. Bakersfield has the stupidest looking mascot I've ever seen. It was impossible to tell whether he was supposed to be a cow or a Dalmatian. I asked some of the guys in the bullpen what they thought and the vote was split. I also reminded Christenson not to try and have sex with it.

"Fuck you, Brett," he said.

84

We had a day off after returning home for a series with Rancho Cucamonga. Duerson and I went to the Inland Center Mall. He wanted to get some clothes and I had nothing else to do. It was odd. Kids kept stopping Jon for autographs and ignored me completely. After getting Jon's autograph, one asked me, "Are you somebody?"

"My mom says I am," I said.

I consoled myself by thinking that since I was wearing a polo shirt and jean shorts I'm only recognizable in uniform and hat.

While Duerson went into the Casual Male Big and Tall, I went to the Comic Shangri-La. I needed some Batman reading material. I found some things of interest and bought them. Then I went to the Casual Male Big and Tall to find him. I was wandering around the store apparently looking lost when a pretty redhead came up and asked if I needed help. Her nametag read "Michele."

"Yes," I replied. "I'm looking for a large black man."

She looked puzzled for a second and I saw Jon wandering around the aisles.

"Ah, there he is," I said and walked off.

I'm not someone who shops in big and tall stores. After that I went into Waldenbooks and was looking through the sports section when I felt someone's eyes upon me. It was Michele the redhead.

"Are you following me?" she asked. She was flirting with me.

"Maybe. Is that good or bad?" I said.

"I'm not sure," she demurred.

"I know who your friend is. Jon Duerson from the Stampede. Are you a player too?"

"That depends on who you ask," I cracked.

She chuckled.

"Yes. I'm a player too. Brett Samuels. You heard of me?"

"No," she said.

"Well, why don't you give me your number and you can get to know me," I said.

She moved her head around and said, "I don't knoooow."

"Okay then," I said, "I'll see you later." And started to walk away.

"No wait!" she almost yelled. She caught up to me and gave me her number. She's a twenty-two-year-old student at Cal State at San Bernardino. Hopefully she doesn't mind a younger, more intelligent man.

85

Carlton Gray is a third baseman/outfielder/catcher who had been in San Bernardino for the past two years. He was twenty-five, married with a young son and originally from Boston. He figured that A ball was as far as he was going to get and he'd had quite the interesting career path. His father was such a big Carlton Fisk fan that he named his son after him. He also forced his son to wear number twenty-seven and be a catcher. When Fisk signed with the White Sox as a free agent Carlton Gray's dad shut the curtains in the house and wouldn't speak to anyone for five days. During Little League games Carlton's dad would stand right next to the fence and scream at his son while he was playing. It's not real easy to hit when someone is screaming at you. It's not easy to do anything when someone is screaming at you.

Carlton had several scholarship offers out of high school but was drafted in the thirty-eighth round by the Philadelphia Phillies. His father wanted him to go to college, but Carlton signed. Mostly to get away from dear old Dad. He spent two years in the rookie leagues for the Phillies. Then he was sent to A ball in mid-season and then traded to the Dodgers as a player-to-be-named-later. He was stuck and said he was still playing so he wouldn't have to get a regular job. He says lots of clever things. He made me appreciate my father not pushing me. It's hard to enjoy success with the pressure that Carlton had to endure. Especially if every accomplishment is diminished in one way or another.

Carlton has also mastered the art of getting girls to notice him every time he plays. In the first game of the Rancho Cucamonga series there was a popup near the third base dugout. It was clearly out of play, but Carlton ran over and jumped over the dugout steps and wound up hanging by one arm on the roof. If you had seen the look on Mickey Martin's face. After the inning, Carlton sat on the bench and I gave him a suggestion. "Next time, why don't you just hop up on the top of the dugout completely and start doing a striptease? Or maybe just stand there and flap your arms like you're trying to fly."

He snorted a laugh.

"My wife gets mad if I do it so obviously."

"Good point," I said.

86

My record ran to 1–3 with a not bad/not great performance against Rancho Cucamonga. We were losing 2–0 in the bottom of the sixth when Christenson homered with a man aboard to tie it. I started the seventh by drilling the first batter and then got two outs before giving up a two-run homer of my own. Maybe Mickey should have yanked me after the single. Just kidding.

I was disgusted with myself because I gave up the homer on a bad forkball. Lately it seems like *every* forkball I throw turns out to be a bad forkball. I started to worry that they were going to send me back to Great Falls. Better wake my ass up, I thought.

87

We salvaged the third game of the series against Rancho Cucamonga and our record was 9–10 after nineteen games. Sitting in the clubhouse before the opener of the series against Stockton I was chatting with Frankie Scarsi trying to decide where to take that Michele chick on the date that I'd set up for that weekend. He suggested a trip to the store in which she worked for a round of anal sex. As lovely as that sounded, I passed on the advice. Introducing anal sex on the first date wouldn't be starting on the right foot. Across the room, Rod (Kareem Akeem) Woods was telling Brooks Simon and Homer Burns about the joy of joining the Nation of Islam. He was talking about Malcolm X and the honorable Elijah Mohammed and what wonderful men they were. Then he started in about Louis Farrakhan and I had to open my mouth.

"Why don't you talk about the rabid anti–Semitic nonsense that Farrakhan is always spewing?"

"The Nation of Islam is not a racist organization," Woods (Akeem) said. "It is an organization dedicated to the upgrading of the black community."

"What about the anti–Semitism? Is that a necessary part of 'upgrading the black community'?"

Guys were stopping their activities to listen to this. It was getting pretty heated.

"I have never heard Minister Farrakhan make any derogatory comments about the Jews."

"*What?*" I exclaimed. "Are you deaf as well as dumb?"

I started calling him "Rod" and he was getting mad.

Finally, Coach Willie Tavarez stepped in and told us to knock it off. That was where it ended.

I was really pissed though. How dare he sit there and say that Farrakhan has never said anything derogatory about the Jews. I remember when Farrakhan went on the *Arsenio Hall Show* and had a free forum to rant and rave about how the Jews are "bloodsuckers" holding the black man down. To endorse an organization led by someone like that and trying to recruit young, impressionable people into it is unconscionable. I couldn't listen to that and not speak up. If anything good came from the appearance on the *Arsenio Hall Show* it was the effective ending of Arsenio Hall's career. At least there was something salvageable.

88

Duerson homered again to win the opener of the series with Stockton. Walking into the clubhouse the next afternoon for the second game, I was greeted by a nice surprise.

"Hey, Mac," I said in greeting Wes McCormack, the Dodgers' roving minor league pitching instructor.

We shook hands and I asked what he was doing there.

"I'm here to straighten out Durst," he said.

"Bonus babies get all the attention, I guess."

"It's no guess," he said, "it's a fact."

He asked how I was doing.

"I'm 1–3. Does that tell you anything?"

"What's the matter?"

I told him of mistakes in pitch selection and the Mickey Martin incident against High Desert.

"Awww, don't let Mickey bother you. He's harmless," he said, trying to console me. Then with a smirk he asked if I'd met Mickey's wife yet.

"Not yet," I said.

"Hoo boy. Just wait. I think everybody fucked her. She used to be a waitress at Hooters in Georgia. She made the round of the league, but Mickey went and married her."

"I heard she looks to bang one player a year," I whispered.

"Oh, yeah. That's true. I wouldn't touch her though. She's been with a lot of guys. I mean a *lot* of guys."

For the record, McCormack's presence didn't help Durst any as he got pounded again. The guy is 6'4", 225 pounds, is great looking and has been compared in raw ability to Roger Clemens. None of that was doing any good on the mound, though. If he keeps this up he'll only have about seven more years of slack left. Such is the status of the bonus baby. If that were me, I'd be packing my bags for Great Falls ... or Brooklyn.

89

Shagging flies in the outfield during batting practice, I found myself trapped in a bear hug. I couldn't move my arms and was trying to turn my head to see who it was when I heard Christenson asking me how I did on my date the previous night with "that broad" I met.

"Did'ja fuck her?"

"Lemme go," I whined.

"No. You gotta fill me in first."

"Yeah, I fucked her. Now get off."

"That's my boy," he said, releasing me. "How was it? And what does she look like anyway?"

"Hey man, I don't go with rejects from the zoo like you do," I said.

"Hey Jon!" he called to Duerson. "What's Brett's girl look like?"

"She ayight." He responded in Ebonics.

"So," he said returning his attention to me. "How was it?"

"It's sex man. It's always better than jacking off. I'm a little worried about getting her pregnant though."

"Didn't you use a condom?"

"Yeah, but still," I said.

"Typical Jew," he said, walking toward the dugout. "At least you got some pussy," he called back over his shoulder.

I didn't have any real reason to worry, but did anyway. The last thing I needed at twenty was a kid. I could always resort to the Tony Taglianetti tactics of resolving an unwanted pregnancy. First, try and convince the girl to have an abortion. If that fails, throw her down a small flight of stairs. If that doesn't work, throw her down a larger flight of stairs. If *that* doesn't work, chase her with a coat hanger and fix the situation yourself. I never asked him if he'd actually performed any of the above acts because I was afraid of the answer.

90

We lost the last game of the series against Stockton and our record stood at an un–Dodger-like 10–12. We had to head straight for the bus for the ride to San Jose, so we had our bags packed and ready before the game. As we were waiting for departure, I spied for the first time, the wife of our fearless leader Mickey Martin. Circulating amongst the players, Nikki Martin (that's right, Mickey and Nikki Martin) was saying hello and seemingly looking us all up and down. Most of the guys were staring at her pretty hard. Some were doing it discreetly using their peripheral vision. (Baseball players' peripheral vision is highly developed because of the skills necessary to play this game.) Others were out-and-out staring. She has short dark hair, blue eyes, a slight tan, and enormous breasts. I was sitting on the ground reading a magazine when something blocked my sunlight. I looked up slowly. Standing directly over me was Nikki Martin.

"Hi," she said sweetly.

Uh oh.

I smiled faintly.

"What's your name?" she asked.

I swallowed and looked around, hoping for someone to help me. No help was imminent so I had to think fast. After a long pause something finally popped into my head. I looked directly into her eyes over my sunglasses and said, "No hablo ingles," hoping that she didn't speak Spanish.

She shrugged, smiled and walked away.

Whew.

Carlton Gray came over, having heard the exchange.

"That was quick thinking," he said.

"It was lucky thinking," I said.

"You got more willpower than me. If I weren't married I'd be in there right now. In fact, I still might," he said.

"Better you than me," I said.

91

The ride from San Bernardino to San Jose is around 400 miles. That's nine hours providing the bussie (ballplayer slang for bus driver) doesn't get lost. You must find ways to keep yourself busy during these trips. In Great Falls there were no outrageously long rides. On the long trips you have few things to do. You can play cards, which I hate. You can sleep which is hard to do on these rides. Some buses have TV and VCR, but they don't always show movies that interest me. You can talk, but that can be hard to do with this group. I was keeping busy by reading the Batman comics I bought at the mall. Mike Queen started in.

"Lookit, Breutt's readin' a comic buu-uuk. Haw haw."

"I got tired of reading about your mother in *Hustler*," I said. "And don't get me started about the photos."

"Fuuuuck yew," he said.

"Fuck your *mother*," I said.

He stood up and had an angry look and as he took a step toward me, everyone told him to sit down. He'd started it.

After that I started a buswide debate because Brooks Simon asked me if I read Superman and I announced that Batman would beat Superman in a fight. The argument, involving everyone on the bus including the coaches and the bus driver, went on all the way into San Jose.

92

The bus rolled up to the front of the Gateway Inn in San Jose a little after midnight. Some guys sneaked out to look for some action, but I chose not to join them. I wasn't in the mood. I called my parents and we talked for a while despite my forgetting about the time difference between the west and east coasts. They said they might visit San Bernardino soon.

I pitched in the first game of the series. The San Jose Giants were our archrivals simply because they are an affiliate of the San Francisco Giants. From the minors to the Majors the Giants and Dodgers hate each other. This is a rivalry in which Juan Marichal once clocked Johnny Roseboro over the head with a bat. That touched off a brawl so fierce that the cops had to come onto the field to restore order. I didn't do a good job against the San Jose Giants. I did a *fantastic* job against the San Jose Giants. Nine innings, no runs, five hits, no walks and eight strikeouts. Mickey and Marky Martin stayed away from me the whole game. If that was the reward for pitching like that, I knew I'd have to do it more often.

Christenson knows people all around California and since we had an afternoon game for the second game of the series, he used his connections to finagle five tickets to the San Jose Sharks–Detroit Red Wings second round playoff series. The tickets cost $43 each. Supposedly that is what regular season game tickets cost and Christenson's friend got us that price for playoff tickets. I refused to believe it until my ass was planted in one of the seats. Mickey gave us permission to miss curfew to go to the game. It didn't matter because we would have gone regardless of whether we had permission or not. Me, Christenson, Scarsi, Duerson, and Gray hopped into a cab to the San Jose Arena. The seats were actually pretty good. Hockey is by far the best sport to watch live. We sat in the upper level, section 226. We had a diagonal view of the ice. The Red Wings won in overtime. I didn't remember hockey being as chippy as it was in that game. Usually they're more cautious during the playoffs for fear of taking bad penalties. Then it occurred to me why I stopped watching hockey in the first place. The game has gotten so *violent*. I like the good, hard hitting as much as the next guy, but the attempt to ban fighting has made stick infractions worse. They seem to be genuinely trying to hurt each other. I once saw two brothers fighting on the ice. Where is the line drawn? It has gotten disturbing to watch. Besides all that, the players are much bigger than they used to be. On average, hockey players used to be my size: 5'10"–6'0", 170–200 pounds. Now they're averaging around 6'2", 215 pounds. Bigger guys, bigger collisions. Add all that to the malicious intent and you have hockey today.

After the game a couple of guys wanted to go looking for Mexican food. Evidently San Jose has good Mexican food. I reminded everyone of the Tommy Gianelli story. Scarsi still wanted Mexican food, but no one else did.

Christenson and I went to the IMAX Theater in San Jose. We saw some crappy pseudo-comedy that sucked. I wanted my money back. It was marketed as an outer space exploration film, but it wasn't. Christenson was pondering what porno would look like in IMAX. It would probably be interesting.

We lost the last game of the series in San Jose and headed to Visalia. That's a 200-mile, five-hour ride. All you get to eat on the road trips are rest stop fast food. It's a good way to save money, but a bad way to stay in shape. I tried to bring my own food sometimes to save my stomach.

93

Visalia is a small town without much to do. The team is an affiliate of the Oakland Athletics. The Athletics have a philosophy of drafting really tall pitchers. Inevitably when we played them we faced a group of guys between 6'4" and 6'10". They wouldn't want me over there. I wonder if they're aware that just because you're tall that doesn't mean you can pitch.

Wes McCormack had straightened out Durst for the time being. He pitched extremely well in our 5–1 win, evening our record at 13–13. Jon Duerson caught fire in the second game, hitting a 430-foot homer. Is it possible that big pitchers can't get out big hitters?

Masato Fujinami took over for Jose Alvarez in the starting rotation. Fujinami is a twenty-seven-year-old righty and unlike Makatoshi Hakatoshi is *from Japan*. The earlier joke that I tried on Hakatoshi probably would have worked on Fujinami. Oh, well.

The Japanese pitchers have really unusual motions. They try to get more hip thrust and leg drive into their pitches. Fujinami seems to throw directly overhand and has a great split-finger. When you talk to him he nods a lot.

I pitched the last game of the series in Visalia. Let the linescore tell the story: two innings, five runs, six hits, one walk and no strikeouts. Needless to say, I didn't have it. We were behind 5–0 when Mickey came to the mound to drag the carcass back to the dugout to rot. Selfishly, it made me feel better that Alvarez got shelled too. We were behind 9–0 when Duerson hit a grand slam to make it 9–4. He singled in the sixth to drive in another run. Then in the ninth he hit a three-run homer to make it 9–8. We didn't score any more runs and lost 9–8. My record dropped to 2–4 and after the game we got on the bus for the ride to Modesto. Our record: 14–14.

94

The ride from Visalia to Modesto is only three hours. We had a fascinating discussion on the worst television show ever written. I had to choose between *Baywatch* and *Beverly Hills 90210*. I decided on *Baywatch* but, in my eyes, they're equally as bad. Brooks Simon had the nerve to nominate *Seinfeld*. Had he lost his mind? There are so many awful shows that it would be hard to narrow the list down to one. *Baywatch* was a solid choice though.

While we were on the subject, I went into my riff of a pre–*Friends* Jennifer Aniston. She was: a Nutrisystem diet girl, on the TV version of Ferris Bueller (blechhhh), on a sketch comedy show called *The Edge* and in a movie called *Leprechaun*. There was a scene in the commercial for *Leprechaun* that was unforgettable. The lovely Jennifer gets her face licked by this seedy, repulsive looking leprechaun as she looks at the camera and screams. Lucky she found those *Friends*. Why I have all of this information stored in my head is beyond me, but now you're stuck with it too.

Speaking of Brooks Simon, he has a funny move. Did you ever see someone flip their hand into someone else's face and say, "Talk to the hand"? Well, he puts his own twist on that by dropping his pants, turning around and saying, "Talk to the ass." It's more effective if you ask me.

For some reason, the Athletics have two teams in the California League. Maybe their farm system is so packed with nine-foot-tall pitchers that they need two teams. Modesto isn't a large town. Its population is around 180,000. George Lucas used to live in Modesto and has a plaza named after him at the five point's intersection. I used to watch *Star Wars* endlessly and copy the dialogue to re-enact the movie with my action figures. Once *Star Wars* became the subject of the conversation everyone was chipping in with their opinion of which film was the best of the three. There is no argument. *The Empire Strikes Back* is the best of the three.

We arrived at the Vagabond Inn. An appropriate name for the existence of a minor league baseball player.

95

I was keeping the pitch count in the first game in Visalia and came to the conclusion that keeping the pitch count in a blowout is a form of purgatory.

The three games in Modesto aren't much to talk about unless you want to talk about us getting our asses kicked. We got swept three straight. After witnessing Miguel Santana getting hit in the nuts with a one hop shot in a 2–0 series opening loss, I decided to take my jockstrap and cup from the back of my locker, wash them and start wearing them again. Miguel is originally from the Dominican Republic. They play without shoes there, so expecting the guy to wear a cup was asking a lot. He writhed around on the ground for ten minutes before he was able to get up. He left the game and suffered the hard luck loss. He wasn't severely injured.

We lost the next two games 8–5 and 3–2. On the ride back home (which took nine hours) Mickey looked ready to explode, but held himself together.

What he does is very healthy. He takes his rage and pushes it deep into the pit of his stomach. As it tries to rise, he forces it back down with more rage accompanied by alcohol and cigarettes. More people should respond to adversity the way Mickey Martin does.

Tick, tick, tick …

96

I saw Michele the night I got back and was trying to decide if she got on my nerves or not. She seemed to drink an awful lot, which is her business. But I wasn't interested in getting involved seriously and I think she *was* interested in getting involved seriously.

We lost the first game to the Valley Division's last place team, the Lancaster Jayhawks. Lancaster is the single A affiliate of the Seattle Mariners. Mickey kept bringing up that they're in last place. So? We were in last in the Freeway Division. Mickey was looking for an excuse to have a tirade. And he did. After the game, he came charging into the clubhouse and tossed the two reporters that were covering this debacle out. He slammed the clubhouse doors shut and sprinted toward the food table. With a leaping kick he sent the whole postgame smorgasbord all over the room. Then he took a bunch of bats and fired them into the middle of the clubhouse and started ranting and raving like a lunatic.

"YOU WANT ME TO SET ALL THOSE FUCKIN' BATS ON FIRE? YOU AIN'T FUCKIN' USIN' 'EM!"

He was waving his arms around like a chimpanzee and his face was turning all the colors of the rainbow. I thought that I saw smoke coming from his ears but may be mistaken.

"YOU FUCKING FUCKS!" (Nobody ever said Mickey wasn't imaginative.) "YOU FUCKING GUYS HAVE PLAYED BASEBALL FOR YOUR WHOLE FUCKING LIVES? JESUS FUCKING CHRIST, ALMIGHTY! I'VE NEVER SEEN SUCH A GROUP OF PATHETIC LOSERS IN ALL MY LIFE!" (Try the mirror, Mick.)

Then I think he started making up curses.

"FUCKITY FUNGY GRUISGH FACK!"

We were trying desperately not to laugh, but it was almost impossible. Everyone sat at their locker not sure what to do.

"I HAVE TO PUT IN MY FUCKIN' REPORTS ABOUT YOU FUCKS! IF IT'S UP TO ME, NONE OF YOU MOTHERFUCKERS ARE GONNA BE HERE FOR TOO FUCKIN' LONG! YOU GUYS ARE NOTHING BUT CUNTS AND PUSSIES! ANYONE WANNA FUCKING VOLUNTEER TO BE A FUCKING CUNT OR A FUCKING PUSSY? STAND THE FUCK UP!"

I wanted to point out to Mickey that he was the only one standing, but thought better of it.

"YOU FUCKING FUCKS MAKE ME WANNA PUKE!"

(The feeling is mutual, Mick.)

Then he kicked the door to his office open and slammed it shut behind him. Marky Martin looked around the shell-shocked room.

"Well," he announced, "that's a crappy way to start a homestand."

The whole room fell on the floor laughing.

What I wanted to know was why Mickey threw the press out of the room. He was screaming loud enough that they heard him in San Francisco. What good was closing the clubhouse doors going to do?

I was pitching the next game. After the meeting I walked around to several guys and asked them if they'd ever heard some of the curses that Mickey invented. Nobody had.

97

I managed to stop the losing streak with a seven inning, five hitter. I gave up two runs and was helped by another Jon Duerson home run. The man did not belong in A ball. My forkball wasn't working, and then problems with the twister arose. It was just gliding into the hitting zone. I almost gave up a couple of homers that went foul. What's wrong? I wondered.

An interesting exchange during the fourth inning made me think. Gray was playing third and there was a hot shot hit at him. He fielded it cleanly and was getting ready to throw to first when he yelled, "Duck, asshole" at me. I'd forgotten to duck. Carlton Gray fired the ball to first and missed my head by maybe two inches. Let me explain. When a ball is hit to the third baseman, the pitcher has to duck to give the fielder a clear path to the first baseman. Usually I remember. When I was in Little League, I played third base. I was considered a slick fielder without much of an arm. That was not the case. I had a strong arm. The problem was that the pitcher never ducked to give me a clear path to throw and I was too polite to ask him to. The coaches were always wondering why I threw bullets to first during practice but not during games.

Mentioning Little League brings back memories. I have memories of anti–Semitism during my time in Little League. It may not have been clear-cut anti–Semitism, but it had leanings. Like Pat Buchanan. When I was twelve I played in a local church league that all my friends played on. There were a couple of Jewish kids in the league. One day, my team was having a team meeting and the coach singled me out.

"Now just because Brett may be a little different from us, we're all part of one team."

One of the other kids looked at me funny and I mouthed to him that I'm Jewish. It didn't bother me then, but as I got older it started to bother me a great deal. We were kids playing baseball. Why call me different? What was different? Did I have green blood like Spock? And even if I was different, how is that relevant? My parents are named Samuels. The other players' names were Bucci, Rosetta, and O'Brien. So what? Why bring differences up?

Perhaps this is the reason that I find Bible-thumping in the club-house so distasteful. Many of the players who are walking around talking about Jesus are worse hedonists than Dave Christenson. I know because I've seen it. They're looking for an image or a holier than thou way to deal with the money and pressures that come with playing baseball professionally. There's supposed to be a separation between church and state. That is quickly evaporating. How about a separation between church and ballpark?

98

I was sitting at home watching *The Real World* from Boston on MTV. I was desperately trying to figure out how someone who uses the word "supposably" could get into Stanford, which is exactly what one of the cast members did. It sounds ridiculous when people misuse or mispronounce words. Stephen Jones has an enormous power vocabulary and understands every ten-syllable word that he uses. It's just that no one else does.

Perusing through the *San Bernardino Sun*, I spotted an article detailing how terrible we've been through the first thirty-three games. The beat writer, Marvin Lerner, was trying too hard to be controversial. I know the difference between trying to stir shit up and *really* stirring shit up. I grew up in the tabloid capital of America. *The New York Post*, *The Daily News* and *Newsday* play the game of writing provocative stories to sell newspapers. This Lerner character is an instigator in training. He didn't even rip me. He said that I'd pitched well for the most part. He also said that Jon Duerson has been doing a superior job. Everyone else got shredded. Lerner saved the best for last when he got to Mickey Martin:

"Martin appears to be more concerned with running the Stampede as his own personal steppingstone to a higher level than focusing on how to win. Witnessing some of his violent tirades is at the very least disturbing, at the most it is frightening."

Looked right on the money to me. I brought the paper into the clubhouse so everyone could see it. I especially wanted to see Mickey's reaction. I wasn't disappointed. Mickey stormed around the clubhouse swearing like a trooper. I don't think he was angry about what was written. I think he was angry because what was written was true.

99

Miguel Santana was freaked out by getting hit in the nuts and was tentative during his next start. He wasn't following through because he wanted to be in a better position to catch a shot hit back at him. Naturally he got pounded and we lost the last game of the series to Lancaster 8–0. Marky Martin is not the guy to go to for the straightening out of mechanical problems. And he certainly isn't the guy I would want to straighten out a psychological problem. Wes McCormack had to make a return trip. A pitcher can't be scared any more than a hitter can be scared. In many ways a pitcher is more vulnerable than a hitter. Think about it. A hitter has a helmet. A pitcher doesn't. A pitcher has his glove, but if the ball leaves the pitcher's hand at ninety miles per hour and the hitter hits the ball right back at the mound on a line the speed has increased to 110–115 miles per hour. There's no way to avoid it sometimes. And that's with the wooden bat. Imagine if the hitters were using aluminum as they do in high school and college. Admittedly the professional hitters make better consistent contact, but the danger is still there at any level. Add in the strength of the hitters today compared to the past. And you can add the muscle enhancing drugs that many players use and you have a war zone on the mound.

Speaking of muscle enhancing drugs, I was one of the last guys in the clubhouse after the Lancaster game. In a low whisper I heard, "Brett."

I looked around. Nobody there. I heard it again and started to get nervous. Hearing voices is one of the first signs of insanity. Was I hearing voices? Was my old partner Jacob Marley coming back to haunt me to enlighten me on the importance of Christmas?

Finally after hearing it again, Dave Christenson popped his head out of the trainer's room and motioned me in.

"What the hell's the matter with you? You scared the crap out of me," I said.

"You're not gonna believe this," he said.

"Believe what?"

"Nikki Martin showed up at my apartment last night ..."

Uh oh.

"And?" I asked.

"I fucked her brains out," he said with a certain pride.

"Real smart, Dave," I said. "Real smart."

"I couldn't help it man. You know how it is. You wouldn't resist her either."

"I already *did* resist her, man."

"Yeah, well. I just needed to tell somebody," he said. "Don't tell anyone else, okay?"

"Sure, Dave," I said and walked out.

As I was leaving the clubhouse I got an eerie vision of one day reaching into the ballbag and pulling out Christenson's severed head. Courtesy of Mickey Martin.

100

If you looked at the standings you'd see that Visalia was the only team worse than we were. They promptly came into town and won the first three games of the four game series. We looked horrible. We played horrible. We had to attend meetings before every game. There were pitchers' meetings and hitters' meetings where we went through scouting reports and other minutiae. It was quite claustrophobic and felt something like torture. Meanwhile the coaches in San Bernardino weren't too swift and their observations were usually wrong. To every hitter, it seemed, Marky Martin had the same scouting report: "Don't give him anything good to hit. Hard stuff inside, breaking balls away."

For the tougher hitters, the scouting report went like this: "Hard sliders away."

Great preparation, Marky.

I went onto the mound with the team's record at 15–22. I managed to gut my way through the game and won, evening my record at 4–4. Kareem (Rod Woods) Akeem led the game off with a homer. I ignored Marky's scouting reports and got through eight innings, giving up two runs without my best stuff. I was tired and had thrown a lot of pitches when Mickey pulled me and put Strock in. After giving up a run in the ninth he held them off. I was pitching much better and my confidence was returning. While warming up I discovered something interesting. There was a softball in the bullpen and I found that holding onto a softball between innings stretches the fingers and makes the baseball seem smaller. That makes you feel as though you have more leverage helping you to get more power into the ball. Even if it's only mental, every little bit helps.

101

Modesto was in town for three games. They too were wallowing in mediocrity. The only teams in the league in either division playing well at all were Lake Elsinore, Stockton, and High Desert. We still had a chance at the playoffs if you can believe that, given how crappy we were playing. Then we went for the playoffs by going out and getting swept three straight by Modesto. They didn't kick our asses completely if that's any consolation. The standings showed the San Bernardino Stampede at 16–25. If this were the big leagues, Mickey would be cleaning out his office. How they would handle the situation in A ball, I wasn't sure. We'd heard some rumblings that the management was not happy. Could be some changes coming, we pondered. Stephen Jones was said to be on his way. Exacerbated, as he would say.

102

A nice long road trip always breaks losing habits. We headed to Stockton. That's only four hundred miles. A nine-hour ride. On that ride I became irrevocably convinced that Frankie Scarsi is a moron. He was talking about the TV show *Sweet Valley High*. It's about twin blondes who are identical in appearance but polar opposites in personality. He started singing what he thought was the show's theme song.

"Sweet Valley Hi-i-i-igh. Sweet Valley Hi-yi-yi-gh."

I listened for a minute and couldn't place the tune. After a moment, I did. I turned in my seat and said, "Uh, Frankie, that's not the tune for *Sweet Valley High*. That's the tune for 'Snoop Doggy Dogg.' Y'know, Snoop Dog-gy D-o-o-o-o-g?" He stopped singing.

We won the opener in Stockton. It was a good sign because it was the type of game that we usually lost. We scored once in the eighth to tie the score and Christenson homered in the ninth to get us the win. I pitched the second game and was horrible, but won anyway. Six innings, four runs, seven hits, two walks and three strikeouts. I gave up two more towering homers on bad forkballs. Time to put the pitch away for a while. I could get by with my other pitches. I was over .500 at least at 5–4. This was a bizarre team. While the doormats of the league pushed us around, we played well against the better teams. We finished a sweep in Stockton when Miguel Santana, his head on straight and cup in place, looked like a young Pedro Martinez leading us to victory.

The GM of the Stampede Nelson Coonts was on the trip to see what was going on. I think that both of the Martins' jobs were saved by the sweep in Stockton. I think that both of them thought that we played just a bit harder because we knew that their jobs were in jeopardy. They were wrong, of course. Nobody knows why teams suddenly start playing well. Teams in baseball beat each other no matter how good or bad one or the other is. A bad team can't just beat a better team; it can beat the hell out of the better team. It all depends on what you have that particular day. Nevertheless, Mickey Martin bounced around the clubhouse after the final game.

"Great work, men," he said.

103

Stockton to Adelanto is a nine-hour shot, but we were only forty miles from home when we got to Adelanto, so it wasn't too bad. This hopping back and forth between Northern California and Southern California was growing tiresome. Now tell me if this makes sense: We traveled to Adelanto to play High Desert three games. Then we turned around and went home to play a three game series with … High Desert. Are the schedule makers *looking* for fistfights? When two teams play each other things happen, both intentional and inadvertent. Sometimes guys get hit. Sometimes guys get spiked. Sometimes things are said during the heat of battle. Disagreements happen. And when you have a Billy Martin–type nut like Mickey Martin (no relation) managing your team, trouble can brew.

The first three games in Adelanto were uneventful. We took the first one for our fourth win in a row. Jack Kray was masterful in a complete game three-hit shutout. There's no way to tell which Kray is going to show up for any given game. He can beat anybody and he can lose to anybody. After that, we lost the next two games. No major incidents occurred, but there were little things to be filed away for later. If anything was going to happen I figured that it would be back in San Bernardino.

Back home, I pitched the first game and went eight innings, giving up two runs. The game was tied when I was taken out. I had no problem with the decision. I was tired. Strock came in and got the win when Duerson hit a shot over the left field wall to end it. There was palpable tension between the two teams. I thought that the next hit batsman would start the fireworks, but there wasn't any hit batsman.

In the third game of the series High Desert had Craig Steffan on the mound. Steffan was a well-known hothead who got rattled if you rode him from the bench. Hearing this I, being in one of my more obnoxious moods, started getting on him as soon as I saw some emotion. There was no problem until the fifth when Duerson hit one out. Way, way out over the center field wall. Steffan was pissed and we started letting him have it. After the ball cleared the county, Steffan glanced at our dugout and I came up with a great line.

"Hey, did they serve dinner on that flight?"

That, in baseball circles, is considered a poison barb. Everyone on the bench was laughing pretty hard. At this point, Steffan, rattled, angry and immature, decided to take his frustrations out on the next hitter. Another emotional soul by the name of Dave Christenson. Steffan is big and bitchy. Christenson is big and bitchy. Steffan's face was red and his teeth were clenched as Dave dug into the batter's box. Steffan looked in for the sign but we had a pretty good idea what he was going to do. Steffan brought his arms over his head, lifted his leg and swung his right arm around. The ball left Steffan's hand and headed *behind* Christenson's head. Now that is serious. When a pitcher throws behind the batter's head he's trying to injure him because the instinct is to duck. If you duck, you're ducking into the ball. I would never do that. I just couldn't live with myself if I really hurt someone. (Granted I don't throw hard enough to seriously hurt anyone.) Apparently Steffan has no such qualms. At any rate, Christenson hit the dirt and avoided the missile traveling at ninety-plus miles per hour. Then he got up and stared at the mound. Steffan, glaring at Christenson, was ready to fight. He opened his arms and said, "Don't just stare. Come on out and do something you fucking bitch."

Christenson, no shrinking violet, seemed to be considering a visit to the mound before that comment. After the comment it was all over. Christenson dropped his bat and charged the mound. The umpire tried to get in the way of the chemically enhanced outfielder, but Christenson ran right around him. The High Desert catcher chased after Christenson, but couldn't catch him before he got his hands on Craig Steffan. Christenson punched Steffan with a good shot on the side of the head as both teams running onto the field engulfed them like an ocean wave. Fights started breaking out all over the field as both bullpens ran in and started pushing and shoving on the outskirts of the pile. I was somewhere in the middle pulling guys off and making sure no one from our team got sucker-punched. Duerson was playing cop and his 6'5" frame received the respect it deserved. Guys were screaming and cursing. This went on for about ten minutes before the umpires were able to restore some semblance of order. I would classify this as a mild to severe baseball fight. Most bench clearing brawls are anything but. Just guys dancing, grabbing, holding, pushing and shoving. The two guys that started the fight are usually the ones that are the angriest and that subsides after a few minutes with fifty other guys piled on top of them. The umpires decided whom to eject after a small conference. From our team, Christenson, infielder Willie Hernandez, pitchers Melvin Sanders, and Jack Kray (a soft-spoken guy most of the time who apparently goes off during a fight, because he was acting like a lunatic) all got tossed. Mickey Martin got the boot too.

The rest of the game went on without incident. The worst part is that before the fight we were leading 3–0 and after the fight, they scored eleven unanswered runs and beat us 11–3.

Just a moment to touch on the phenomenon of baseball fights. There are three types of guys in baseball uniforms. Some guys like to fight, some guys try to break up fights, and some guys look for someone on the other team that they are familiar with to utilize as a dance partner. The dancers show team loyalty by joining their teammates on the field, but show their prudence by not getting in on the action. I consider myself one of the guys trying to break things up. I've never had anyone charge the mound on me. I've had opposing players make comments that I've responded to, but nothing developed. I like to think that I would have stood my ground.

104

We went to Lancaster for three games trapped in the basement of the Freeway Division with Visalia. The league was reviewing the umpires' reports regarding the fight with High Desert to decide if there should be any disciplinary action. You never know what's going to happen when the league reviews a situation. There could be fines. There could be suspensions. Or there could be nothing. Many times guys who should be suspended aren't and guys who are completely innocent get suspended. We were told to expect word after the first Lancaster game.

There were some sights to see in Lancaster. What is it about these small California towns that they have so many things that my parents would enjoy? In Lancaster there is the Aerospace Walk of Honor and a sidewalk monument to Edwards Air Force Base test pilots. Several people are honored every year. That's my dad's kind of stuff. And for my mother there's the Antelope Valley California poppy reserve featuring wildflowers. I went to the sights and took pictures. Maybe I can get Dad inducted into the Walk of Honor. Do you think they would accept a troublemaking staff sergeant?

We beat up on Lancaster 8–2 in the opener. Durst started and finally showed why he was the Dodgers' first round selection. He'd be deadly if he ever put it all together. I'm the exact opposite. If I don't have it all together when I get out there I'm deadly all right ... to my own team. Right after the game we heard from the league regarding the fight. Christenson was suspended for three games and fined $100. Kray, Hernandez and Sanders got one game apiece. They have the right to appeal the suspensions but I didn't know if they would. Appealing doesn't do much good. The one thing that is good about an appeal is that you can play until you receive a hearing. They needed to make a decision.

After losing the second game, I started game three. After eight innings we were ahead 5-1 and I was rolling along. Duerson had homered again. I had allowed one run, four hits, two walks and had eight strikeouts. I was sitting on the opposite end of the bench from Mickey and Marky Martin. I make it a point to stay as far away from Tweedledum and Tweedledummer as is humanly possible. Out of the corner of my eye I saw Mickey ambling towards me. He stopped directly in front of me and grandly announced in front of one and all, "Samuels, I have decided to allow you to finish this game."

I looked up at him, forced a grin and said, "That's truly benevolent of you, Mick."

Was he kidding? How many other managers would allow a pitcher who hasn't complained about being tired to finish a game in which he was breezing along? Let's see ... about 99 percent?

And how many managers would the length of the dugout to announce such a bold strategic maneuver? Answer: One. Mickey Martin.

I had a one, two, three ninth. Mickey Martin — benevolent genius. My record improved to 6-4 and the team's record was 24-29.

105

When I walked into the clubhouse back in San Bernardino before the first game with San Jose, I noticed a photocopied piece of paper on my stool. Everyone had received one. I picked it up and began reading. It had a heading that said, "The Nation of Islam." Right underneath that it said, "What Muslims Want."

Oh Rod, what are you up to now?

The devout Muslim, Rod (Kareem Akeem) Woods was now giving out lists of demands. Here is the synopsis of "What Muslims Want":

139

1. Freedom
2. Justice
3. Equal Opportunity
4. People whose grandparents were slaves should be allowed to establish separate state or territory on this continent or elsewhere. Land must be fertile and minerally rich. Whites must maintain and supply needs for 20–25 years or until Muslims can do it themselves.
5. Freedom for believers in Islam held in Federal prisons. Freedom for black men and women under the death sentence in the North and South.
6. Immediate end to police brutality and attacks against blacks.
7. Equal employment opportunities.
8. Exemption from taxation.
9. Equal education but separate schools up to age sixteen for boys and eighteen for girls. Black children educated by their own teachers.
10. Inter-marriage and race mixing prohibited.

After all that there is a list of the Muslim beliefs:

1. One God: Allah.
2. Holy Qur'an and scriptures of prophets of God.
3. Truth of the Bible. Today's Bible has been tampered with.
4. Allah's prophets and scriptures.
5. Mental resurrection of the dead. Blacks are mentally dead and should be resurrected first. They are the chosen people.
6. Judgment of God.
7. Separation from whites.
8. Equal justice. Whites are not equal.
9. Integration is hypocritical.
10. Muslims take no part in wars and taking lives unless receiving land as compensation.
11. Women are to be respected and protected.
12. Allah appeared in person as Master W. Fard Muhammed. Allah is the only God.

I read this whole list twice. Now there are some things in here that make sense and are reasonable requests. Ending police brutality and the equal opportunity stuff are good things. Others are patently ridiculous.

I rested my chin on my palm and wondered why someone would bring this into a locker-room. I was about to make the list into a paper airplane and throw it across the room in the direction of Rod's (Kareem's) locker but didn't. Instead I folded it up and put it into the back pocket of my Levi's. I would bring it home and formulate a response.

After losing 4–3 to San Jose, I went home and sat in the living room with a bunch of notebook paper, a pen and the list of Muslim demands. On the top of a blank sheet I scribbled, "Brett Samuels' list of responses to Muslim demands." Point by point I came up with an answer to every one of the things the Muslims supposedly (supposably?) want. I started writing when Duerson came over to see what I was doing.

"What's this?" he asked. Then he looked at my sheet of paper, read it and calmly ripped it to shreds.

"Brett," he said, "I can't let you do this. You're only going to get your ass in trouble with the other niggers and I'll have to bail you out. You're my friend and this is only going to give you trouble."

"Come on Jon. I'm just playing. He shouldn't be bringing this stuff into the locker-room." I said.

"It's only gonna cause trouble. You know I'm right."

I did know he was right. It would have been misconstrued. I abandoned my project.

The saddest thing of all this is that unless Rod (Kareem) started hitting like Ken Griffey, Jr., he wasn't going to get very far in this game. He is the best outfielder I've ever seen. In my last start in Lancaster, he jumped over the wall to save a home run. But the politics are not going to play any better in a big league clubhouse than they do in the California League. The brass isn't going to want the aggravation of having someone bringing lists of Muslim demands into the room. Whether Rod (Kareem) cares about all this I don't know. I just know that it is a shame to waste the ability that he has trying to politicize a baseball team.

106

We split the next two games with San Jose and then High Desert came back to town for the rematch. Tensions were still high. Carlton

Gray was walking around saying, "Let's not take any shit. If anything starts make sure you get in the first punch."

That led me to query, "Who are you, Don King?"

During batting practice both teams were eyeing each other cautiously. There wasn't the usual pregame chitchat amongst the teams. Baseball is unlike other sports in that there is lots of fraternization. Guys talk to opposing players before, after and even during games. We were all ready for more action, but once the first game started tensions seemed to deflate. There were no staredowns, no beanballs, no nothing. That may be because the umps warned both benches and managers before the game that any more trouble and there would be stiffer fines and more suspensions. (Speaking of which, the San Bernardino players' suspensions were upheld. They started serving immediately and they were staggered so we weren't left too shorthanded.) We lost the game 5–3.

I pitched the second game and was great. It's just that Craig Steffan was better. He got his revenge against us by throwing a complete game shutout and we lost 1–0. I gave up the one run on a triple and a sacrifice fly and gave up three hits total. I can take that. If I pitch that well every game, I'll win most of them.

We salvaged the last game on a Carlton Gray homer in the bottom of the ninth. In Carlton's words: "There's nothing better than a walk-off home run."

I'd love to hit a walk-off home run. It's got to be more fun than giving one up.

After the game the majority owner of the Stampede, Billy Bickley, came into the locker-room to give out cigars. His daughter had just had a baby. I don't think he knew any of our names, but most of the guys couldn't care less about that. As long as he signs the checks. To them, that's what's really important.

107

To entertain the troops in the clubhouse at Rancho Cucamonga, I started doing my Michael Jackson imitation. It's just me using a high voice and acting like "Shaft." The guys were either laughing at the imitation or laughing because I'm such a horse's ass. I think it may have been the latter because Brooks Simon looked at me and said, "That is the worst Michael Jackson imitation I have ever seen in my life. Bar none."

They should learn to appreciate what I'm trying to bring to the clubhouse. A little levity goes a long way.

As far as the games go, something odd happened. We started winning. We won the first game. Then we won the second game. Then we won the third game. And finally we won the fourth game. A clean sweep! I pitched the fourth game and had an easy time because we scored seven runs in the second inning. There weren't even any homers. Lots of doubles though. Craig Strum (the Australian on the team) doubled with the bases loaded to bust the game open. I went seven innings and gave up two runs. I wasn't great, but I worked my way into and out of trouble. My "cutter" was all over the place. Combine that with the fact that my forkball was getting tattooed and I was rapidly running out of pitches.

On another subject entirely, you must remember that I'm from New York and there are no earthquakes in New York. The Rancho Cucamonga team is called the "Quakes" and the ballpark is named the "Epicenter." Why would you name a team and a ballpark after a disastrous occurrence such as an earthquake? Especially in California where they are so prevalent. The name started really freaking me out so when we left I breathed a paranoid sigh of relief. And the sickest part is that I have no such phobias in San Bernardino, which is only twenty miles away from Rancho Cucamonga. Anything that hit them was probably going to hit us. Maybe I'm just wacky.

108

Winning the first game against Lake Elsinore brought us to within two games of .500. You have to crawl before you can walk and you have to walk before you can run. So, getting to .500 would be major progress. Our confidence was improving as our record was improving. The playoffs started to look like a viable possibility. Duerson suddenly started hitting again after a brief dry spell. I wasn't ashamed to announce to anyone and everyone within earshot that the man didn't belong in A ball.

"How long can they keep him down here?" I thought out loud.

Our win streak ended with a 7–3 loss, which was followed the next night by a 5–4 loss. How inconsistent could we get? Mickey looked like he was trying to be pissed but really wasn't. We could usually tell how angry he was. His face was like a mood ring. It just wasn't the right color after the last loss. He had a brief team meeting. I wasn't listening, but then he said something that caught my attention.

"You fucks play like *you could care less.*"

Would someone please explain to me what that saying means? I hear it all the time and it's meaningless in the context in which people use it. To say that someone could care less implies that they care to a degree to begin with. Take the phrase apart and define it. Care means to be concerned. Could is to express possibility. The proper phrasing should be: "You fucks play like you *couldn't* care less."

I would have corrected Mickey if I thought he would have responded positively to my critique. I doubt he would have though. He may have broken a bat over my head. I decided to keep my mouth shut. I thought to myself, "Maybe one day during a quiet moment..."

109

Visalia was our last stop for the first half of the season. The All-Star break had descended upon us. The selections would be announced after the first game at Visalia. I hoped I'd make it. The game, played at Lancaster, was on the next Tuesday. This was my first legitimate shot to make an All-Star team at any level. Sitting in the bullpen watching Duerson go deep twice to lead us to an 8–1 victory behind Masato Fujinami, I became wistful. I started thinking back to my Little League days. When I was eleven and on the previously mentioned church league team, our team was in last place. The way the All-Star selections worked meant that the teams got a certain number of selections based on what place they were in. First place got four picks, second place and third place got three picks and fourth place (last place) got two. The game was played after the regular season and after the league's "World Series." There were three kids on our team worthy of being All-Stars. Since we had only two spots, one would be left out. With about three games left in the regular season, a beer swilling, tattooed slob named Harvey pulled me and one of the other candidates off to the side and told us we were the All-Stars. Harvey had no kids on the team so I have no idea why he was there. He never tried to fiddle with me because one of my parents were always with me at games and practice; but who knows about the other kids? I remember telling my dad as we walked to the car that I had made the All-Star team. I was so happy and excited. At least until the season ended. After the last game of the season, the coaches were saying that a deserving player was going to be left off the All-Star team because we had only two spots. I knew immediately that there was trouble. The coaches stood off to the side and argued for fifteen minutes. I had already been told that I was an All-Star. Finally, they called us all together and named the All-Stars. Needless to say Brett Samuels wasn't one of the names called. I started crying like a baby. My mother came over and asked what happened. She knew that that piece of trash Harvey (who conveniently wasn't there that day) had told us who the All-Stars were weeks before. She started screaming. Weeks before, the other kid who was picked that day concurred with what I said. I went home crying. My mother called the head coach that night, and he said that Harvey said, "I told them that they were in the *running* for the All-Star team."

He was lying through his teeth. And if that were the truth, why did he only call the two of us over? I could have caused a huge problem, but my mother, rightfully, didn't want them to take the kid who replaced me off the All-Star team. I never returned to the team. That may sound selfish, but hey, I was eleven. And I think a grown man calling two eleven-year-old kids liars is more selfish. And destructive.

110

Winning the first game in Visalia was secondary to finding out who was going to the All-Star game. Duerson, playing and hitting as if he needed to solidify his case, hit two more homers. How much longer could they keep him in San Bernardino? At least until after he started the All-Star game. Mickey Martin stood in front of the team and announced, "All right you animals, here are the All-Stars: Starting — Duerson; Reserve — Christenson; and pitchers Strock and Samuels."

Yes!

You couldn't have punched the smile off my face. I was ecstatic. My first All-Star game. I ran and called my parents who were thrilled. The game is shown on ESPN 2 and I told them to get the VCR ready. I had to calm down for my next start the next day.

I won my start but pitched like crap. Marky Martin suggested that the All-Star selection was going to my head. I do believe he was kidding. Here's the line: Six innings, four runs, seven hits, two walks and five K's. Crap. The important thing, as they say, is the "W," but I'd like to pitch well. My record heading into the break stood at 8–5. We split the final two games at Visalia to end the first half with a record of 34–36. Right after the last game, Duerson, Strock, Christenson and I headed to Lancaster for the Single A All-Star game.

111

There's much pomp and circumstance around any All-Star game and we enjoyed every minute of it. The game is played on the traditional Tuesday just like in the Majors. It's just that we play a month earlier than they do. We arrived and checked into the visiting team hotel with the other All-Stars. We, the Freeway Division, were playing against the Valley Division. We met the managers at the workout the day before the game. Kenny Beck from Lake Elsinore was managing the Freeway Division and told us that he would try to get us all into the game, but it can be difficult regarding pitchers. ESPN 2, covering the game, had Harold Reynolds and Dave Revsine there to broadcast the action. Reynolds used to play for the Seattle Mariners and Baltimore Orioles. I met him and he seemed like a pleasant guy. *USA Today, Baseball America* and the local teams' beat writers were around to cover the game. I tried to remember to keep my usage of "I mean" and "y'know" to a bare minimum so I wouldn't sound like a total idiot. We wore our road uniforms since Lancaster was in the other division. Thus, the Valley Division was the home team. We had the workout day on Monday and everybody was trying to have a good time and not take the game too seriously. Duerson put on a batting practice show and his gaudy numbers were generating lots of attention from the media. I couldn't get myself arrested. Beck asked all the players how they felt because he didn't want to be responsible for an injury to another organization's property. The night before the game, most of the All-Stars just hung around together in a couple of local bars. Beck had given us a time to be back at the hotel, but what was he going to do if we weren't back? Fine us? We didn't cause too much of a ruckus.

Game time came about on Tuesday and I was scheduled to be the third pitcher in. Duerson, showing off for the national audience, went deep in the first with a man aboard. The first two pitchers for the Freeway Division were rolling along when I was called in with us leading 3–0. It was the start of the fourth inning when I heard my name announced. "Now pitching for the Freeway Division, from the San Bernardino Stampede, number fifteen, Brett Samuels."

I got chills and my stomach was churning with nervousness. Duerson was still behind the dish so I wouldn't have to work with an unfamiliar catcher. I abandoned my "cutter" because the word was getting around the league that I loaded the ball up somehow and the other guys were sure to be watching me closely. Some might even be creepy enough to go through my belongings. We can't take any chances, now can we? Eager to impress, I told Duerson that I wanted to throw twisters if we got two strikes on any hitter. He reluctantly agreed. So, I stepped onto the mound in my first All-Star game, nervous as ever, without a great history of pitching well in pressure situations and managed to get two strikes on every hitter ... and struck them all out.

112

The Freeway Division won the game 5–1. Christenson went oh for one. Strock pitched a scoreless eighth. The four of us were in the lobby getting ready to head back to San Bernardino when Duerson was called to the desk.

"You guys are gonna have to carry on without me," he said when he returned.

"What? Why?" I shrieked, sounding like a girl.

"Headin' to San Anton'," he said.

"Whattaya mean?"

"They're moving me up."

The Dodgers decided to send Jon to Double A. I kept on opening my big, fat mouth about how he didn't belong in A ball and someone listened to me. I was happy for him, but miserable for myself. I was losing my roommate, catcher and friend. I was being a selfish baby by pouting, but it didn't help.

"You gonna start stamping your feet and holding your breath soon?" Strock asked, noticing the look on my face.

"Nooo," I whined.

Jon was coming back to San Bernardino with us to get some bare essentials and would then head immediately to join his new teammates on the San Antonio Missions of the Texas League. I was acting more like a baby on the way home and kept quiet. A rarity. When we got back, Jon packed some stuff and caught the next flight to San Antonio. The big club wanted him there as soon as possible so they said they would take care of the shipment of his car. He shook my hand and apologized for leaving me alone in the two-bedroom apartment. I told him that he had no reason to apologize.

"Maybe soon you'll be there too," he said.

"Yeah, maybe," I grunted with a sour face on.

He took his stuff and hopped into the waiting cab. I was alone in a two-bedroom apartment. Michele suggested that maybe she could come and move in to keep me company. An idea that I immediately nixed.

"Not happenin', babe," I said.

It had gotten to the point that she was even irritating me when she was naked. I didn't need to see her any more than I was already seeing her. Even that was becoming too much. The time to move on was rapidly approaching. As far as affording the apartment goes, that wouldn't be a major problem. If the new guy that the Dodgers brought in was normal, then maybe he could move in with me. I considered getting Christenson to give his apartment to the new guy and move in with me, but decided against it. I wouldn't want to be caught in a mood swing. After much consideration I decided that I should at least try and live alone. How bad could it be?

With Duerson gone to Double A, someone had to take his place on the roster. Whenever a player transaction is made, it affects a number of other people. One move sets a series of other moves into motion. For example, someone may get released from the big club. If the Dodgers promote someone from Triple A to the Majors, someone has the join the Triple A roster. That may be someone from Double A, then someone has to replace *that* guy. So on and so forth. It's a domino effect. Of course, they may just sign a released player from another organization as filler so they don't have to do lots of shuffling and reshuffling. That way, they also don't have to give a guy a raise when they move him up.

A day later the Dodgers signed pitcher Jesse Williams from the independent Atlantic League's Bridgeport Bluefish to join us. Back-up catcher Fernando Villanueva moved into the starting lineup. His English is spotty. I would've loved to be on the mound during a conference between him, Masato Fujinami and Mickey Martin. Mickey could shout obscenities while Fernando and Masato nod and look perplexed.

113

Stockton came back in to play the now powerless San Bernardino Stampede. There was hope for us yet, though. We won the opener 5–2 and the second game 5–3. Those two victories evened our record at 36–36. Considering how bad we were, that felt pretty good. On a lighter note, the San Diego Chicken slummed from his coop in the Majors to entertain the denizens of A ball and their fans. I watched him for a long while and came to the conclusion that he's not particularly funny. Sort of like Adam Sandler in a chicken costume. For a brief moment, Mike Strock and I considered pelting him with various objects from the bullpen, but didn't. We didn't want to get sued.

"Why don't we just pluck 'im, stuff 'im and cook 'im?" Strock suggested.

"Or we could tie him up and leave him in the desert," I replied.

Do you think that the vultures would eat an annoying, decomposing man in a chicken suit? Well, there's only one way to find out.

I pitched great with Villanueva behind the plate. He's a better thrower than Duerson, whose arm is his only weak point. Villanueva is a defensive ace. Of course, we missed Jon's bat, but we'd have to find some way to score. We won the game 4–2. I went eight innings and regained control of my "cutter." Villanueva looked at the ball and at me funny a couple of times but caught on quickly and gave me a strange smile in the dugout. He's kind of chubby. I'm sure the scout that signed him refrained from calling him fat. Preferring to use "stubby" or "squat" as the adjective. To us, though, he's fat. My record improved to 9–5.

114

Our season record stood at 37–36 as we went to Rancho Cucamonga. Since this is a split-season league we would still get to the playoffs if we were to win the second half. Never mind the fact that we were horrible in the first half; we could still get to the playoffs. We had gotten off to a decent start for the second half. Leading 8–6 in the first game in Rancho Cucamonga, Martin brought Mike Strock in to pitch the ninth and he promptly gave up three runs to blow the game. Mickey Martin made a sound I'd never heard before. It sounded like, "greaewr-rgrearrgreehhgrhh." Like the sound an animal would make. Is that worse than making up your own curses?

There's a girl in Rancho Cucamonga that the guys call All-Night Annette. (That shouldn't be confused with "No, No, Nanette!" which was the show that former Red Sox owner Harry Frazee sold Babe Ruth to finance.) Everybody in the league knows All-Night Annette because she hangs around at the ballpark wearing short skirts and no underwear and will screw any player that asks. Guys bring her into the clubhouse and she'll blow or fuck them, whichever they prefer. She accompanies the teams back to the hotel and tries to accommodate as many of them as possible. She's taken on entire rosters in one night. I was sitting in my room when Strock came by and said, "Dude, you gotta see this."

Off I went to Tony Hatcher's room and saw things that I had only seen in porn. All-Night Annette was taking on five guys at once and there appeared to be a line waiting to get their turns.

"You gonna get in on this?" Strock asked.

As tempting as the offer was, I declined.

"Why not? Why're you being a pussy?"

"Look, man, I'm not Mr. Romance, but this just isn't my deal," I said and left.

In spite of the things I've seen since I've been playing professionally, I still don't believe many of them. I cannot believe that All-Night Annette is actually someone's daughter.

As for the games on the field, we won the next two in Rancho Cucamonga and left town at 39–37.

115

Arriving in the hotel at Lake Elsinore, there was a message for me at the desk to call Jon Duerson in Wichita, Kansas. I bought a prepaid calling card and called him back as soon as I settled into my room.

"H'lo?" he said, sounding terrible.

"Jon! What's going on?"

He told me what was going on. What was going on was that he homered in his first two games playing for San Antonio. In the third game he faced a guy throwing 98 miles per hour. A pitch ran in on Jon and as he fell backwards to avoid getting beaned, he got hit right on his left hand.

"It's busted," Jon said. "Out for six weeks, at least."

"Wow. That sucks." I said. "At least it didn't hit you in the head. It was lucky in a way."

"Yeah, real lucky," he said in a sarcastic tone.

I suggested that he keep up his running so he wouldn't get fat. He appreciated my concern.

That's just bad luck. I sent him a set of business cards to hand out to avoid the continuous questions regarding his hand because I thought it was clever.

It said: 1. My hand is broken.
2. My hand hurts.
3. No, I don't need surgery.
4. Yes.

That covered all the bases as far as I was concerned.

116

We won the first game in Lake Elsinore 14–5. I pitched the second game and got the hell kicked out of me. Four and two thirds innings, seven runs and eight hits. Two of the hits home runs. Mickey Martin mercifully waved the fight over and dragged me back to the dugout with two outs in the fifth. This fucked up my ERA, but good. Strock walked by my locker afterwards and cracked, "Ace, my ass."

We won the third game of the series on a shutout by Miguel Santana.

Completely miserable on the bus back to San Bernardino. I was lonely, depressed and pitching like garbage. Tony Hatcher, whose father was a blues guitarist in clubs for years (and indeed still is) was strumming his own guitar in the silence of the night. Wanting to express my own misery, I asked him if he knew "Lodi" by Credence Clearwater Revival.

"Hell, yeah," he said, and started strumming the tune on his guitar. As he did, I started to sing. I can sing pretty well. And I sing the bittersweet song about traveling the back roads of small towns trying to make it as a musician especially well. The lyrics can also apply to our situation in some ways.

After Hatcher and I were finished, everyone seemed to sit reflectively as the bus rumbled along the interstate through the dark California night. We headed home and I felt a bit better after expressing the sorrow that I was feeling through that song.

117

High Desert was back in town. It got tiresome playing the same teams over and over again. Mostly it's the same players too. There were so many games in the league and not that many teams. It got tedious. We won the opening game of the series and lost the last two. So inconsistent. Jeff Durst, for all his ability, looked lost out there. I know the feeling. I had been under the impression that players from large college programs assimilate more easily. But in Durst's instance that wasn't the case. The new guy, Jesse Williams, got into the second game and looked good. He's 6'5" and 180 pounds. Complete with a long nose and face and long skinny body, he looks like a rat. I didn't see a tail. He can bring it pretty well with a fastball in the low nineties.

This was a short homestand as we headed right back out on the road to Lake Elsinore. I finally terminated the relationship with Michele. I just couldn't take it anymore. I started getting itchy when she showed up at my apartment unannounced. I'm not good at breaking up with girls, but for some reason I had no problem this time. Between sobs she asked me why I was dumping her. I was honest. I said that I couldn't take her anymore. Simple enough.

The two-bedroom apartment was getting awfully lonely for the three days and nights. It wasn't as if Duerson and I had long talks or anything, it was just that there was someone there. And now I was alone. I woke up in the middle of the night and was unable to fall back asleep. I went into the living room and switched on the TV. There was nothing on except infomercials about the "Body by Jake Ab-Rocker" and Ron Popeil's rotisserie oven. I started to get paranoid. I looked out into the empty, quiet street. What if I don't get any further than A ball? What if I, God forbid, have to go and get a real job? My God. What could I do? What was I *qualified* to do? Nothing. I have some things going for me. I'm young, attractive and intelligent. Still, I worry. Imagine what I would be like if my record were 6–9 instead of 9–6.

118

Interesting conversation on the way to Lake Elsinore. The guys were having a debate about which woman they would want to have sex with if they could have any woman in the world. I heard the names of the usual suspects: Carmen Electra, Mariah Carey, Tyra Banks and Pamela Anderson. Well, I announced, you can have all of them. My choice is and always will be Laetitia Casta, the French supermodel. Take a look at one photograph and tell me how you can beat that choice.

I managed to straighten myself out in Lake Elsinore, winning 8–1. Seven innings pitched and one run. Villanueva hit a home run. Do you think it has anything to do with me that the catcher I'm pitching to always seems to hit home runs? Maybe I throw such crap that it gives them confidence when they get to the plate.

After the game I went out on the prowl with a couple of the guys. I managed to pick up a chick with dark, shoulder length curly hair and all sorts of piercings. She had on a belly shirt displaying a navel ring and when she opened her mouth I saw a tongue ring. I was all excited about having a really wild time, but much to my dismay, when I got her clothes off and climbed on top of her she just laid there like a lummox. I always expected these pierced girls to be nice and slutty and was terribly disappointed. Ah, well. At least I got laid.

The next night, as is my wont, I barged into what I thought was Carlton Gray's room. Surprised to see that it wasn't, I was even more surprised by what I did see. I think I finally discovered the nature of Jeff Durst's problem and why he was getting raked all around the field. He and Frankie Scarsi were sitting in the room with huge lines of cocaine on the table. I stopped dead in my tracks, as they looked at me terrified.

"Whoops," I said. "Sorry boys. I didn't see that." And did a 180 and marched right back out the door in much the same way as I came in. Scarsi came running after me.

"Brett, Brett!" he called.

"What?"

"You're not gonna say anything about this, right?"

"Hey man," I said, "what you do is your business. Not mine."

I honestly didn't care that they were doing drugs. I think that if a guy wants to do drugs, let him. If you think that because nobody from baseball checks into rehab then there are no addicts you're sadly mistaken. Nobody gets busted because there is no drug testing in baseball. The union doesn't allow it. Look at it this way: Baseball is filled with immature men who get pretty much whatever they want whenever they want it simply by asking. They're also very rich. Draw your own conclusions.

While I'm on the subject, I have a way to diminish the use of drugs. Legalize all of them. And don't think I'm some libertarian nut. And it's not because the drugs will go out of style. It's because the drug companies will make the prices so outlandish that no one will be able to afford them save for athletes and Hollywood celebrities. And that's who's using anyway. (I say these things having never sampled anything stronger than Advil. Not even pot. That is the 100 percent truth.)

119

We returned home after taking the last game against Lake Elsinore to play ... High Desert. Is it my imagination or had we just played High Desert at home three games ago? We left home to go to Lake Elsinore after playing High Desert just so we could turn around and come back home to play High Desert again? Perhaps I should volunteer to create a sensible schedule.

Jeff Durst's cocaine use wasn't helping his pitching any. He lost to High Desert 5–3. In the second game, Mike Strock entered a 4–4 game and gave up a game-losing double. That happens with short relievers sometimes. It's not something to get too uptight about. It's part of the job. Feast or famine.

Michele left five messages on my answering machine. Did we have a fatal attraction here? Am I that irresistible? I called her and told her to knock it off though I didn't know what good it'd do. I pitched the final game of the series with High Desert and won again. Seven innings, two runs, six hits, two walks and six strikeouts. I managed to wiggle my way out of a bases loaded and nobody out situation in the second inning with no runs scoring. That is no small feat. When you have the bases loaded and nobody out it's hard *not* to score. Somehow High Desert managed it. I like to think that I had something to do with that. My forkball was working again and my "cutter" was cutting again. I raised my record to 11–6 and the team's record to 45–43. I thought I had acquired a cool new nickname, but the whole team refused to adopt it. I asked Villanueva how my curve looked after the game and he said in his Spanish accent, "Wicked, boy. Esta muy bueno."

Wicked boy, I thought. That's a better nickname than "Chia-head." I mentioned it to Strock.

"I have an even better one," Strock said, "how about ass-face?"

"I think I'll stick to 'Chia-head'," I said glumly.

120

We had a much-appreciated day off before traveling to Modesto. When we took off for Northern California, guys were really starting to bitch about Mickey's lineup juggling and bizarre decisions. Baseball players are only happy when they're complaining so I don't put too much stock in what they say. Mickey is a deeply disturbed individual. Once I accepted that, he and I got along much better.

We got to Modesto and won the first two games of the series. We were hovering around first place for the second half. Playoffs here we come? Who knew? What I do know is after the third game I saw the worst explosion yet from the irrepressible Mickey Martin. By all rights the guy had reason to be upset. We blew a 5–1 lead by making three errors in the seventh inning and two more in the eighth. We lost 8–5. After the game, Mickey was a sight to behold. Not only did he topple the food table, but he started flinging equipment around the room. It was like being inside a pinball machine. Guys were ducking projectiles all over the place. Mickey, unlike most coaches, wears spikes. Why? I have no idea. Most wear coaches' cleated shoes. Anyway, after he was done throwing things he ran toward the wood paneled wall and threw a kick. His spikes got caught in the wooden paneling and he was unable to free himself. He stood there, hopped on one foot cursing a blue streak trying to get his leg free. Everyone just started laughing without trying to hide it. Oblivious to everyone laughing at him, Mickey managed to free himself, did a pirouette and fired his cap in the air and stormed into his office. Our fearless leader. He should wear the coaches' shoes. It's much safer to kick things with those. Afterwards, discussing Mickey's tirade, mutiny was being considered. Frankie Scarsi showed that drugs kill brain cells by coming up with this gem: "Maybe we should go to him as a group and say, 'Give me liberty or give me death.' Like that guy Alan Hale."

"Uh, Frankie," I said gently.

"What?"

"That was Patrick Henry that said that."

"What'd Alan Hale say?" he asked in full sincerity.

"Well, *Nathan* Hale said, 'I only regret that I have but one life to lose for my country'." I replied.

"What'd Alan Hale say then?"

"Whatever he said he said it as the Skipper on *Gilligan's Island*."

121

After Masato Fujinami dominated the Rancho Cucamonga Quakes at the Epicenter (yeesh), I started the second game of the series. According to the linescore I got shelled, but linescores are misleading sometimes. The home plate umpire, Eddie Karn, was squeezing the strike zone all game. He's been that way with me ever since the time early in the season when he suggested that I was holding my curve too tightly. On occasion umpires make friendly suggestions to players. I'm always hearing comments and suggestions regarding my unusual overlapped finger grip. I'd had enough that day and snapped, "I'll handle the pitching, thanks." Since then his strike zone has been tight. And if you don't think some umpires hold grudges against certain players and use their power against them, wake up! I was struggling in the game, working into and out of trouble. I had runners on second and third and two outs in the third. The count was two and two and I threw a great curve on the outside corner. The pitch was a strike. I was already walking off the mound when I realized that Eddie had called the pitch a ball. I rolled my eyes and made a face, cursing Karn under my breath. The next pitch got ripped into the corner for a double and two runs. I was enraged. I was jawing at Karn and he removed his mask and told me to shut up. Just as I was about to respond, Mickey Martin came out to the mound to hook me. I'd given up five runs. Mickey asked Karn what the problem was. Karn replied that I had an attitude problem.

"I don't blame the kid for bitching, Eddie. Your zone has been horseshit all game," Mickey said in an even voice.

"Are you arguing balls and strikes?" Karn demanded.

I was standing there listening to this, yapping at Karn over Mickey's shoulder, seething.

"What if I am?" Mickey asked.

"Are you?"

"What if I am?"

That is one redeeming thing about Mickey Martin. He defends his players no matter what.

"If you are, you're outta here," Karn said.

"Is that a threat?" Mickey's fuse was almost up.

"No. It's a fact," Karn said.

That was it. Mickey Martin lost it.

"YOU WANT ME TO FUCKING ARGUE BALLS AND STRIKES, YOU FUCKING COCKSUCKER? OKAY, I'M ARGUING BALLS AND STRIKES, YOU FUCKING CUNT! YOU BEEN STICKING IT UP OUR ASSES ALL SEASON. YOU'RE GONNA BE STUCK IN FUCKING A BALL YOUR WHOLE FUCKING LIFE UNTIL THEY FIRE YOUR FUCKING ASS!"

"SO ARE YOU!" Karn screamed back. Then he made a throwing motion with his hand and yelled, "YOU'RE OUTTA HERE, MICKEY!"

Martin lit into Eddie Karn with both barrels, screaming and yelling. For five minutes he stayed out there, kicking dirt and gesturing. He was finally dragged back to the dugout by the other umpires and his coaches. Back in the dugout he chucked the Gatorade jug onto the field followed by a number of helmets and bats. Finally he stormed into the runway to the clubhouse and broke every light along the way. I sat quietly on the bench. Carlton Gray sat next to me.

"See what you started?" he asked.

122

Carlton Gray must have felt sorry for this poor, pathetic soul living by himself because he invited me to his house for dinner. His wife, Mary, is a great cook. I went over there and hung around. I watched Carlton's three-year-old son dribble a basketball better than I could and shoot it even better than that. After explaining what happened between me and that redhead (Michele) we had dinner. Mary looked at me halfway through and asked point blank, "So, I hear you throw a scuffball."

Far from it, babe.

123

I called Duerson before the next day's game and he sounded miserable. I told him about the blowup with Eddie Karn. He said that Karn is an asshole.

"How's the hand?" I asked.

"Broken," he replied quickly.

I told him about my new possible nickname.

"If you think I'm gonna call you 'Wicked boy' or whatever the fuck you just said, you can forget it, 'Chia-head.'"

It's a good thing I didn't tell him about the "ass-face" crack. Finally, I asked him about the competition in Double A.

"Well, let me put it this way: about three guys in ten can hit a decent curve. So you'll do well when you get here."

I appreciate the confidence. He might have said "if" I get there.

Rancho Cucamonga was in town to complete the inane home-and-home series. Christenson hit a two-run homer in the first and took his sweet time getting around the bases. The Quakes didn't appreciate it. Homer Burns hit one out too and we were blowing them out 9–0. They brought in reliever Jason Smith. Smith can really bring it. The teams were feeling tense with each other. Christenson came to the plate again and Smith brushed him back. The ump, a big guy, held

Christenson back before he could run out to the mound. Christenson completed his at-bat by popping out. The inning ended and Jack Kray strolled to the mound. The ump hadn't warned the benches and it didn't take a genius to realize what Jack was going to do. He ripped a ninety-mile-per-hour fastball at the first batter on the first pitch. The ball hit the guy on the left shoulder blade. Immediately he dropped his bat and charged the mound. Kray flipped away his glove and raised his fists. As the batter arrived at the mound, Kray grabbed him under both arms and flipped him to the ground. Then Kray started pummeling him. Both benches emptied and Christenson stormed around looking for Jason Smith. When he found him they started fighting. I was hanging around the pile watching that no one did anything stupid. One of their guys popped Mike Queen right in the side of the face while Queen wasn't looking. I have no love for Queen, but that cannot be allowed to happen. I went over and for the first time in my pacifist, Jewish life, hit someone. I punched him right in the jaw and he fell backwards. One of their other guys grabbed me and we started wrestling on the ground near third. Another pile covered us. Being at the bottom of those piles is no fun. All you get is stepped on, sat on and yelled at. This went on for fifteen minutes and was more brutal that you generally see as baseball fights go. The umps told both benches that they didn't want to see any more of that shit.

No kidding.

If they had warned Smith after he threw at Christenson then none of that would have happened. I suffered my first ejection of my baseball life. I was proud of myself though. The other guys seemed impressed too. Brooks Simon came over and said, "I've never seen a Jew actually hit someone." And then he patted me on the shoulder. We won the game 10–3. The fight looked like it made us play better because we won the next two games, 9–7 and 2–1. I pitched the last game of the four game series and gave up three runs and five hits in eight innings. But lost. I make myself sick. There were no more incidents throughout the series. I got fined and suspended for one game for the fight. It wasn't a game I was pitching, so I would watch the game from the stands. It would be like a night off. Our overall record was 52–46 and our record since the break was a solid 18–10. We were tied for the division lead in the second half with Lake Elsinore. I was 11–7.

124

Hungry for updates regarding his relationship with Nikki Martin, I went to Christenson regarding said relationship. "What happened with you and that slut?" I asked confidentially.

"Which one?" came the response.

I forgot whom I was talking to.

"Nikki Martin," I said.

"Aha, *that* slut. Well, I fucked her the other night ... wait a second, I thought you weren't interested. That's what you told me."

"I never said I wasn't interested. It's a well-known fact that being Jewish has made me into a busybody and I need to know everything that's going on. It also makes it easier for me to be a clubhouse lawyer."

(A clubhouse lawyer is someone who gets involved in things that aren't his business and tries to either instigate or straighten things out. Most leaders are clubhouse lawyers.)

"I see," Christenson said. "Well, I see her once in a while, but it's casual. I know she's fucking other guys besides me."

"Other players?" I exclaimed.

"Nahh. Just other guys."

Oh.

If Dave Christenson ever got off the bulking concoctions he would have movie star good looks. He has the Florida-bred tan and the sculpted goatee and a style in his dress. After a few years maybe he'll stop.

That night we lost the opener of the series with Bakersfield 5–1. Miguel Santana started and pitched well into the sixth inning. The score was 2–1, Bakersfield. Santana walked the leadoff batter and then gave up a single. There were runners on first and third with nobody out. Now, if anyone out there can explain the next set of strategic moves made by Mickey Martin, please do. The two-place hitter in the lineup, a righty, was batting. Mickey had Santana walk the guy intentionally to pitch to the third place hitter, a lefty, with the bases loaded, wanting to set up a force at every base. I'd never seen this done unless it was the bottom of the ninth or extra innings and one run would lose the game. In that case you have no choice. In this situation, there were a million things that Mickey could have done. He had action in the bullpen so he could have yanked Miguel. Or if he insisted on leaving Miguel in, he could have conceded the run and gone for a double play. Or he could have played the infield halfway and told them to come home on a sharp grounder. These are just coming off the top of my head. What he did do, there's no explanation for. Mark Mattera would know not to do something so strange. And, as I knew he would, the third place hitter doubled home three runs. Mickey's managing career was destined to die in San Bernardino, and rightfully so. Then I thought about it and reconsidered. There are plenty of managers in the big leagues who don't have the first clue as to what they're doing. Why not one more?

We got shutout the next night, 2–0. Jack Kray was the victim of the lack of run support this time. He did pitch well though. We salvaged the last game of the series in a semi-slugfest 8–5. We fell behind 5–1, but homers by Christenson and Willie Hernandez led us in a comeback. Jesse "The Rat" Williams won in relief. I named him "The Rat." He didn't seem to mind. It made him feel wanted.

125

Back on the road to Adelanto to play High Desert. I know this is all sounding painfully repetitive, but think how we feel having to live through it as opposed to reading about it. If we were traveling by plane in first class like they do in the Majors, well that would be tolerable. But we weren't. We were traveling by bus into quiet little towns. And the Dodgers are a first class organization from top to bottom. I'd hate to see what it's like in some of the cheaper organizations. It was only the beginning of summer in Adelanto and it was already over 100 degrees. The oppressive heat is impossible to play in. Not too hard to break a sweat though.

We had a special guest for the series. Dodgers star third baseman Jared Kemerrer (the guy they traded The Superfreak for) was down here on a minor league assignment rehabbing from a pulled hamstring. That meant Carlton Gray had to DH for the series and he was none too happy about it. Some guys have trouble getting into the flow of the game when the only thing they're doing is waiting for their turn at bat. And if they fail, they can stew about it until their next at-bat. I was expecting Kemerrer to be a Major League asshole, but he wasn't. Not only did he encourage us, but also he tantalized us with the luxuries that Major Leaguers are surrounded by. Then he started talking about the women. "You guys don't have any idea how close you are to getting Big League pussy," he said.

Guys played more aggressively after that.

The renewed vigor didn't help us any. Masato Fujinami lost the opener 2–0. We got shutout the next game too. I was that victim and got the loss. Maybe they should try and let the pitchers hit. My record fell to 11–8. Afterwards Kemerrer took about fifteen of us out to dinner and paid for the whole thing. That cost a nice chunk of change, but it's not like he doesn't have the cash. He was making $7.5 million that season. I would be free with my money too if in that tax bracket. During dinner he mentioned my curve and slider.

"I don't call it a slider. I call it a 'twister'," I corrected him.

"Good idea, kid. Be colorful," he said. "And what about that scuffball?"

"It's a 'cutter.'"

"Yah. Right," he said with a roll of the eyes.

He was full of useful information *and* he bought us dinner. We briefly considered holding him down and yanking his other hamstring out of its insertion to keep him down here for a while. Then we realized that the Dodgers would probably frown on such behavior and thought better of it.

In the third game of the series, we finally busted out with some runs. Miguel Santana was the recipient of the generosity. But we got shut out again in the last game of the series. That made it four shutouts in six games. Mickey said there would be extra batting when we got home, but he didn't go berserk like we expected. Maybe he's taking Prozac. I wondered what extra hitting was going to do. If you're not hitting, all extra hitting is going to do is ingrain bad habits into you. If there is a problem, it must be corrected. I think we just ran into some good pitching more than anything else.

126

Back into town came Visalia. I was not only getting sick of seeing my teammates' faces, but the other teams' faces as well. Our record was slipping back again as we fell three games behind Lake Elsinore. Guys sat passively in the clubhouse playing cards or watching TV. I'm continuously amazed at some guys' lack of concern for winning. Some of the guys are so intense that it's scary and others just roll slowly along. Maybe the laid back atmosphere of California had something to do with it. New York is so much more hectic. A hectic atmosphere adds urgency. Maybe that's what we needed. The few times I've driven in California, the other drivers looked at me as if I was the "Night Stalker" every time I touched my horn. In New York my hand is perpetually on the horn.

We lost the opener to Visalia 8–3 and the second game 11–3. We were fading fast. Frustration was setting in and Mickey's temper was shortening, if that was possible. I was expecting a food shower after the 11–3 ass kicking, but there was none. Standing in the center of the clubhouse, seething, Mickey said through clenched teeth, "If you guys don't give a fuck then neither do I," before slamming the door to his office.

Pitching the last game of the Visalia series I wasn't expecting much run support. I, however, was determined not to lose again. I didn't overthrow; I just took one pitch at a time and was able to concentrate more than usual. What resulted was the best game I have ever pitched in my life. Nine innings after the first pitch, I fired the last pitch — a twister. The batter swung and missed and I had a two-hit shutout. For one night at least, Mickey and Marky Martin didn't exist. A relatively bad year for the team didn't exist. Christenson homered to get us an early lead and I retired the first fifteen batters to face me. We added a couple of runs later and had a 4–0 lead. All I had to worry about was pitching. And that's what I did. No runs, two cheap hits (one an infield hit, the other a bloop over short). I shook my fist in victory and broke into a huge smile after the final out was recorded. Villanueva slammed the ball into my glove and grabbed me in a blubbery hug. Afterwards I was interviewed by KCKC 1350 AM radio. This was my night and no one could take it away from me.

127

The next day was a much-needed day off after which we would head to Stockton for three games. I was in my apartment, sound asleep, when my ringing phone awakened me. Stumbling over in the dark to answer it, I banged my shin hard on an end table. It hurt enough to make me yell a curse. I still wasn't fully awake when I got to the phone and was unable to enunciate my usual "Yello."

"Unglihjd?"

"Brett? Is that you? I didn't interrupt anything, did I? You got a girl there?" the voice asked.

"Uhhdjha." I was speaking in tongues.

"Brett! Wake up!"

"I'm awake," I said, shaking the cobwebs out. "Who in hell is this?"

"Mickey Martin. How you feeling? I asked if you got a girl there."

"Unfortunately no," I said. "Whaddaya want, Mick?" I was getting annoyed.

"Listen, I wouldn't have called so late, but it's important. The Dodgers have made a trade," he said.

My heart leapt into my throat.

Have I been traded? Oh, shit. Where are they sending me?

My head started pounding.

"Brett, you still there?"

"Have I been traded?" I stammered.

He didn't answer. He just kept going on with his own agenda.

"The Dodgers traded a couple of guys from the big club and a couple of minor leaguers to Philly."

I started to get really pissed because he wasn't answering me.

"Goddammit, Mickey! Have I been traded?"

"No, no, no. Didn't I already say that?"

"No, Mickey."

"Oh. Sorry. Well, anyway. There's some moves being made. Stephen Jones called me and asked how you did tonight and I told him about the shutout. One of the guys traded was at San Antonio and they need a replacement up there on the roster. You're flying to Texas tomorrow."

165

I was having trouble fathoming what was happening.

"What?" I said in a low voice.

"They want you in San Antonio."

"You're kidding."

"Nope. You're going to Double A, kid. Good luck."

128

They were sending me to Double A. What next? I called the front office the next day at 9:00 A.M. They had everything ready for me. I was flying at 7:00 the next morning to El Paso, Texas, to join the San Antonio Missions in the midst of a road trip. I asked what I was supposed to do about my apartment and they said they would take care of it. I started to think that they were being very generous until I realized that they *had* to do that. It was in the contract. I was getting a raise too. Up to $1,800 a month. There was a lot to do. I had to call my parents hoping that they hadn't planned their trip to San Bernardino. I had to get to the ballpark and get my equipment. Then I had to pack all my stuff in the apartment. I was very excited and hadn't even thought about the fact that I was only two steps from the Majors. I got hold of my parents and luckily they hadn't planned their trip yet.

"I was stationed in El Paso," Dad said.

"I'm just joining the team there. I'm playing for San Antonio," I said.

"El Paso's nice."

"I'M NOT PLAYING FOR EL PASO, DAD! THAT'S WHERE MY NEW TEAM IS RIGHT NOW," I yelled.

I'm starting to understand why Mother is always yelling at him. The man doesn't listen.

129

I wasn't sure where I was going to stay in San Antonio. Duerson was living in a hotel, so I figured I'd do the same. No point in finding an apartment with a month left in the season. One of the assistants for San Bernardino gave me a ride to LAX. It's only sixty miles from San Bernardino to Los Angeles. I lugged my stuff into the airport and checked in at the America West counter. I found out that the coach ticket I had received from the team cost only $126. The Dodgers were feeling extremely generous. I shouldn't complain though. They could have sent me by bus. That would be a thirty-hour trip. Flight 2421 from Los Angeles took off slightly late at 7:18 A.M. I got stuck next to a fat woman that wanted to talk throughout the whole flight. I tried my "no hablo ingles" routine, but she spoke Spanish too. I looked at her and said, "I'm sorry, I'd love to chat with you throughout this flight but I have an important test coming up and need to study for it." She said okay. Then I went to sleep.

The plane touched down at 11:27 A.M., Texas time. I exited the plane and was greeted by a coach, Rich Uribe, of the Missions' staff. Managing and coaching in the minors is hard work. They have to do *everything* and don't make much money. We loaded my stuff into a rented car and took off to join the team mid-series versus the El Paso Diablos.

130

After being bored to tears hearing the life story of Rich Uribe, I marched into the visiting clubhouse at Cohen Stadium (Hey! A stadium named after a Jew) and felt like an alien as all the guys playing cards and doing whatever looked at me like I was an unwanted interloper. I usually have to open my mouth before receiving that reaction. This time I was off to an early start. Duerson, his hand in a cast, hadn't heard the joyous news of my arrival.

"What the hell are you doing here?" he asked.

It's always nice to feel welcome.

"I missed ya," I said in a smart-ass tone.

"I knew they had to bring somebody up. I didn't think it'd be you. Why you?"

My pal.

Some guys nodded hello. Others didn't. One came by and introduced himself.

"Hi. I'm Frank Stein," he said.

Frankenstein?

I looked at him, shook his hand and grinned.

"Uhhhhhhhh!" I said, waving my arm straight out in front of me. "Fire baaaaaad. Uhhhhhhhh!"

He frowned at me and looked at Uribe.

"Where'd you get *this* asshole?"

I think he was joking. There was a uniform waiting at my locker without my name stitched across the back as all the other uniforms had. I was a surprise addition. They gave me number twenty-two. It wasn't my customary number fifteen, but it's okay. Twenty-two is a pretty good pitcher's number. Jim Palmer wore number twenty-two. The uniforms have what I think is the Alamo on the front with "Missions" in block lettering underneath. San Antonio Missions manager Jimmy Strait poked his head out of his office and waved at me to come in.

131

Jimmy Strait is a stout man of sixty-four with a potbelly. He sat behind his desk and asked me to sit. Strait, originally from Tennessee, had been in baseball since age seventeen. His claim to fame is that he has never drawn a check from anyplace other than baseball. He's balding with a buzz cut. Where the buzz cut ends and the baldness begins is anybody's guess. He put his glasses on the end of his nose and looked down at what appeared to be a stat sheet.

"Looks like you did pretty well in California," he said.

I nodded.

He looked up at me. "Well, I heard some good things about you from James Witherspoon."

"What about Mickey Martin. Did he have anything nice to say?"

"Ah, Mickey," he said and started laughing. The laugh lasted for a long moment. "Mickey's harmless. How many food tables did he tip over?" he asked, not expecting an answer and laughing some more.

After that Jimmy Strait got down to business. I was going to be the fifth starter. That was fine with me. Jimmy Strait is exactly what he seems to be. He's had a fascinating career. He played in the Majors for three years before moving into coaching. He's been a player, a scout, a coach, a manager, and a general manager. The man has perspective. He enjoys managing at Double A because he likes to have hungry kids in his charge clawing their way to the Majors as opposed to spoiled millionaires already in the Majors.

I must admit, I'd like to be a spoiled millionaire.

Jimmy managed twice in the Majors. A successful stint for the Montreal Expos in the late seventies and early eighties ended when they said that they wanted to find someone to bring them to the next level. He went to the Dodgers as a coach and stayed for several years before the Baltimore Orioles came calling with another managing job. He lasted for a year. The Orioles' tyrannical owner, billionaire Aristotle Komistopolous, fired him in his yearly staff purge. Komistopolous had owned the Orioles for five years and been through six managers. Komistopolous would call Strait in the middle of the night to discuss strategy and Strait would hang up on him. Strait was also asked to meet the owner for a weekly lunch to discuss the state of the team. Strait refused, citing his practice of never discussing business while eating. All of this infuriated Komistopolous. Despite Strait's leading the Orioles to ninety wins and their best finish in years, he was fired. Komistopolous had his flunky/son do the dirty work over the phone. Jimmy Strait immediately got up and marched into Komistopolous' office building, pushed past the secretary and barged into Komistopolous' office. He demanded to be fired to his face. The word on the street is that Aristotle Komistopolous shit himself right there and then.

Jimmy Strait is my kind of guy.

Strait gave me the basic rap. The "You wouldn't be here (in Double A) if the organization didn't think you were ready ..." kind of thing. He talked to me for a few minutes and let me leave to get settled. As I was exiting his office, he called to me.

"Oh, and Brett, one more thing. Make sure you learn the signs. Sometimes I use my pitchers to pinch run."

The signs? Pinch run? Me?

Later Rich Uribe was showing me the signs and futilely trying to get them through my thick skull. Finally I said, "Y'know, not for nothing Rich, but when I was in high school we had the greatest set of signs. They never failed. Nobody missed one. Never."

"Yeah? What were they?" he asked.

"Well, when the coach wanted us to steal, he'd stand in the first base coaching box and whisper 'go, go, go!'" I said, pantomiming a sweeping motion with my hand. "And when he wanted us to bunt he'd hold his hands in the bunt position and call our names."

He stared in response. Uribe is a serious guy.

"They worked," I said. "We won."

"That's not the Dodgers' way of doing things," he said.

Well, la de da.

132

Equipment manager Tony Donaldson asked me what my hat size was.

"Seven and an eighth," I said.

"Is that with or without your hair?" he cracked. His lips curling into a sardonic smile.

I hadn't gotten a haircut since my GI in January. I had returned to resembling something akin to a tumbleweed. Spying Tony's bald head, I said, "I wouldn't be making any *hair* comments if I were you. Unless you're talking about the '*Hair* Club for Men.'"

He shut up and gave me my hat.

There wasn't much left to be decided in the Western Division of the Texas League. San Antonio won the first half by five games and led the second half by thirteen games with a month to play. A first round bye was in the cards for the Missions. The El Paso Diablos were the team in second place. Unless I infected this team with some serious bad luck, El Paso would be no problem.

They play five game series in the Texas League. There are only eight teams in the league, which means familiarity. Sitting in the dugout during the second game of the series (my first game in Double A),

Duerson sat next to me and said, "By the way, I hope you like bus rides."

"What's that mean?"

"Nothing," he said.

Then Frank Stein came over.

"Oh, and by the way smartass, you'll love the bus rides we take here. Heh, heh, heh."

Throughout the game I kept asking what those cryptic comments were supposed to mean. Nobody answered me. We won the game 5–1. This is a good team, I thought. I just went back to my hotel to rest. The other guys seemed to have more freedom than we did in A ball. Jimmy Strait seemed like a fun guy to play for. The pitching coach, Chris Shavers, told me that I would pitch the last game of the series. I charted pitches before that game. We won 3–1. That was the seventh straight win for the Missions. I didn't want to be the one to halt the win streak with crappy pitching.

133

My pitching wasn't crappy, but I did halt the winning streak. I pitched well enough to win but lost anyway. I went seven innings and gave up three runs on five hits. I walked two and struck out five. I was simply outpitched. Oh, well.

As for the other players on the Missions, the shortstop Billy Everly looked terrific. He was the number one pick three years ago. At age twenty-one you may as well write superstar on the back of his uniform. He's one of those famous five-tool guys. Except he can actually play. He homered in the game I lost and after seeing him for only three days I figured that he would be a September call-up for the Dodgers.

I learned why the guys were making snide comments concerning the bus rides and why they play five game series in the Texas League. The trip from El Paso to San Antonio is 554 miles! That's an approximately twelve-hour ride. I wondered if it would be possible to be sent back to San Bernardino until the Dodgers deemed that I was ready for the big time. Maybe I could just appear in home games. How about a special plane? Have I achieved that superstar status?

I guess not.

134

After twelve gruesome hours and numerous meaningless chats, we rolled into San Antonio, exhausted. I was basically homeless. The team had generously found me a room at the Holiday Inn. I can't describe that bus ride. Blecchhh!

We had a day off to recover before opening the series with the Wichita Wranglers. They were vying for the mantle of the worst team in the league. There were a couple of really bad ones. I used the day off to get my head and body straight. San Antonio looked like a lively town. Much more so than Great Falls, Montana. I'd find out once I was settled in. I did see lots of pretty girls around even when I wasn't looking. I couldn't wait until I started to look.

The thing about the five game series set-up is that in a five-man rotation every starting pitcher will start a game in every series. Games in Texas start at 7:05 P.M. on weekdays and Saturdays and 6:05 P.M. on Sundays. In Texas the heat and mosquitoes get so bad that it is impossible to play in the afternoon. Believe me when I say that the heat isn't diminished much in the evening. There are just fewer mosquitoes.

I arrived at Nelson Wolff Stadium and my uniform with my name across the back was there. Very nice. Duerson got his soft cast off and was allowed to hit off a tee. He was given some scientific medical advice: "Take it easy." It's a good thing they're so cautious with their top prospects.

Wichita may have been at the bottom of the standings but you'd never know it by the way they played us. It feels funny to say "us" since I've been a Mission for only a few days. Wichita beat us the first game 7–6. We played terribly. Maybe it's me. There's an interesting dichotomy between Jimmy Strait and Mickey Martin: Jimmy is calm and Mickey is deranged. Jimmy doesn't yell or ever seem to get upset.

We won the second game 5–2. Our pitcher, Dick McNally, is the ace. He's a 6'5" lefty from Florida and has a long slow motion and then unleashes bullets. The quality of play in the Texas League is a step up from the California League. Double A is the litmus test for the scouts and executives to see which players are true big league prospects and which should go home and work in the "Gap." Double A has players from all A ball teams merging since there is only one Double A team in every organization. It's like a five-lane highway merging into one. That causes serious traffic jams. You have players from San Bernardino, Vero Beach and Yakima joining Double A. You also have the guys from Cuba, the Dominican Republic and the Orient. I'd know soon if I was kidding myself.

We lost the third and fourth games to Wichita. Boy, was I an inspiration to this club.

I pitched the last game of the series and got my first Double A win. I went seven and two-thirds innings giving up two runs and six hits. Strait yanked me after I gave up two singles with two outs. I had no real problem with the decision. Closer Dave Jenkins saved it for me.

135

Another bad team, Midland, arrived. I wondered if there were any good teams in the Texas League. I was settled in so I was ready to look around San Antonio. After the bus ride it took several days. I saw the Alamo, the San Antonio Riverbank (which is a collection of stores and such) and the San Antonio Zoo. There are lots of strip joints there (they call them gentlemen's clubs). I also found out that one of the team's sponsors is "Hooters"—Southern belles with huge breasts appealed to me greatly. As for the games with the Midland Angels, we won three of the five. Our pitcher in the first game was Lin Weng-hsung, a twenty-four-year-old righty from Taiwan. He throws ninety miles per hour sidearm and is murderous on right-handed hitters. He speaks very little English, but I didn't try my joke of cursing him out. Fool me once, shame on you; fool me twice, shame on me.

Lots of girls hung around the ballpark. Other than the inhuman heat and the bus rides, San Antonio seemed like lots of fun. On a good note, Duerson was cleared to play. He wasn't going to catch the rest of the way, but he could hit. So he would DH. I was masterful in the final game of the series but got a no-decision. The hitters seem to have trouble with the good breaking stuff. I left after the ninth having given up no runs, five hits, no walks and six strikeouts. Dave Jenkins lost it in the tenth.

136

Onto the buses for the trip to Wichita, Kansas. Are you ready for this one? San Antonio to Wichita: 628 miles. That's fourteen hours. Fourteen! I could read *War and Peace* in that allotment of time. The talks are just as stupid in Double A as they are in Single A and Rookie ball. The conversation turned to music. There were a couple of glam-rock fans on the team if you can believe it. Dylan Torrey is a fan of Poison. I never knew of any guy that was a fan of Poison that wasn't considered homosexual. I started in about Poison lead singer Bret Michaels. He was on VH1 being interviewed claiming his music was as good as R.E.M. He was puzzled about the pronunciation of R.E.M. lead singer Michael Stipe's name. "Steep, Stipe, Steep, is it Stipe?"

Michaels has started making movies now. Bad, bad movies that he writes and directs. At the very least he has stopped torturing people with his music.

We arrived at the Clarion Hotel Airport fourteen and a half-hours after departure. What a nightmare. Duerson was the recipient of the pleasure of rooming with me again.

"I can't get away from you, can I?" he asked.

No, you can't. No one can.

137

The guys on the team accepted me quickly. I found this out because an elaborate practical joke was played on me. Duerson must have been involved because he left for several hours. I was sitting in my hotel room watching TV when there was a knock at my door. I opened it and saw a fat woman. She turned out to be a Russian prostitute whose services had been procured for me by an unnamed culprit. She pushed her way in.

"I am Irina. I am gift forrr you." She had a deep Russian accent and was rolling her R's.

I looked at her with my eyes bulging out of my head as she sat herself on my bed.

"Yourrr friends sent me to pleasurrre you. I understant that you vant to eeet my pooosy?"

Yeuchhh.

I almost passed out at the mere thought.

"You gotta go," I said, shaking my head and pointing toward the door.

"Ohhhh, no. Your friends tolt me that you vere shy. Dey tolt me not to leaf no matter what you dit."

I had to think. Curfew was coming soon and along with curfew was bed check.

"Um, well, um…. Okay. Just let me clean up," I said and disappeared into the bathroom.

Okay, asshole. How you gonna get outta this?

She knocked on the bathroom door.

"Arrrre you comink out?"

"Uh, one second. I'm uh, um … I'm taking a crap," I said and shrugged at my reflection in the mirror.

I looked at the bathroom window and got an idea. I turned on the shower and climbed out the window, barely fitting through. I went to the pay phone in the lobby and dialed my room. Thankfully she picked up.

"Helloooo?"

"Brett," I said quickly, "listen, the cops are raiding the hotel. Get that girl outta there. This is no joke. Hurry."

I hung up and spied my room from outside. The door opened and she quickly left. She must have been arrested numerous times. I got back to my room, breathed a sigh of relief and plotted my revenge against the bastards.

138

I strolled into the clubhouse at Wichita and everything appeared normal. Everyone was doing his own thing. The card games were being conducted as usual. I scanned the room looking for laughter. Duerson was unable to look me in the face. Frank "Uhhhhh —fire bad" Stein was hiding his face in a towel. Dylan Torrey had a newspaper in front of his face, but it was shaking up and down. And finally, pitcher Jim Miller was laughing too. That looked like all of them. They weren't making too much of an effort to be anonymous. Duerson looked at me and asked, "So how was your evening, Brett?" and burst out laughing hysterically. He was laughing so hard that tears were coming out of his eyes. The other culprits soon followed suit.

"All right, all right you sonsabitches," I announced. "I have a mental note of all of you that were involved in this hilarious joke and shall respond accordingly." With that I grabbed the newspaper from Dylan Torrey, took a package of baby wipes from my bag and disappeared into the bathroom.

As far as the games go in Wichita, we won the first game 4–3. Duerson was the DH and looked rusty. He had the right to be rusty since he'd been out for six weeks. It should take a few days to get some semblance of timing back for him. In the second game of the series we had the chance to clinch the division and an automatic spot in the championship round as a reward for taking both the first and second half titles. Dick McNally started and didn't disappoint. He pitched a complete game and won. We mobbed him on the mound celebrating our automatic spot in the championship round. A champagne soaked celebration followed the game. I had a lot of fun during that. I'd never been part of one. I enjoyed having champagne dumped on my head. I was drinking a lot and wondering why I wasn't feeling any effects. Dave Jenkins straightened me out, "You idiot. That's not champagne. That's sparkling cider."

I thought I was becoming an alcoholic.

139

I went out and pitched the last game against Wichita. I still wasn't sure I was ready for Double A. Duerson pulled me aside before the game and told me that I was giving the hitters too much credit. "They aren't any better here than they were in San Bernardino. Just throw the ball."

That's exactly what I did. Nine innings later, I had a shutout. It wasn't that pretty. I gave up seven hits and two walks, but it did wonders for my confidence. Attitude can be just as important as ability. My 5–0 victory got my mind in a better frame. Maybe I did belong in Double A. After all, why would they send me there if they didn't think I could do the job. That night I did do the job.

140

The ride to Midland from Wichita: 659 miles. There are cots on the bus to sleep, but it's nearly impossible. Guys started talking movies, specifically comedies. Pete Crocker, a twenty-five-year-old catcher/first baseman, started talking about Adam Sandler. Most of the guys started talking about how funny he is. I can sit here and say with total sincerity that Adam Sandler has never made me laugh. When I elucidated this generation X blaspheme the other guys looked at me as if I'd just announced that I was a homosexual.

"How can you say he's not funny?" Frank Stein asked in a condescending way, as if I just didn't get it.

"You find that baby talk funny, Frank?" I asked.

Then I started imitating Sandler.

"I just a widdle boy. I maky poopy in my pants. Oh, boy. A widdle biddle piddle."

"What the fuck is that?" Dylan Torrey asked.

"Adam Sandler," I said.

"He don't do that stuff," Stein said.

"Ah, bullshit," I said.

"Well, who do you like?" Jim Miller asked. "Pauly Shore?"

"I'll tell you this," I said, pointing a finger, "Pauly Shore *has* made me laugh which is more than I can say for Adam Sandler."

There was no way to win the argument because no one listens. Adam Sandler is just not funny. And I think that it is a sick world when a talented comedian like Jon Stewart is stuck on *The Daily Show* and Adam Sandler is getting $20 million a film.

I felt like shit as we arrived in Midland. I went straight to the hotel and slept. Then when we went to the park I slept on the training table for another hour. I knew I was taking a risk sleeping so much around this crew, but if I don't get enough sleep I get cranky. It had to be done.

141

From a team standpoint the remaining regular season games were relatively meaningless. We had already cemented our position in the championship round so Jimmy Strait was resting his regulars and playing the backups more than usual. Duerson, trying to get his stroke back, was DH'ing every day.

Pitching coach Chris Shavers, a 6'4" blonde, blue eyed man of forty-three with a terribly bad back, was watching me throw in the bullpen between starts. I threw a few forkballs that would have been lit up. The forkball is primarily a moving change-up. The ball is held deep in between the index and middle fingers and thrown just like a regular fastball. Mine moves around like a knuckleball as previously mentioned, when it's moving at all that is. Lately it hadn't been. Shavers seemed to have an idea what he was talking about, so when he suggested that I move the ball a little further toward the end of my fingers and throw it harder like a split-finger fastball, I agreed to try it.

"You don't throw that hard, Brett. They'll adjust to the fork up there," he said, referring to the Majors.

After being insulted, I decided to try it. I'm not un-coachable. I put the ball toward the end of my fingers and let fly. The ball flew over the catcher's head and toward the dugout.

"It's gonna take some work," Shavers said.

I appreciated the difference between Chris Shavers and Jeff Finestra.

The Midland series didn't mean squat to us but we beat them four out of five anyway. I went out there in the last game trying not to give the hitters too much credit. One problem: You have to give the hitters a certain amount of credit or you'll get creamed. Which is exactly what happened. It wasn't *that* bad, but it wasn't that good either. Five innings, five runs, six hits, two walks and three strikeouts. We scored seven runs early, so I escaped with a no-decision. I gave up a 460-foot home run to their clean-up hitter Walter McCrary. It was still looking for a place to land when we left the ballpark. The main reason that I give up some tape-measure home runs has nothing to do with my 86 mph fastball. It has to do with the fact that I throw a "light" fastball. It's called a "four seam" fastball and has a straight spin and is held across the horseshoe part of the ball with the index and middle fingers. As it's traveling toward the plate, the ball doesn't appear to have any seams at all. Guys who throw really hard make the ball rise. The reason for this is called Bernoulli's Law. The Swiss scientist Bernoulli discovered that as the speed around a gas increases, the pressure decreases. The sharp rotation placed on the ball overcomes the gravitational pull and makes the ball rise. I don't throw hard enough to make the ball rise. I've had people suggest that I switch to throwing a sinker. But when I try and throw a sinker, the ball doesn't sink. Good sinkers are like hitting a cannonball. Maybe I could work on something like a sinker with my "cutter."

142

I was reading *Baseball America* on the ride from Midland to San Antonio. That ride is only 366 miles and nine and one half hours. I turned to the individual team section and found something that caught my eye to say the least. Under the Dodgers' team insignia it had details of a trade rumor that had been floating around:

"The Dodgers have expressed interest in Montreal Expos' free-agent-to-be center fielder Roger Creighton. The Expos are said to want

179

young talent in return with the asking price believed to be stud catcher Jon Duerson and Double A pitcher Brett Samuels plus cash. A team source said that the Dodgers want to replace someone for Duerson in the deal. Talks are expected to continue up until the August 31 deadline."

"What the fuck is this?" I asked no one in particular. The guys started asking what the matter was. When I showed them it was like dangling a steak in front of a lion.

"They're getting rid of you, Brett" was the gentlest comment I heard for the rest of the ride home. I shouldn't have said anything. The article got me paranoid. I didn't want to be traded.

At the ballpark before the first game of the last regular season series of the year, I walked into Jimmy Strait's office to see what was going on with the offending article that I held in my hand.

"What can I do for you, Brett?" he asked, removing his pipe from his mouth.

"Well Skip, I saw this in the paper and didn't know what to make of it," I said, handing the article to him. He read it and looked up at me.

"You're upset about being included in trade rumors, right?"

"Well, yeah."

"Listen, son," he began, "I don't know what they're thinking up there. If it were up to me, I wouldn't trade you. But you have to understand in this era, with the haves and have-nots, they're going to trade young players for high-priced veterans. You with me so far?"

I nodded.

"The Dodgers are in a pennant race so they'll try and upgrade and improve any way they can. If they make a trade they're going to have to give up some kids. If you're successful down here you'll have to accept being asked for in trades. They may not want to trade you at all. Sometimes writers make things up. That's why you have to be careful with the newspapers. They can always hide behind that 'one source said' crap."

"Should I forget about this, then?" I asked.

"Look, I don't want to say they're not gonna move you and then feel like a fool if they do. They may have no choice in order to get the player they want. If they ask my advice I'll tell them to hold onto you.

Other than that you have to accept these things when you sign the contract."

"Okay, I guess," I said, getting up to leave and not feeling much better.

"Listen kid, don't worry about things you can't control. You see this head of hair?" he lifted his hat to reveal the baldness blending into the buzz cut. Or was it the buzz cut blending into the baldness? "This is from worrying too much. Just do your job and don't worry about the other stuff."

So much for easing my apprehension. At least he was honest though. Mickey Martin would have said, "They're trading you over my dead body." The next thing you'd see is me packing my things for wherever Montreal wanted to send me.

This stuff comes with the territory. The worst thing is that I had to sweat it out until midnight, August 31.

143

Our playoff situation settled, we played the final five regular season games with El Paso. I wasn't scheduled to pitch until the last game of the season, so I was free to execute my revenge against the pranksters who sent the bloated Russian prostitute to my room. I got a great idea when I was in Jimmy Strait's office asking about the trade rumors. Jimmy Strait is a big country and western music fan and he knows just about everybody still alive from old Hollywood. He has numerous photographs in his office with various famous people. It's not a mural but there are a great many of them. After the first game with El Paso (we lost) I executed my plan.

The next day when Jimmy walked into his office, he yelled, "Now what in the hell is this?" The clubhouse, half full, went over to see what was going on. It seems that all of Jimmy's pictures had disappeared along with his furniture. All that was left were pictures of Jon Duerson, Dylan Torrey, Jim Miller and Frank Stein. The guys in the photos automatically looked at me. I put on my most innocent face.

"I'd better get my pictures back and soon," Strait announced. He didn't appear annoyed. He knows how players are. But he did want his photos back. Stein and Miller interrogated me and were soon joined by Duerson and Torrey. I denied all knowledge of wrongdoing.

The night before I stealthily hung around the clubhouse until everyone had left and executed my plan. I hid the desk in the opposing clubhouse's storage closet. It was a hassle dragging it that far, but it was worth it. I hid the photographs in Duerson's trunk. The LAPD couldn't have done a better job in framing an athlete. The visiting clubhouse attendant found the desk and returned it. As for the pictures, nobody knew where they were. A frantic search was conducted with no results until Duerson finally went into his trunk before the fourth game of the series and found the pictures. I was sitting in my hotel room when I heard him yell, "Brett, you prick!" I started laughing hysterically.

The pictures mysteriously returned to Jimmy Strait's office that night. I never admitted guilt. Until now.

144

I started the final regular season game against El Paso and won, pitching seven and one third innings and allowing two runs. It didn't matter regarding the playoff rotation. I was headed to the bullpen. Strait was using four starters for the championship series and that left me out. It wasn't that insulting. I hadn't exactly lit up the universe since my arrival.

The regular season in the Texas League was over. Strait gave us two days off before we started workouts for the championship series. We didn't know whom we were going to play. The Tulsa Drillers were playing the Jackson Generals to determine who would play us. They had a best three of five series and we sat waiting, lying in the weeds. Since we had some time to relax, a few of us went to several local bars to drink and meet women (not necessarily in that order). Frank Stein, George Vines, Dave Jenkins, Billy Everly and yours truly were the night crawlers. I had several vodka sours and started to ramble nonsense, I'm told. I don't remember. I woke up the next morning without a hangover and with lipstick on my collar. I hope a female put it there.

After two days off we started workouts for the championship series. I had forgotten all about it, but August 31 had come and gone and I was still a Mission. The player that was the object of their affections, Roger Creighton, was traded to the Braves. Christenson called me and told me that Mickey Martin almost attacked him. Oddly enough it didn't have anything to do with Christenson screwing Martin's wife. It seems that Dave had missed a cut-off man. Time for the rubber room, Mick.

The Dodgers made no moves by the deadline. One thing minor leaguers have to worry about is the dreaded "player to be named later." That could be anybody. Years ago the Braves made a trade with the Indians and one of the players to be named later was Brett Butler. The problem was that someone had leaked the information, so Butler knew for the whole last month of the season that he was going to Cleveland the next year. I was glad to still be bleeding Dodger blue. Okay, maybe not, but I was still a resident of the Alamo.

145

Tulsa swept Jackson so we had a date with the Drillers. That's a great name. The Drillers. It must be a great way to pick up girls. "Hi baby. I play for the DRILLERS." It just might work.

I stationed myself in the bullpen. I hadn't pitched in relief in a long while. I don't mind the bullpen because it's always an adrenaline rush when the phone rings and you're told to get loose. We were huge favorites over Tulsa. We had won ninety-four games and they only eighty. We hoped to take them out in four straight. Game one was a breeze for Dick McNally. He went the distance on a five-hitter. We won 6–2. Texans are notorious front-runners and we were in front, so we had a nice crowd. Game two was my first postseason appearance since the disaster in Great Falls. I wasn't as bad but I was close. We were leading 8–3 after the sixth when Strait brought me in to relieve Weng-hsung. I got the first two guys on pop-ups. The next guy walked and the next singled. I threw a twister that didn't twist and the batter tattooed it over the center field fence. Just like that it was 8–6. My only contribution was to make the game closer than it should have been. Its stuff like that that gives you a bad reputation as a choker. It's a reputation that I was quickly earning.

We went to Tulsa for game three. That was a delightful thirteen-hour bus ride. We wanted to sweep the series there. Apparently the Drillers had other ideas. They beat us 4–3 to get back in the series. Duerson was still favoring his hand and hitting without authority.

Game four was a pitcher's duel. Steve Baker pitched a shutout for us and Billy Everly homered with two outs in the eighth. We led three games to one and had the sparkling cider on ice ready to dump on each other's heads after game five.

Unfortunately the cider was going to be traveling back to San Antonio with us. We lost game five 4–3 when Dave Jenkins came in with the score tied in the tenth and promptly gave up a walk-off home run. At least I wasn't the only one stinking up the place. Ballplayers think like that. Misery loves company. Tulsa was playing us tough. Apparently no one told them that they were supposed to lose to us in four straight.

Back in San Antonio the hotels were beginning to wear on me. I'd been living in hotels both at home and on the road for the past month. We put the cider on ice in the clubhouse before game 6. It wouldn't be very good to have to sell the cider to Tulsa at a reduced price. We had two games to do the job. Lin Weng-hsung started and went eight innings, giving up two runs. The game was tied when he left. Three relievers followed and the game remained tied into the fifteenth. With two outs, Ray Rhett loaded the bases. Jimmy Strait needed a reliever. He chose me. There was a righty batting. When I arrived at the mound from the bullpen, Jimmy handed me the ball.

"Your game, kid. I'm counting on you," he said and walked off.

Catcher Pete Crocker told me to relax. "You can do it," he said.

Am I that fragile that everyone has to give me positive reinforcement?

I looked in for the sign and saw a curve put down. I threw it in the dirt for ball one.

Crocker called a fastball and the guy ripped it foul.

Ho-kay, I said to myself. I've had just about enough of this bull-shit. I looked in for the sign and saw another curve. I rocked and fired. The ball broke so much that the guy swung and hit it like a cue ball. It dribbled toward first and stayed fair. Aaron Beck picked it up and tagged the batter out. I was out of the inning. I didn't choke.

Strait pulled me aside in the dugout.

"I brought you into this game for a reason," he said.

Yeah. You had nobody else.

"I want you to learn to pitch in a high-pressure situation as well as you do in the regular season. This is your game. You're the man," he said and smacked my ass.

We didn't score in the next two innings and neither did they. I started rolling along. The bottom of the seventeenth, Billy Everly singled to start the inning. Aaron Beck bunted and the ball rolled between the pitcher and the charging first baseman. Everybody safe. Runners on first and second with nobody out. Dylan Torrey was batting. He squared to bunt and the pitcher threw the ball directly at him. That is a strategy in a bunt situation since it's hard to bunt a ball thrown directly at you. The ball hit Torrey on the thigh. Bases loaded. At the plate: Jon Duerson. Tulsa brought the infield and out-field in close. They had no choice. All we needed was a little fly ball and we were the Texas League champions. This was the perfect time for Duerson to bust out of his funk. Tulsa's pitcher, a lefty, pitched from the wind up. We were all at the top of the dugout steps. The pitch came in. Jon swung. He lined it between third and short. The third baseman and shortstop dove through the air. The ball was suspended. Time stopped. Everyone watched, hoping that the ball would get through.

The ball got through.

The left fielder stationed right behind short tried to pick it up and throw home in one motion. He missed it. Duerson raised his right fist as he ran to first. Everly pumped both fists in the air as he headed home with the winning run. The whole dugout charged the field. I jumped into the air making big circles with my arms and must have looked like an idiot. There were two big pileups on the field: one around Everly at the plate and the other on top of Duerson, who was yelling, "Watch the hand! Watch the hand!" The fans were going crazy. It was a joyous scene at Nelson Wolff Memorial Stadium. Everyone was climbing on each other in one big pile by now. We were the champions and I got the win. I didn't even choke. I almost did. But didn't. This was my first championship at any level and I would indeed receive a ring. Nobody ever forgets their first championship. Dave Jenkins stood on top of the pile of young men screaming, "WHOO-HOOOO-HOOOO!" sounding like Daffy Duck. The celebration had begun.

I have vague memories of that night. I was muttering incoherently about my championship ring. That's what I was told. Before I was totally smashed I wandered into Jimmy Strait's office. He was wearing a cowboy hat, a "Missions" T-shirt and still had his uniform pants and coaches shoes on. He was sipping a can of Budweiser. The photos were back in their rightful place. He was taking things in stride since he's won championships before. He enjoyed watching the young kids celebrate.

"Kid," he told me, "I left you in that game for a reason. You have to learn how to get out of certain situations if you're gonna be a success. When you're getting your ass kicked, you keep walkin' around like you own the fuckin' place. Keep that attitude no matter what."

One final note on the celebration: I have a memory of two "Hooters" girls. What happened with them is anyone's guess. I don't remember whether it was one of my fantasies or reality and no one else seemed to know either.

146

There was a huge story in the *San Antonio Express News* about our gripping victory. I was able to read it and cut out the article because I was just about the only guy on the team without a hangover. Within the next couple of days we had to pack our stuff and get out. I needed some rest. It was a long season and my final stats look quite good. Here they are: Wins—15, Losses—9, Innings Pitched—193, Hits—149, Runs—71, Earned Runs—66, Walks—50, Strikeouts—137, Games—

29, Games Started — 27, Complete Games — 5, Shutouts — 3 and Earned Run Average — 3.08.

A few days after the season, Jimmy Strait announced to us in his final team meeting that he was retiring from managing to become a scout. He was sixty-four and wanted to spend more time at home. I was curious as to why he didn't want to manage in the Majors. I asked him.

"Kid," he said, "I managed up there twice. I prefer working with the younger kids for two reasons. Number one: I like having a real impact on a kid. Teaching him something that will not only improve his baseball playing but also improve *him*. Number two: I was more of a babysitter up there than I could ever be down here."

I gave him something of a perplexed look.

"I know that may be hard for you to understand, but if and when you get up there you'll see. You'll know what I mean after ten minutes in a big league clubhouse."

I'd like to learn firsthand.

I went home to New York waiting to see what the Dodgers wanted me to do. I had thrown a lot of innings during the season and needed a rest. The Dodgers' director of minor league operations, David Cryer, called me in mid–September and told me that because I threw so many innings, they wanted me to rest until December and then report to Vero Beach to work on some ancillary aspects of my game. My pickoff move was crap and they wanted me to can the forkball and work on that split-finger that Chris Shavers had started working on with me. I was somewhat relieved because there were many places that they could have sent me such as Venezuela, Puerto Rico or the Arizona Fall League. I wasn't paranoid about not being sent anywhere.

I would soon be twenty-one. Maybe I'd get invited to the big league camp. *The big league camp!* Who would have considered such a thing just a year and a half before?

147

I had some free time and because I barely spent any of my salary during the season, I didn't get a part-time job. I didn't envy guys like

Carlton Gray who during his off-seasons has done such jobs as delivering pizzas and working in a shoe store. I rested for two weeks before beginning light workouts on my own. No throwing. Just trying to keep my legs in shape. There were no edicts from the team about gaining weight, so I canned the Met-Rx. I was left to my own devices for the most part because Tony Taglianetti had been traded to Cleveland right after the season and they immediately sent him to play in Venezuela. He was playing for the Oriente Caribbeans.

"How is it?" I asked being there was a good possibility that I would end up there one day.

"It's fucking horrible, but it could be worse," he said.

Your guess is as good as mine regarding what that means. He was playing third every day, so that was a plus.

Jon Duerson called me from the Arizona Fall League where the Dodgers sent him to play for the Peoria Javelinas. His manager was former Dodgers catcher Davey Hunter.

"What's a Javelina?" I asked.

"How in hell should I know?" he asked.

He told me that his hand was getting better. I had him pegged for Triple A Albuquerque or maybe, just maybe *Los Angeles*.

Since I had some time off I tagged along on my parents' trip to Europe. I was able to amuse myself with women in both England and France. I ran to try and stay in some semblance of shape.

148

I reported to the Instructional League in Vero Beach on December 3. There weren't many guys there. I was staying for two weeks and then going home. Then I had to report to the *big league camp* with pitchers and catchers on January 27. In Vero Beach was minor league pitching coordinator Tex Charles. Tex wasn't even from Texas. I don't know where the name came from. He's from Missouri and always has his head covered. He was only thirty-nine but must've been totally bald. I never saw him without a hat. He was up to 250 pounds. He pitched at 200. I looked it up.

I started to realize that it must not be that difficult to get a job in baseball. Some of the guys I've run into don't have the first clue as to what they're doing. Some do, but they seem to be in the minority. It reminds me of when I was playing in the Parade Grounds and I would get a new catcher. Everyone would have their own theories of where your legs should be, where your arms should be, how high to lift your leg, when to break your hands, what target to focus on, etc., etc. When you're young and impressionable and don't have much confidence you try and incorporate everyone's advice. That's what I used to do and wound up all fucked up. I was learning to filter new information and deposit what I didn't feel I needed into the trash. It's not hard to tell who has a clue and who doesn't. When he played, Tex Charles had a great pickoff move. I took his advice in that area. He was a good teacher despite his fat stomach getting in the way of his leg lift. I needed help with going from the stretch position also. Charles was able to help with that too.

There wasn't anybody I played with there and I was rooming with a Dominican kid that barely spoke English. My basic knowledge of Spanish helped me communicate, but I prefer having a roommate with whom I can go out and troll for chicks (of which I found plenty). My instruction in the Instructional League completed, I went home for a few weeks before I had to return for spring training.

I bought a copy of the *Baseball Digest* prospect issue. In it is an article discussing the best prospects in every organization and after that there are lists and brief scouting reports of other prospects. I scanned the article for my name ... unsuccessfully.

Duerson's name was in the article though. I tried the next section. I turned to the Los Angeles Dodgers and found under Double A San Antonio ... "Brett Samuels—Pitcher, Age 21." There was a brief scouting report. "Great curveball, great slider" (they wouldn't know to call it the twister), "good cutter" (HA!), "should increase velocity with maturity."

As for the guys I knew, also listed were Duerson, Christenson, Strock and Santana.

I gave the magazine to my dad before I left for spring training.

149

Taglianetti got back from Venezuela right after the New Year. He said the place isn't that bad, but you have to be careful because they gamble on the games and if you fuck up you might get shot. That's scary. We went to a couple of hot spots in Manhattan. I didn't say we got in to a couple of hot spots. We just went. We went to a club called "Life" and to our disbelief ... got in. Don't ask me how because the transvestite at the door used to work at other clubs and would never let us in. What happened? I don't know. I met a nice looking Spanish chick there. I hung out with her a few times before I left for Vero Beach. We tried to get in to the club a couple of more times before spring training with no luck. Who knows what the criterion is? I made a mental note that if I were ever famous I would go back there and let the owner know my feelings on the door policy. But then I thought it over and decided that if I was one of the people who were let in regularly then I wouldn't want guys like us in there either. The old axiom applies: I wouldn't want to join any club that would have me as a member. Late January rolled around quickly. I had to report back to Dodgertown as a nonroster invitee to the big league camp.

♦ PART III ♦

150

It was nerve-racking to think that I would be walking into the big league camp, and for the time being would be in the same locker-room with all the Major League pitchers and catchers. I was sure to be the victim of some hazing. The guys with the big mouths are the biggest targets. I vowed to keep my mouth shut, but I've tried that before and it hasn't worked.

On the flight back to Florida, I tried to remember the things that Jared Kemerrer told me during his brief stay in San Bernardino. It went something like this: "If you ever get to the Show, one thing I can tell you is that you don't have to put up with the rookie initiation bullshit. If you stand up to it initially without looking like a fag you'll escape it for the whole year and the guys will respect you for it. They might get pissed, but they'll respect you. If you let them get away with it though, you'll be carrying bags and stereos and put up with all sorts of shit all year. Trust me, I know. I stomped it down early in my first year. I saw other guys who didn't and they dreaded coming to the ballpark it got so bad. Remember that."

151

I checked into Dodgertown and I went to my room. My roommate for the spring was John Sanderson, who was twenty-two and had
been drafted from Georgia Tech in the fourth round two years before.
Sanderson is a 6'2", 200 pound right-handed pitcher. He has a crew-
cut and dark brown eyes with one eyebrow looking like a caterpillar
going straight across his forehead. I walked in and said hello.

"Grughms." He said.

Uh oh. A mumbler.

"I looked at him and asked, "Whatdja say?"

"Ufnfnjjn," he said.

"Oh," I said. Either he didn't speak English, was a mumbler or
didn't want to talk to me. The next day, Sanderson invited me to breakfast, I think. He said, "Trjslj kfd bkdadsayt?" And then we went to eat.

We walked into camp and saw lots of guys around. We went into
the locker-room and changed into our uniform pants and royal blue
Dodgers warmup jerseys. I saw "legendary" Dodgers manager Lou
D'Angelo. Never have I heard such torrents of obscenities come from
another human being's mouth. But he's won two World Series and been
to three more and has been managing the Dodgers for seventeen straight
years. An amazing accomplishment these days. D'Angelo ignores the
minor leaguers as is his wont. From what I've heard he won't speak to
them during the regular season either. He doesn't want to learn any
more names than he has to. My guess is that his body is too busy con-
verting all those carbohydrates he consumes into glucose for his brain
to be functioning correctly. Everything that passed his lips seemed to
be bread or pasta. He's a large man and looks like a New York City
police detective. He has dark hair flecked with gray, a Roman nose and
a paunch. Every time I saw the guy he was shoveling food into his
mouth. As for the workout, we stretched as a group, ran and went to
the mounds to loosen up. Duerson was there and noticed my yearly
haircut.

"Is this an annual thing?" he asked.

"How's the hand?" I asked in response.

"Better," he said. Jon was in improved spirits.

Over near the dugout I saw James Witherspoon for the first time in a year.

"Hey, hey," I said.

We shook hands and chatted for a moment. They were sending him to San Antonio to replace Jimmy Strait.

152

Spring training is so dull. But less so when you're working out with the big leaguers. And the women are *incredible*. We were doing our sprints and getting into "baseball shape," whatever that is. After a few weeks of this, the regular players started ambling in. As they arrived I got to pitch batting practice to them a few times. The batters are always behind the pitchers early in spring training, so it isn't that difficult to look good against them.

We traveled by bus to Port St. Lucie to play the Mets. I got to go but wouldn't pitch. It didn't look very promising for me to pitch in any of the games. It wasn't a bad thing though. I relished hanging around at the ballpark with the big leaguers. They hadn't invited me to drink with them or anything. I guess they hadn't heard that I'm the life of the party. There hadn't been any hazing yet, but it started in Port St. Lucie. Dodgers ace pitcher Lee Black from Dallas, Texas, universally known to one and all as one of the biggest pricks in baseball and armed with a degree in kinesiology from Stanford and a $120 million contract, walked up to me.

"Lookit what we have here," he said.

I looked up at him from my chair without expression.

"I just found the rook that's gonna carry my bags," he announced to one and all and tapped me on the shoulder for emphasis. I felt like I was in prison and he was claiming me as his bitch. I sat stonefaced as I watched his hand move from his side to my shoulder and back again. I stared into his face and he walked away. Everyone was looking and I felt like an idiot.

Remember what Jared Kemerrer told you.

After that afternoon's game, during which I thought about how

193

to combat Lee Black, the players' equipment bags marked "Los Angeles Dodgers" were packed and left in the center of the clubhouse. Most everyone was in the shower and I decided to follow through on the idea I had formulated to combat Lee Black. I found the bag marked "#43 — L.Black" in script. I picked the bag up. I was fully dressed in uniform pants and a gray LA Dodgers T-shirt and shower shoes. I marched into the shower with Black's bag slung over my shoulder. All the guys looked at me and started laughing. I scanned the shower room and located Lee Black. He was buck naked with shampoo in his hair as I stopped directly in front of him. He's a big guy, 6'4", 200 pounds, lean and muscular. I wouldn't want to fight him. The bag and I were soaked by now. I dropped it at his feet.

"Where do you want me to bring it?" I asked with a friendly, helpful grin.

He stared back at me with his mouth open in disbelief. When he didn't answer after a few seconds I shrugged and left the bag with him in the shower. The other guys, many of them veteran Major Leaguers, laughed raucously. Later, Jared Kemerrer came up to me.

"That," he said, "took a pair of *balls*." And patted me on the back.

Lee Black, on the other hand, never bothered me again.

153

"I don't get it," I said to Dave Christenson out of earshot of the coaches. "I mean, why bring me here if you're not gonna put me in any games?"

"Just enjoy it while it lasts," he said.

There had been a week and a half of games, both regular and split-squad, and I still hadn't seen the light of day other than to pitch batting practice. All I'd been doing was working out with the team, throwing BP, sitting in the bullpen and watching the millionaires drive off in their sportscars to play golf and fool around on their wives.

On a brighter note, I was signing autographs by the stands when a blonde came over with a baseball in her hand. She had on a belly shirt and short white shorts with strappy shoes. She looked at me and asked me to sign her ball. I looked into her eyes and said sure. I signed my name and wrote the phone number of my room. What the hell? Why not?

After the game, in which I did not appear, I went back to my room. A short while later, she called. I invited her to the room and asked Sanderson to scram. He agreed ... I think. He said, "Hsjfgjdi." And left.

She walked into the room and immediately stripped. We took care of our biological needs and afterwards she started telling me all about her boyfriend, a linebacker for the Tampa Bay Buccaneers. I didn't need to hear about that. But by that time, who cared?

154

Finally in a split squad game against the Marlins at Vero Beach, I got into a game. I pitched one inning and gave up one hit. Then I got into two more games in the next three days. I gave up a total of four hits and no runs in four innings. I threw to some established Major Leaguers and wasn't too intimidated. That means I was able to throw strikes and not embarrass myself. The next day the first cuts came. A whole slew of young guys were shipped to the minor league complex, me included. Christenson, Santana, and Frank Stein were sent down with me. Duerson was still in the big league camp. He was crushing the ball and I started to think that they might keep him up there to get two hundred at-bats and learn in the Majors. Roommate Sanderson was broken up about my departure. "Mfjadijnmlda," he said.

Christenson showed me something intriguing. He had stolen Lee Black's Dodgers jacket. He displayed it proudly as a memento of his experience in Dodgers camp.

There was something that disturbed me about Lou D'Angelo. He had time for every Hollywood suck-up or opera singer that showed up, but refused to talk to guys without a year in the Majors under their belts. That's not the way to make a young player feel comfortable in the clubhouse (or the dugout, or bullpen, or hotel, or bus, etc., etc.) Not only that, I didn't like the way he handled the cuts. I know, I know.

Who am I to complain? Well, I'm nobody to complain but that's never stopped me before. D'Angelo doesn't handle the cuts himself. He sends his right-hand-man (or his lackey if you prefer) Rocky Bocchino to inform the condemned that they're on their way down. Bocchino seemed to relish the chore. He was known around camp as the Grim Reaper. "Did the Reaper get you?" is a familiar question around camp.

155

The first day at the minor league complex I ran into Carlton Gray. "What are you doing here?" I asked. "Why weren't you in Dodgers camp?"

"I've become a player-coach at San Bernardino," he replied.

I looked puzzled. "You don't wanna play anymore?"

"It's not that. I've been stuck in A ball for fifteen fucking years. I like San Bernardino and so does my family. That's where I'm gonna stay."

"Good luck," I said.

He'll make it as a manager someday. And a better one than Mickey Martin.

We started playing the minor league games and toward the end of the spring I started to wonder where they were going to send me. I'd pitched well. I was hoping to go to Triple A Albuquerque. When I found out where I was going I was in for a rude awakening. They were sending me back to Double A San Antonio. I was disgusted. The only saving grace was that I was playing for James Witherspoon again. When I saw him I expressed my frustration.

"Just pitch as well as you can and shove it up their asses. Show them they made a mistake. They'll move you up soon enough."

156

One guy not victimized by the Reaper and sent back to the minor league complex was Jon Duerson. He made the Major League roster and went west with the Dodgers. He made it to the Show at twenty and I'm intensely jealous.

Some disturbing news. My black Pro-8 glove broke. I can get it fixed but decided that perhaps it was time for a new glove. I'd get it fixed anyway, but would use one of the multitudes of free gloves that I had collected from Rawlings. They'd given me two gloves a year for the past three years and I insisted on using the same one I used in high school and college. I had one of the Trap-eze models I mentioned earlier broken in and ready. It was still traumatic. I'm superstitious and if I'd gotten off to a bad start, the black Pro-8 would've been back before you could blink.

Before we left for San Antonio, Stephen Jones gave his speech. I assume that he didn't want to make the trek to Texas to do his verbal gymnastics so he gave it to us before we left. I'd grown to love these speeches. He was dressed casually for this one. No expensive suit this time. He had on a short-sleeved golf shirt and casual dress pants. Hair perfectly coifed as always.

"Gentlemen, your environment has you poised to actualize what has been your endeavor. Double A is the litmus test for you sportsmen."

Sportsmen. We're *sportsmen* now. I looked at Christenson and frowned when I heard that. He had his eyes half open and was chewing his nails.

"You will either be contemplated as a legitimate prospect or a marginal to dubious prospect. There are sportsmen from a triform of aggregation amalgamating."

I glanced at Miguel Santana and couldn't help but wonder what was going through his head during this. His English is okay, but he couldn't handle this stuff.

"There are sportsmen from external stations. Now you must toil laboriously. The scrutiny is tremendous. Concentrate on your pursuit and commit to excellence. Commendatory occurrences will eventuate. Godspeed, gentlemen."

I don't know if my vocabulary is improving or Jones' is diminishing because I had a pretty good grasp of what he said. Should I be worried? I wondered.

157

Arriving back in San Antonio with James Witherspoon and Wes McCormack in charge along with many familiar faces made me feel better about not being sent to Triple A Albuquerque. Having played with both San Bernardino and San Antonio the year before was an advantage. I knew most everyone on the roster. Christenson broached the subject of sharing an apartment, but I declined. I've never lived alone for more than a couple of months. I thought I'd try and see what it was like. The team made suggestions about finding apartments. I wasn't too worried about being able to pay for an apartment by myself since the cost of living in Texas is next to nothing compared to New York. I found a place on Wurzbach Road for $450 a month about eleven miles from Nelson W. Wolff Stadium. Having grown tired of not having my car I asked my mother to look into getting my car shipped. She did and said it would cost $750 to ship my Saturn SL1 from New York to San Antonio.

"Do it," I said. "And I'll give you the money back."

"We'll have it shipped to you. Don't worry about the money," she said.

I didn't argue with her. I was actually getting organized like a real life grown-up. I didn't spend too much time looking at sites during my first tour of duty with the Missions. Now I was more settled in and figured that I may as well experience some landmarks.

158

A few days before Midland came in for opening day we had a work-out at the ballpark. I was sitting in the locker-room reading the *San Antonio Express News* when I noticed quite the interesting article. It was a season preview of the San Antonio Missions. One question caught my eye. It said, and I quote (I am not making this up): "Is Samuels the next Koufax?"

Oh, they're kidding.

It was brief. It said, verbatim: "Brett Samuels has been putting up numbers that make some believe he may be the Dodgers' next version of Sandy Koufax. There may be another Jewish hero on the horizon for the Dodgers, Brett Samuels, the winning pitcher in the championship clincher last season, has been making everyone take notice with his outstanding record over the past two seasons. He's one to keep an eye on."

I read that and announced to everyone in the room that it was now official. I was the next Sandy Koufax. Most guys ignored me. The ones who didn't asked what I had been smoking or had the nerve to ask who Sandy Koufax was. Many players today have no sense of history. The writer of the article has a point though. There are many striking similarities between Koufax and me. Koufax is 6'2". I'm 5'11". He has huge hands and threw gas. I have moderate size hands (with long fingers) and can barely pump gas into my car, let alone throw it. Sandy Koufax once struck out 382 in a season. Checking my own stats says that I've been a professional for two years and have a grand total of 218. I may make 382 in my third year as a pro. Koufax is a lefty and I'm a righty. Other than that we could pass for carbon copies of each other. That writer really did his homework. I'm sure he noticed one trait we have in common and that justifies his writing that stuff.

We're both JEWS!

That is as good a reason as any to compare us.

159

There were two born again Christians on this team. I had missed having them around. Andy Ramirez is from Brooklyn and is always talking about Jesus and salvation. He grew up playing on the Parade Grounds just like I did. He played for the Youth Service League, which has and will continue to send numerous players to the professional ranks. He and I played against each other but didn't know each other. At least Ramirez was laid back and nonpreachy about his convictions. Danny Bell, on the other hand, grew up in a conservative home in Missouri. His father is a minister and drilled his beliefs into his son. Not only is

Danny an evangelical Christian à la Pat Robertson, but he's an ultra-conservative moralist à la Alan Keyes. Listening to him yammer about life, politics and religion was liable to drive one to strangulation. Witherspoon heard all this stuff and, knowing of my penchant for arguing about that stuff, asked me to keep my mouth shut about it. I said I'd try.

Witherspoon told me that I was going to start the opener against Midland. That's more like it. It was three days away and I was already getting pumped up. Oddly I didn't miss Mickey Martin.

160

Nothing beats the feeling of expectation on opening day, especially if you're the starting pitcher *and* you were a member of the championship team the year before and are getting your ring. There's always a good crowd and everyone gets their adrenaline flowing as they get introduced to the crowd. It's a great way for girls to notice you. The diamond-studded ring I had to adorn my finger isn't a bad way either. The reserves got announced first and then the starters. I was warming up in the bullpen so when I was announced, I wasn't on the foul lines. I heard my name. "Aaaand pitching, warming up in the bullpen, number twenty-two, Brett Saaaaaaamuellllls." I stopped warming up and tipped my hat even though that is bad form. Rico Etchesteria was warming me up in the bullpen and had no reaction when his name was called. He's very calm.

Midland wasn't real good the year before and the scouting reports for this season weren't much better. I tried to keep from getting overconfident. The first 450-foot bomb I surrendered would cure any overconfidence. I strolled out to the mound and was comfortable knowing most everyone on the field had played behind me before. Etchesteria was behind the plate, Christenson at first, Homer Burns at second, Queen at short, J. J. Kent at third, Ben Carter, Kareem Akeem, and Makatoshi Hakatoshi from left to right in the outfield. I completed my warm-ups and gave Etchesteria the signal to throw the ball to second. The leadoff batter, John Reiser, stood in. I've never had much luck with leadoff batters. Let's change history, I thought. I threw two curves to get ahead and finished him off with a straight fastball. I changed my pattern of pitches and got off to a good start for once. I retired the first seven guys to face me before giving up a single in the third. Mike Queen homered in the fourth to give me the lead and I held it into the sixth when I gave up the tying run on a double and a single. Makatoshi Hakatoshi doubled with two runners on and gave me a two run lead in the sixth. I gave up a home run that barely got over the 310 sign in left field with two outs. I got the final out in the seventh and Witherspoon took me out. I don't argue with James Witherspoon as I did with Mickey Martin. We scored an insurance run in the eighth that we needed as Mike Strock gave up a solo homer in the ninth but still got the save. I got the win and finally got off to a good start.

I called my parents after the game. They said that they were going to try and come up toward the end of May. We had a long homestand then. The word from Los Angeles: Jon Duerson hit a pinch home run in his first Major League at-bat against the Arizona Diamondbacks. The man is going big time. I knew him when. Speaking of the Dodgers, their bullpen blew a 5–1 lead in the sixth inning and lost 11–5.

161

I saw the San Antonio Missions winning another championship. Of course, I was hoping to be in Albuquerque winning a championship, but that's beside the point. We beat the hell out of the Midland Rockhounds. The *Rockhounds*. I nudged Frank Stein with a confused look on my face. "Hey man," I said, "weren't they the Midland Angels last year?" I hadn't noticed the name change until the second game.

"Brett," he said, "you're like five days behind everyone else."

Well, I'm two days behind everyone else at the most.

"They have a new affiliation and a new nickname. They're with Oakland now."

I should have known when I saw the eight-foot tall pitchers.

We won the first four games by scores of 4–3, 10–3, 4–1 and 6–0. They beat Jack Kray in the last game 5–2.

It was nice to have my car again and not to have to depend on others for transportation. I was also able to get lost in a completely new state. My sense of direction leaves something to be desired at times.

After the drudgery of spring training and the prospects of the long season and the bus rides looming, we needed to let loose a bit. So, Christenson, Stein and I went to a bar and got half-sloshed. After that we needed something else to occupy what was left of our minds, so we went to the movies. We decided somewhere along the line that it would be fun to play "Mystery Science Theater 3000" during the film. For those of you unfamiliar with "Mystery Science Theater 3000," the basic premise is that a guy and two robots pick a terrible science fiction film and sit in the front of a theater and goof on the film. We picked the perfect film for it too: Dee Snider's *Strangeland*. We sat in the front row of the theater on the right side. Christenson was the robot "Crow," Stein was "Mike Nelson" and I was "Tom Servo." As soon as the film started, we unleashed a torrent of insults and merciless obnoxious comments all through that godawful movie. Why do these has-been rock stars insist on punishing their loyal fans by butchering other mediums? We managed to entertain ourselves and it made it worth the price of the tickets. The other patrons didn't seem to mind. That may be because there *were* no other patrons. Dee Snider's *Strangeland* was not a box-office success. In fact, when we went to buy the tickets the teenaged girl in the booth furrowed her brow and said, "*Really*?" when we told her what film we wanted to see.

Yeah, really.

162

It was off to El Paso for the prerequisite five game series. That, you will recall, is a twelve-hour trip. For approximately eleven hours and fifty-nine minutes I listened to Danny Bell ramble on about family values, prayer in school and abortion. It felt like Robert Bork was on the bus. To make matters worse, Bell has a speech impediment where his S's come out sounding like SCH. So, when he says, "This is the day to start being accountable for your sins," it sounds like "Thisch isch the day to schtart being accountable for your schinsch."

I was keeping my mouth shut at the behest of my manager, but how long I could continue I didn't know. I almost said something when Bell started going on and on about how everyone should drop all the other sham religions and come happily to Jesus.

And don't think for a schecond that I'm above making fun of his schpeech impediment.

It's really great being a number one starter in the Texas League. The five game series pretty much guarantees that I will be the starter in the first game of every series. After the long bus ride, we had time to check into the Quality Inn and rest a few hours before heading to the ballpark. Warming up, I felt like crap. I had nothing. No curve, no splitter, and my "cutter" was all over the place. Not only that, I was throwing pus (baseball parlance for not throwing very hard). The game began and Akeem (I give — I'm not going to call him Rod anymore) led off the game by hitting one over the wall. We scored another run on a double by Christenson. I went to the mound and hoped to bluff my way through and not embarrass myself. I managed to squeak through the first inning, giving up one run on three straight singles. After that I started to feel a bit better. The innings passed and I got my stuff together. My velocity improved, as did my breaking pitches. By the time Witherspoon pulled me with two outs in the eighth, I had a 4–1 lead. Mike Strock pitched the ninth and I had my second straight win to start the season. I started to think they'd send me to Albuquerque soon.

An interesting thing happened to Mike Strock. He always threw hard, as I believe a closer should, but now he's bringing it in at 95–97 mph. In years past he topped out at 91–92. I asked what the secret was and he told me that he parades around his hotel room in women's undergarments and then stands on his head and clucks like a chicken. I do believe he was joking.

163

We went looking for things to do in El Paso. El Paso is on the border of Texas and Mexico so there are lots of Mexicans around. I felt like I was back in New York. There was a museum that I wanted to go and see but not for the customary reasons. The Centennial Museum is on the campus of the University of Texas El Paso. I wanted to look for college girls and I dragged Dave Christenson with me. Unfortunately for us it was spring break time and there weren't many people around. We went to the El Paso zoo the next day. There's a casino in the area but I managed to stay away.

We won four of five in El Paso. It was a good series baseball wise, but a costly one injury wise. In the second game, J. J. Kent got hit on the jaw with a 90-mph fastball. Kareem Akeem was on first and Kent glanced his way to see if he was stealing while the pitcher was in his motion. When Kent looked back toward the pitcher he lost sight of the ball as it came out of the pitcher's hand. It crashed into Kent's jaw with a sickening SMACK! The whole dugout groaned as Kent went down. We felt the pain just from the *sound*. Imagine how Kent felt. He was lying at home plate for ten minutes before they let him walk off to a nice ovation, spitting a trail of blood along the way. The diagnosis: J. J. Kent had a broken jaw and was out for two months.

In the last game of the series Jack Kray was rolling along into the sixth inning with a shutout. On the third pitch of the bottom of the sixth he let go of the ball and let out a piercing screech. Kray grabbed his arm, fell forward and rolled onto his back kicking his legs and crying. Dave Christenson ran over from first base and held Kray in place so he wouldn't do himself any more damage. Witherspoon and McCormack and team trainer Will Densmore ran out. After a few minutes the stretcher was brought out to cart Jack off the field to await an ambulance. The hospital X-rayed Jack's arm and the news wasn't good. Jack Kray's arm snapped in two like a twig. He was out for the season and his career was in jeopardy. It was a depressing way to end a series and a miserable ride into Wichita. Kray took off for Los Angeles for surgery to repair his damaged livelihood.

J. J. Kent returned to the team in Wichita with his jaw completely wired shut. It was difficult for him to talk. This prompted Frank Stein to ask if it would be feasible to have my jaw wired shut too.

No, it wouldn't.

164

Our bus was on Gateway Boulevard on the way out of El Paso when we passed a group of kids with punk hairstyles, clothes and multiple piercings. Twenty-five-year-old Cliff Rose, an infielder from Minnesota, seated in front of me, started yelling at them out the window.

"Get a normal haircut and a job, you fucking freaks!"

I leaned around the side of the seat and told him to knock it off.

"What's it your business?" he asked.

"You're saying it in front of me and that makes it my business."

"What? You like those fucking freaks, Samuels?"

"I don't like it or not like it. It's not my business. And it's not yours either."

"Well," he said, "I don't like it and I'm not gonna keep my mouth shut about it. I don't like freaks or fags."

"You don't like freaks or fags? You're from Minnesota, Cliff. The frigging governor is a pro wrestler for Chrissakes," I said.

This went on for a few minutes. I'll never understand why everyone has to comment on everyone else. Why does everyone *care*? I personally do not care what two consenting adults do in the privacy of their own homes or with their own bodies. As long as they're not forcing their ideas on me, who cares?

To display my social liberalism, I told the story of the time in a nightclub when a guy came up to me and asked if I was homosexual. I didn't beat the hell out of the guy and I didn't get pissed. Why should I have?

"Didja fuck him?" Frank Stein asked with a smirk.

"Aww, shuddup Frank," I said.

The ride from El Paso was remarkably long and painful. Twenty-one hours on a bus filled with smelly guys climbing on each other. Guys started talking about sex and I was reminded of a story from college. Kingsborough was traveling to upstate New York when outfielder Craig Tucci started describing his fantasies. Our coach, Lou Roessler, seated nearby turned around and told Tucci, "Your parents would be disappointed."

"Coach," I said, "look who you're talking to. They're *already* disappointed."

To this day, I'm the only one to evoke that kind of hysterical laughter from Lou Roessler.

165

We were exhausted and completely sick of each other as we arrived in Wichita. Waiting for us at the Broadview Hotel were the two players brought in to replace Kent and Kray. Infielder Trey Craft from North Carolina and pitcher Mel White from Washington were rested and relaxed from their plane rides. We looked like we'd just come out of the dryer. Mike Strock was stalking the lobby wondering why they called the hotel the Broadview when he couldn't see any broads.

We went to the ballpark and I warmed up and walked to the mound ready to pitch when the skies opened up. We sat in the clubhouse waiting out the rain delay for two hours before the umps called it. Witherspoon asked if I would be able to start the first game of the doubleheader the next day despite warming up the day before.

"No problem," I said.

The next day, I started the first game of the doubleheader. The Wichita Wranglers hadn't improved from last year. The previous day's warmup was not a problem. In fact, after my performance against the Wranglers I may make a day-before-my-start warmup a regular part of my routine. Check this out: seven innings (doubleheaders are only seven innings each game in the minors), no runs, five hits, no walks (!), and eight strikeouts. I struck out the last guy in the bottom of the seventh and turned to the left punching the air. My record improved to 3–0.

166

Checking the newspapers revealed that Jon Duerson was ten for his first thirty in the bigs with two home runs. The man can flat out hit. It was only a matter of time before he was in there every day at first base or behind the plate. Even though Lou D'Angelo doesn't acknowledge rookies, I was sure that he'd be able to force himself to write Jon's name on the lineup card. And considering the start the Dodgers were off to, some wholesale changes may have been on the way up there anyway. Things were a mess. Stephen Jones was destined for apoplectic seizures (as he would say).

A couple of guys were going to play golf and invited me. I declined. I don't have the temperament to keep from flinging clubs all over the course. Instead Dave Christenson and I went looking for sights to see in Wichita. We wound up at the Kansas Wildlife Exhibit. I had wanted to go to the Children's Museum of Wichita, but Dave refused. The day after that I went to the Kansas Aviation Museum with the extremely quiet J. J. Kent and took photos for my dad.

Strock and I were playing "Highlander" before one of the games and sword fighting with quick-stick bats. Quick-stick bats are really thin bats designed to help increase concentration. Witherspoon caught us. (We weren't trying to be discreet. We were doing it in the outfield.) He didn't exactly tell us to stop, but said that if either of us got hurt he was fining us $250 each. We stopped shortly after that.

After the fourth game of the series I barged into Frank Stein's room as I sometimes do. I saw what perhaps is the most embarrassing thing I'd ever heard or seen a ballplayer do. In the room were Frank Stein, Homer Burns, Cliff Rose, Aaron Beck and Steve Baker. What they were doing *shocked* me. No, they weren't doing drugs as I'd caught a couple of guys doing in San Bernardino. They were doing something that, in some circles, would be considered worse. They were sitting there and watching … *Dawson's Creek*!

My mouth hit the floor. For one of the few times in my life I was speechless. Finally some words formed.

"Oh, you're kidding," I said.

"Shudd-uu-up," Stein whined.

I guess he didn't want to be interrupted during the castration scene. I've seen the show. I'm still waiting for the episode in which Dawson comes out of the closet. They're high school kids with the vocabulary of Stephen Jones. I can't watch it for any reason other than to goof on it. I was in the room laughing at them for three minutes before I was forcibly removed. The men of the San Antonio Missions are not to be interrupted while watching *Dawson's Creek*. The pansies.

207

Dawson must have inspired Frank Stein because he homered in the top of the tenth of the last game in Wichita to win it for Strock in relief.

On the bus back to San Antonio I started reading excerpts of the Mike Tyson *Playboy* interview aloud followed by my witty comments. I was imitating Tyson's high voice complete with the lisp. Here is my favorite part about the alleged rape of the beauty contestant that sent Tyson to jail.

Tyson: "I fuck her, suck her on her ass, suck all over her. *I perform fellatio on her.*" (Emphasis mine.)

My comment: "If the jury had known that he'd sucked her dick they never would have convicted him."

That evoked laughter. I live to entertain.

Homer Burns then asked if I thought that Tyson was guilty of that rape.

"Well, I think that he probably thinks he didn't and the girl thinks that he did," I said.

"What do *you* think?" he repeated.

"My guess is he probably did rape her," I said.

It wasn't the longest ride back to San Antonio, but it was long enough. Fourteen hours. It's no wonder guys are so desperate to get to the Majors. My stomach started acting up from the fast food on the rest stops and I had to soothe it with the Pepto-Bismol and Imodium AD combination. I probably wouldn't poop for several days.

168

Before the opener of the home series with El Paso, I was getting my shoulder rubbed in the trainer's room. Mike Strock was in there too getting treatment on a creaky elbow. Homer Burns strolled in with a copy of *USA Today Baseball Weekly*.

"You seen this, Brett?" he asked.

"Seen what?"

He started flipping through the pages and found what he was looking for. He put the paper in front of me and tapped what I was supposed to be looking at. I did a quick read through. It was the minor league reports. Under the Dodgers banner there was a small box and it said this and that about certain minor leaguers in the organization. It said, "In Double A San Antonio twenty-one-year-old righty Brett Samuels is reminding many scouts of a young David Cone."

I smiled and pondered that for a second.

"Check this out, Strock," I said, "they're comparing me to David Cone. I can see the similarities."

"Why?" Strock asked. "Is he a dick too?"

169

Before the second game with El Paso I was doing my windsprints when Witherspoon strolled by. I called to him.

"Hey Skip, isn't it enough with this running shit already?"

"No, Brett."

And that was that.

I was signing my valuable autograph for a bunch of young kids and their equally young mothers when Dave Christenson bounded from the dugout. Very loudly he announced, "Brett, I just got the most incredible blowjob in the locker-room."

The mothers looked mortified. You have to watch what you say in front of kids. I turned to Christenson, "Dave, jeez. Use your brain for Chrissakes."

He looked annoyed at me even though he knew I was right. It's a good thing that he'd eased up on the bulking concoctions. A year earlier he might have impaled me on the fence.

We lost three of five to El Paso. A mini-slump for the Missions. But James Witherspoon lets us eat the food on the postgame spread as opposed to attacking it like Mickey Martin.

170

Wichita came to town and I was on the mound to try and put an end to the mini-slump. We were in first place by four games, but needed to get back on track. We pummeled Wichita. We scored seven runs in the first inning on a grand slam by Christenson. Danny Bell homered as well, and we were off to the races. I went eight innings and gave up two runs on seven hits. I ran through a stretch of wildness when I lost my release point but managed to straighten myself out. Witherspoon yanked me because I'd thrown 112 pitches. I got the win to raise my record to 4–0. I got clocked at 88 mph for several pitches. Maybe I'd make ninety yet. The sky was the limit.

I was interviewed in the postgame show by broadcaster Gerald Amhearst for KKYX 680 AM, which carries the Missions' games. He was asking me the usual by the book interview questions. Believe me, sports interviews are just as boring for the interviewee as they are for the viewers. His last question gave me the opportunity to have some fun.

"Have you ever in your wildest fantasies thought you'd be doing this well?" he asked in his southern drawl.

"Well, Gerry," I said, "to be honest, my wildest fantasies have nothing to do with baseball. They have to do with every woman in the 'Victoria's Secret' catalogue."

"Um, I, oh, uh, thanks for the interview, Brett."

Stephen Jones was in town watching the troops. I felt like grabbing him and saying, "Triple A is just a phone call away." But didn't.

171

Jack Kray rejoined the team with his arm in a cast and a sling. He said it didn't hurt. He was cranky. I offered to make him some cards similar to the ones I made for Duerson. "Nahh. Bitching gives me something to do," he said.

Miguel Santana got knocked around for a couple of starts in a row. He started to worry about getting sent back to A ball. I didn't think they were going to do that. They'd give him a chance to straighten himself out.

After winning three of five against Wichita we went back on the road to Midland. After Midland we were coming home for Shreveport. Shortly after that, my parents were coming to visit.

On the bus, Danny Bell started in with his diatribe against the values of the president. "He schouldn't be in the White Housche if he can't control himschelf."

What a bunch of crap. The president's behavior was more stupid that anything else. But at least you can say that he never claimed to be anything he wasn't. He never walked around saying that he was Mr. Family Values like Newt Gingrich did. The people knew what they were getting when they elected Clinton. He was a philanderer before and he's still a philanderer. He's a horny guy. Accept it. But Gingrich, oh does he make me sick. He started in with this family values crap and after he left office it became known that he'd been carrying on an affair on his second wife for *six years*. A large number of these conservative Republicans have girlfriends on the side just as the evangelists do. I kept my mouth shut though, remembering Witherspoon's request.

172

I took my first loss in Midland despite pitching brilliantly. I only gave up two runs in a complete game but we only pushed one run across against them. My pitches were all working and I had none of the problems I sometimes have with my mechanics and release point. I started thinking that my new glove was bad luck before I realized that I had been using it all season. I struck out only two in the game and didn't make any smart-ass comments about being sent to Triple A.

Going back to the Holiday Inn several guys were planning on going out for the evening. I wanted to stay at the hotel and be depressed but they dragged me out with them. I had numerous drinks to drown my sorrows and met a girl who I fooled around with in her car. (I hope it was a girl. I was pretty drunk.) The evening wasn't a total loss.

I had four days to stew until my next start at home. There were some sights to see in Midland. Christenson, J. J. Kent and I went to the American Airpower Heritage Museum. Why I insist on going to places more suited to my parents is beyond me. The rest of the time was spent by the hotel pool. I don't swim. I just sit there and read the papers. The Dodgers situation was getting worse by the day. Duerson was playing about three days a week and doing well. The word on the grapevine was that the Dodgers were going to go one of two ways: Write off the season and start dumping salaries, or try and find other teams trying to dump salaries and make some even up swaps. The wild card makes it hard to throw out the season in May. A team is not truly out of it until August or so. If the Dodgers started looking for other teams' stars some minor leaguers could go in the process. Me included.

173

We played like crap the whole series with Midland, and before we left Witherspoon chewed our asses out. We deserved it. He didn't throw food or make up curses. He simply made all the points he wanted to make. He told us that he was treating us like adults and if we continued playing and acting as we were, privileges would start to disappear one by one. If we were going to play like we were in the Rookie League he would make rules like we were in the Rookie League. We went to the buses hanging our heads in shame. Rightfully so.

It was good to get back home. I collapsed in my apartment, exhausted. We had a day off before Shreveport came to town. Again I felt it was up to me to straighten the team's fortunes out. It ain't easy being the ace.

175

Shreveport was another team that had been bad, but improved sufficiently to lead the Eastern Division. We still led the West, barely. I started the game and didn't have my best stuff. I gutted my way through. My twister wasn't working and I couldn't control my "cutter." I just used the fastball and curve and a surprisingly good splitfinger. It also helped that we scored nine runs in the first two innings. Rico Etchesteria and Dave Christenson both homered and it was nice to have some runs to work with. Witherspoon yanked me after seven innings and three runs on six hits. He congratulated me after the game for gutting my way through when it was obvious that I didn't have my best stuff. He looked like he wanted to tell me something else, but didn't.

We won two of the next three games. We were playing the way we had earlier in the season. Before game two, the head of the San Antonio "Hooters" was there to throw out the first ball. They're a club sponsor. He'd brought a couple of girls from the restaurant with him. One of them, a beautiful brunette, asked me what I was doing after the game. I told her that I would break any plans that I had. We went for a drink and back to my apartment. She must have been experienced with ballplayers because when I woke up the next morning, she was gone. How great a concept is "Hooters"?

After the third game of the series, Witherspoon sidled up to me in the locker-room and said, "Listen, I may use you in relief tomorrow. Don't go too nuts tonight."

Huh?

He walked off before I could get the question, "Why?" out.

Later, Frank Stein and Dave Christenson came by my apartment where I bitched nonstop.

"Why's he sticking me in the bullpen? What'd I do to get demoted?"

"He's gotta have a reason," Christenson said.

"Yeah?" I asked. "What?"

Nobody had an answer.

Before the next game I asked McCormack what was going on. He said that they wanted to see me work in relief. I shouldn't read anything into it.

Don't read anything into it? I've been demoted.

I went into Witherspoon's office asking for an explanation. He tilted his head.

"Brett, do you trust me?" he asked.

"Well, yeah. But ..."

"But nothing. Just do as I ask for once without arguing with me. Go to the bullpen and wait until I call for you to warm up."

I opened my mouth to say something and he held up his hand.

"Just do as I ask," he said.

At the start of the game I went to the bullpen. I had pitched once in relief during the championship series, but I hadn't done it regularly since Great Falls. So confusing.

As the game went along we were going back and forth with Shreveport. We had a 5–1 lead. They came back to lead 7–5. We took a 9–7 lead. In the sixth Witherspoon called down for me to warm up. He brought me in to start the seventh. I was more nervous than usual. I tried to take deep breaths to calm my nerves. It eased my nerves further when I struck out the first two batters. I gave up a single and then got the next guy to ground into a force out. The next inning I got them out three up and three down. For the entire appearance, I didn't walk anyone and gave up only one hit, striking out three. I went to the dugout and put my jacket on. Strock pitched the ninth and gave up a run but got the save. We won 9–8. I got credit for a "hold."

Was I out of the frigging rotation now? Nobody said anything to me.

The next day was the final game of the Shreveport series. Was I supposed to sit in the bullpen now? I didn't know. I was sitting at my locker, sulking and thumbing through the newspaper when Witherspoon poked his head out of his office.

"Brett!" he called and waved me inside.

Christenson was playing cards with J. J. Kent, Mike Strock and Joe Wilson.

"What'd you do this time?" Christenson asked without looking up from his hand.

"I dunno, man. First a demotion to the pen, now what?"

I walked into the office. Witherspoon was seated at his desk.

"Sit down," he said.

I sat down.

"You look nervous," he said.

I started whining. "Put yourself in my position. I get sent to the bullpen for no apparent reason and now you call me into the office. What am I supposed to look like?"

"I had a reason for using you in relief last night," he said.

"What?"

"Stephen Jones asked me to. He wanted to see you out of the pen."

"But I've been doing so well as a starter. What, is he gonna trade me? Goddammit James, this isn't right. I think I deserve to know what's going on."

Witherspoon had his fingers steepled in front of his face. He let me moan like a baby for a moment until I tired myself out.

"You done?" he asked.

"Yeah," I grunted.

They're moving you up, Brett."

"Up where?" I asked pleasantly surprised. "Albuquerque?"

"The Dodgers are releasing Richie Jiminez." He was their right-handed long reliever.

"So?"

"You're replacing him," he said.

I frowned and stared in response.

"You follow?" he asked when I didn't say anything.

"Not really," I said.

"You're joining the Dodgers in St. Louis. You're flying out tomorrow."

"This is a joke, right?"

"No, Brett. You're going to the Majors," he said, standing up.

"Congratulations," he said, extending a hand.

My eyes were darting. I was in shock. I stared at his hand before absently shaking it.

"I'm going to the *Majors*?"

He nodded.

HOLY SHIT!

175

I stumbled out of the office. I sat at my locker with my eyes bulging from my head. "What's the matter with you?" Christenson asked as he looked up from his card game.

"They're, um, they're moving me up," I said quietly.

"Yeah, so?" Frank Stein said. "That's great, man. You're going to Albuquerque."

"Not Albuquerque, man," I said.

He looked puzzled. "If they're not sending you to Albuquerque, where else could they be ... oh shit. *Ho-ho-ho shit!*"

I looked just as amazed as he was. I nodded my head slowly.

"They're sending you to the Show man?" J. J. Kent asked excitedly.

"YEAH!" I yelled.

"Get the fuck outta here!" Christenson said. Then he lifted me out of my chair and wrapped me in a bear hug.

Guys started patting me on the head, slapping me on the back and shaking my hand.

"You're gonna be getting big league pussy, dude," Christenson said. I hadn't even thought of that.

"How can they be sending you over me?" Mike Strock asked and then added, "I'm jealous."

It started to sink in. Everyone seemed happy for me. Happy that I was going to the Show. Sad and jealous that they weren't. At least they expressed their feelings to my face. The jealousy is palpable and understandable in situations like that. My head was spinning. I was an undrafted twenty-one-year-old afterthought brought in to fill out the roster. A product of a veteran scout's imagination, I'd taken advantage of my opportunities. It was impossible to believe what was happening. I was going to the Major Leagues.

Brett Samuels from Brooklyn, New York, was going to the Show.

176

I was still freaked out as I left the ballpark. I had so much to do. I had to have my car shipped to me in Los Angeles at the conclusion of the Dodgers road trip. I asked Christenson to handle the car until I could call him and let him know when I wanted it. Considering the way Dave drives that may have been a mistake. I had to pack my stuff and have it all sent to me in LA. Witherspoon gave me the advice that I should pack some clothes and one suit along with my equipment, and once I was settled in after a few days up there I'd send for my other stuff. All I could think of regarding that was what a pain in the ass it would be to get up there, have all my stuff arrive and then have the

Dodgers send me back down. I knew I had to make the most of my opportunity and avoid that headache. I got home and called my parents but they weren't home. They don't have an answering machine either.

The Missions' executive secretary, Mary Worthy, called me that night as I was packing and told me my flight number. Flight 693 San Antonio to St. Louis' Lambert International Airport. First class! Departing 12:40 P.M. and arriving 2:47 P.M. The Dodgers had a night game with the Cardinals. I was in an almost manic state as I ran around my apartment getting my stuff together. I went to bed at midnight but couldn't sleep very well.

I got up the next morning, showered and got dressed. I tried my parents again but they still weren't home. I figured they went away for the weekend. Supposedly they were coming to San Antonio later in the week. I had to tell them to cancel if I ever got hold of them. I'd call them from St. Louis, I decided. I drove to Wolff Stadium to get the rest of my stuff. I left the car outside the locker-room entrance and one of the clubhouse kids was bringing out my stuff as fast as I could shove it into bags. James Witherspoon walked in.

"Why are you here so early?" I asked.

"You all set? You have a ride to the airport?" he asked.

"I'm driving there with Christenson. He'll take my car back with him and watch it until I'm settled."

"Okay. And do me a favor. Don't fuck with Lou D'Angelo," he said, tapping me on the chest with the back of his hand. "Just keep your mouth shut up there. He doesn't like rookies to begin with. The last thing he needs is big-mouthed rookies. Make sure your ass doesn't wind up back here for any reason other than performance."

Witherspoon isn't the emotional type. But he looked like he was about to burst with pride. He was the one who saw something in me that inspired him to give me an opportunity that I otherwise would not have gotten. He shook my hand and turned to leave, but stopped and turned back to me.

"Brett?" he said. "Can I ask you something? And I want you to tell me the truth."

"Sure." I said.

"How do you do it?"

I looked confused. "Do what?"

"How do you cut the ball? I've watched you for over two years up close and personal and I can't figure out how you do it. How?"

He was asking for the secret to my "cutter." I wasn't sure whether or not to tell him. I hadn't shared the information with a single living soul except my cat back home. But other than my parents, this man had done more for me than anyone else. I didn't question whether his word was any good. If he promised to keep it to himself I'd tell him. What the hell?

"I'll tell you, Skip, but you gotta promise me one thing: No matter what, if we're on opposite sides of the field you can't say anything. It could be the seventh game of the World Series and you have to keep your mouth shut. Deal?"

He nodded once with a tilted head and showed me his open hands. An indication to go ahead.

I reached into my bag and found my accessories. Then I found my glove. I dug out a ball and went into my usual routine of rubbing up the ball. I slipped off my glove and showed him my bare glove hand.

"Notice anything?" I asked.

"No."

I slowly removed the plastic magician's thumb tip that was securely on my left thumb. It's used by magicians when they do the disappearing handkerchief trick. It came off with a pop. Underneath was a small piece of sandpaper glued to my thumb and used to deface the ball.

"Abracadabra," I said.

When I take off my glove to rub up the ball, I place it under my right arm to pull it off. If I want the thumb tip to come off too, I hold the glove with enough pressure to pull the thumb tip off along with the glove. The tip stays safely inside the glove. The sandpaper glued to my thumb stays on until I pry it off later. If the umps want to check me, I take the glove off and they can perform an MRI on the thing and they won't find anything. If they want to look at my hand, I just show them my open palms and turn my hand up and down in all my innocence.

"Lemme see that," he said, grabbing the thumb tip. He examined it and looked at me.

"Brett," he said, "you really are a genius."

"Yes," I said. "I *am* a genius."

218

It was time to go to the Majors. THE MAJORS!

I drove my car to the airport. Christenson reluctantly helped me bring my bags into the TWA terminal. He's so lazy. I checked in. Before he left I told Dave to please be careful with my car.

"Don't worry," he said, and winked.

It was exactly that that made me worry. I shook his hand and he wished me luck. I walked through the gate with my carry-on. This was really happening. I was heading to St. Louis to join the Los Angeles Dodgers.

◆ PART IV ◆

177

I boarded my flight and settled into my first class (!) seat. I'd never been in first class before. I was wearing khaki pants and a polo shirt. I brought my one and only suit in a suit bag because I knew I would need it for the flight back to Los Angeles two days later. I tried to read the newspaper to calm down. It took my mind off things until I turned to the sports section and found the list of transactions.

Under the Dodgers it said: "Placed pitcher Richie Jiminez on waivers for the purpose of giving him his unconditional release."

And right under that it said: "Recalled pitcher Brett Samuels from San Antonio of the Texas League."

I looked out the window at the runway and my mind started to wander. It finally started to sink in. I was going to the big leagues. This is really happening, I thought. It's no dream. All those years of being ridiculed and ignored. I was going to the Major Leagues. I couldn't wait for the flight to take off. But, I waited. And waited. And waited. And waited. The captain came on the speaker.

"Ladies and gentlemen, this is your captain speaking," he said in his captain-like voice. "It seems that the National Weather Service has warned us that there are some thunderstorms in the area and our flight is going to be delayed slightly."

The flight was delayed slightly all right. It was delayed for two hours!

So I sat there and started to worry. I was worried that I would get into trouble for being late to the ballpark and they would tell me to turn around and go right back to San Antonio. I was worried about how I was supposed to act once I did arrive. I was worried because I still hadn't gotten my parents to tell them where I was. I was worried because Dave "The Road Warrior" Christenson had my car.

Finally at 2:30 P.M., the flight departed San Antonio en route to St. Louis, Missouri.

178

The plane arrived at Lambert International Airport in St. Louis at 4:40 P.M. I got myself together, popped an Imodium AD and exited the plane with my Los Angeles Dodgers bag over my shoulder. I waited at the carousel for the rest of my luggage (I didn't have much since most of it was being shipped to LA) and went through the arrival area. I looked around.

There must be somebody to pick me up.

I saw a short fat man with a bad mustache and a wrinkled shirt holding a sign that said, "Brett Samuels." I walked up to him and said, "That's me."

He grabbed my hand in his chubby, sweaty paw.

"Hi Brett, I'm Paul Kimball, assistant to the traveling secretary. Can I call you 'Sammy'? I bet all your friends call you 'Sammy.'"

"Uh, no" I said.

"Okay, Sammy. We'll have to go straight to the ballpark since your plane was so late. The car is in the lot."

This is how they greet you in the big leagues?

First we couldn't find the car. Then we finally found it and I threw my bags into the trunk of the Lincoln Town Car and got into the front seat.

"The park isn't far," he said.

We rode through the Saturday afternoon traffic toward Busch Stadium.

Kimball was talking but I wasn't really listening. I was too nervous about what was going to happen to me.

We pulled into the parking lot. He parked the car and a couple of clubhouse kids came out of nowhere and grabbed my bags. They brought them into the visitors' locker-room. There were lots of fans around because batting practice had already started. It was almost 6:00. People were yelling, "Are you a player? Are you a player?"

Kids started running toward me with autograph equipment in hand. Some security guard shooed them away. I walked into the visiting clubhouse at Busch Stadium in St. Louis. I was entering a Major League clubhouse as a Major Leaguer.

There were a few guys in the clubhouse. Most barely acknowledged my presence. It looked like most of the everyday players were out for BP. The starting pitchers who didn't have much to do were sitting around smoking cigarettes, playing cards or watching TV in the players' only lounge. I realized that I could go in there any time I wanted. I'd never seen such luxury. And this was the road! I couldn't imagine what the clubhouse at home looked like.

Equipment manager Pat O'Neill came up to me and said, "How you doing, Brett? Let's get you all settled in." He led me to my locker. All set up for me was a Dodgers road uniform and hat in just the right size. The uniform was facing forward and was brand new and beautiful. It said number twenty-two on the left ribs under the scripted "Los Angeles." This was a major step up from the number seventy-nine that I wore for the brief time I spent with the big club in the spring. I turned the jersey around to look at the back. I saw a larger number twenty-two in Dodger blue. It had "SAMUELS" stitched across the top. I ran my index finger up and down the letters. There were batting practice jerseys and undershirts, long and short sleeved, hanging in my locker. O'Neill called one of the clubhouse kids over and told him to unpack my equipment and set it up.

"Oh, kid. Tom Bratzky, the pitching coach, is in the trainer's room with Lee Black. Go tell Bratzky that you're here." O'Neill turned to walk away and stopped. He turned back around. "Oh, yeah. Welcome to the big leagues, kid."

I went to look for Bratzky. I found him in the trainer's room with my pal Lee Black. Black looked at me, frowned and shook his head before leaving.

"How you doing, Brett?" Bratzky asked, extending a hand.

"Okay," I said, shaking his hand.

"Okay," he said. "What you're going to be doing around here for the time being is long relief. We want you to get acclimated to the big leagues and then we'll see what situations you're best suited for."

"Okay," I said.

"Go get dressed," he said. "And kid," I was expecting him to say, "Welcome to the big leagues." "Don't talk to Lou D'Angelo. He's not much for hearing words from rookies." I nodded, wondering who Lou D'Angelo thought he was.

I got back to my locker and saw all my equipment set up for me. I got into my full uniform. It was almost time to get out on the field. Batting practice was over and the regular players came in. A couple nodded hello. Most ignored me. Jared Kemerrer came in. "Hey kid. Welcome to the big time. We're in last place."

I shook his hand. He whispered in my ear: "Just ignore Lou. He's a real horse's ass. Don't say anything to him."

Does Lou D'Angelo think he's Prince (I mean the artist formerly known as Prince)? I don't buy into this "none must speak to me" bullshit, but I decided to follow the advice. Why start trouble?

Jon Duerson came in. I opened my arms and grinned. "Guess who?" I said.

"Can't you ever leave me alone?" he cracked, and then enveloped me in a bear hug. "You're gonna enjoy it up here. Nothing but women. That's if you stick around, of course."

I hoped to stick around.

I realized that I still hadn't called my parents. Shit. I thought for a second and went to look for a phone.

"What are you looking for?" Jared Kemerrer asked.

"A phone. I haven't called my parents to tell them where I am."

He whipped out his cell phone. "Don't worry about the bill," he said and flipped it to me.

I dialed the number. My dad picked up.

"Yello?" he answers the phone just like me.

"Dad! Where were you the last couple of days?"

"We went up to Pennsylvania for the night," he said. "Where are you?"

"Dad," I said, taking a deep breath, "I'm in St. Louis with the Dodgers."

There was silence at the other end.

"I'm in the Majors, Dad. I'm in the Majors."

179

Game time came around and I strolled out of the clubhouse into the dugout. Lou D'Angelo was in the dugout and he didn't even look at me. I walked out to the bullpen. I felt so proud as I walked across the lush grass of Busch Stadium. I felt as though all eyes were upon me. I tried not to look like too much of a rookie even though I had no clue how to act. I got to the bullpen and the national anthem was played. The game was about to start and I sat in the bullpen trying to make myself inconspicuous. The bullpen guys came over and started saying hello and shaking my hand. I tried to keep my mouth shut. Finally by about the fourth inning, Mark Dane, the Dodgers' closer said, "Hey kid, don't you talk?"

"Yeah," I said. "But I've been instructed not to."

After the game was over (we lost) the reporters were hanging around talking to the high profile guys. One came over and started talking to me. He was the Dodgers' background guy and did little side stories. I gave him the information on the newest member of the big league club. After showering, some guys got on the bus back to the hotel. Others took cabs back. I took the bus. Mostly the guys were talking about which bar they were going to that night. There were also about seven or eight Bible fanatics on the Dodgers. One, Jerry Lott, invited me to team chapel the next morning. As much as I wanted to fit in, I declined. We got to the Hyatt Regency in St. Louis and never had I seen such accommodations. There was a pool and a complete fitness room. Most of the other players were in suites or went to stay in other hotels entirely. There was a curfew. It was two and a half hours after every night game, but it went unenforced. I had a room all to myself with a giant double bed and all the amenities. I looked out the window onto downtown St. Louis and looked at the famous Gateway Arch. I finally realized where I was. I was in St. Louis. I was a Major League baseball player. I was a Dodger.

180

I got to the ballpark the next day and the other players were swapping girl stories from the night before or talking about golf. I had no girl stories and didn't know golf. I had stayed in my room. Duerson came by and hung around. He told me what to expect from the guys. They probably wouldn't mess with me too much because they all knew of the incident with Lee Black in the spring. If they did, just have fun with it.

"Did they mess with you?" I asked.

"Are you kidding?" he replied. He was too big to mess with, I guess.

Sitting in the locker-room, Kemerrer came over and asked where I was staying in LA. I told him I didn't know. Duerson had only a one-bedroom place.

"Well," he said, "I have a guest house on my property. It's really nice. You can stay there if you want. Separate entrance and everything."

"What am I, Kato Kaelin?" I cracked.

"It's up to you," Kemerrer said.

"I'm just kidding. I'd like to. Thanks."

At least I had a place to stay.

All of the team's luggage, including mine, was situated in the center of the room for the charter flight back to Los Angeles immediately following the game. The lifestyles of these guys are astounding. The clothes and shoes in their lockers are exquisite. The jewelry, the cash. I was amazed. I hadn't imagined that it would be like this.

It was a hot day in May. As the game began, the Dodgers, mired in last place with a record of 14–23 got pounded early. Starter Enrique Vasquez got assaulted and two relievers got similar treatment. It was

15–2 as we were batting in the sixth inning when the bullpen phone rang. Bullpen coach Vernon Culsey picked it up. "Yeah? Okay. Okay. Yeah." He hung up and looked at me. "Samuels, warm up."

D'Angelo must think it's safe to put me in.

My adrenaline started flowing. I made sure not to throw too hard too quickly. As I stuck my hand in my glove I felt something funny. It was an envelope. I didn't have time to open it, so I placed it in my back pocket. I was loose in a hurry because it was so hot. My arm felt strong. The combination of the adrenaline rush and my own velocity made me think that I might pop ninety on this day. The phone rang a few seconds later. Culsey held the phone down from his mouth.

"Are you ready?" he asked.

I nodded.

"Okay. You start the next inning."

Oh, shit.

I jogged down the tunnel to the dugout since I was sufficiently warmed up. I sat in the dugout and opened the envelope. It was a note from James Witherspoon.

It said: "Brett, you're on your way. Nothing can stop you now." He signed it, "James." I smiled to myself and placed it back in the envelope and then in my back pocket. The inning ended. I grabbed my glove and headed out onto the field. Center fielder Steve Redfield yelled, "Throw strikes, kid! Ol' Lou hates walks." And then laughed.

Just what I needed. Make me more nervous.

I got to the mound. Most of the veterans had been taken out of the game already. Duerson was playing first. He came over and said, "Just relax. Throw strikes and you'll be fine. Remember. You're Brett Fucking Samuels."

I nodded and he smacked me on the ass.

The PA announcer said, "Now pitching for the Dodgers, number twenty-two, Brett Samuels."

Catcher Pat Olson appeared and asked me the all-important question, "Whattaya got?" meaning what pitches do I throw.

"Fastball, curve, twister, splitter, and I cut the fastball [literally]."

"What's the twister?" he asked.

"It's like a slider," I said.

"Okay. One, two, three, four for the first four pitches. One and then I flutter my fingers is a cutter. Second sign indicator with a runner on second and a fist is a pitchout." He started to walk back to the plate. He turned around.

"Oh, and kid," in a paternal way, he said, "it's fifteen to fuckin' two. Throw the ball over."

Quite the pep talk.

He squatted behind the plate. Matthew Lang was batting for the Cardinals. He stood in and was staring out at me. I'd never seen such concentration. I looked in for the sign.

One. Fastball.

I reached into my glove and gripped a fastball. I stepped back with my left foot. I pivoted on my right. I lifted my leg. I drove off my back leg and released the ball. Even though I knew I should be concentrating on the matter at hand, one recurring theme kept returning to my head. As soon as this ball reached the plate, I would be an official Major Leaguer. My name was going to be in the *Baseball Encyclopedia* from this day until the end of time. If I never threw another pitch, it would always be there. No matter what, it would always be there.

And that's all I ever wanted.